BETWEEN FRAMES

The City Between: Book Four

W.R. GINGELL

For all the people I love, despite their flaws:
Thank you for loving me, despite mine.

CHAPTER ONE

It's always during dinner that stuff happens. More specifically, it's always during the dinners that Jin Yeong picks. Ever since I've been here in this house, a human pet to two fae and a vampire, there's barely been a single dinner I've started to make for Jin Yeong that hasn't been interrupted.

It doesn't happen when I cook for Zero. It doesn't happen when Athelas picks the menu. Just when it's Jin Yeong's turn.

Maybe it's a vampire thing.

Anyway, it was dinner time, and it was Jin Yeong's choice of dinner. That meant I was scrounging the fridge for the remains of the kimchi I'd made last month and chopping stuff like chilli and garlic to marinate the meat for chilli con carne. It's a convenient meal when you don't know exactly when your owners are coming home; it needs to simmer for at least four hours to be tasty, and the longer, the better.

Most pets know when their owners get home by the sound of the front door opening and closing. My owners don't really use the front door a lot unless they're trying to look normal. Me, I know my owners are home when I feel that pull and snap of reality shifting aside to let them into the house.

I was chopping red baby chilli when I felt that particular pull and snap, but when I looked up, it wasn't my owners I saw across the kitchen from me. I saw a Behind creature, all darkness and possibilities.

Oh great. Now they knew how to get into the house?

It could have been male. It could almost have been human, but not quite. I saw myself reflected in the hard silver of its eyes; a skinny human girl, all arms and legs.

It smirked.

Yeah. Just a human. No need to worry. Even the fact that I had a chopping knife in my hand didn't worry it. Just a human. It obviously didn't see that I was chopping chilli.

That was its mistake.

It leapt for me, and I went over with a yelp, brandishing my knife. Lucky for me, it knocked the knife out of my hand, otherwise I probably would have fallen on it. Teeth snapped in my face, fetid breath clinging to them, and I kicked as hard as I could at the thing's torso. The Behind creature didn't shift, but the world around us did, pulling and stretching and somehow merging with that second layer of reality that Behindkind call *Between*.

The mongrel was trying to drag me Between and Behind.

"Zero!" I yelled. "*Zero!*"

The creature snicked its teeth together in what might have been a satisfied smirk and wrapped its long fingers around my neck, throttling the sound out of me.

Oh. Right. Zero was out of the house, anyway.

I snatched at the merging of realities around me, trying to pull myself back into the first layer, the human world; but the Behind creature was stronger, and I hadn't had enough training yet. The world around us—either Between or Behind, I wasn't sure any more—grew dark at the edges and closed in on the creature's face, the one spot of vision remaining.

I couldn't pull myself back into the human world. I couldn't kick the creature again, because it had pinned both my legs. And that vicious face grew dimmer as the creature throttled me without bothering to contain my flailing arms.

Chilli, said my brain.

I know, I told it. *Jin Yeong's gonna be flamin' annoyed.*

No, said my brain. *Chilli.*

I choked on my own saliva, my face hot and red, and stopped flailing. Then I gouged my thumbs into the creature's eye sockets.

See how you like chilli, you mucky tar beast.

For a moment everything stopped, and even the creature's hands froze around my throat. It blinked once or twice, the greasy click of its eyelids tapping against my thumbs like cockroach wings, and began to smile. The fingers around my neck tightened again.

That's when the screaming started.

At first, I thought it was me. Then the creature threw me away from itself, wailing, and tore at its eyes, stumbling in a circle that bled through Between and the human world.

That'll teach it to attack someone who's chopping chilli.

"*Ahshipda!*" sighed someone, from behind the distressed creature.

I hauled in a painful, rattling sort of breath. Great. He must have just got home. My vision was starting to clear up; I could see the slender, besuited figure that was Jin Yeong. Shoes perfectly polished, suit perfectly creased, hair perfectly brushed.

So. Flamin'. *Annoying.*

"*Petteu*," Jin Yeong said, straightening his tie, "*Mwoh hae?*"

"Oh, I dunno," I said hoarsely, scrambling to my feet. "Just thought it'd be nice to be attacked by a Behind creature. You know. For a change."

"*Bae gopa.*"

"Yeah, well I'm hungry, too. I was interrupted before I could put dinner on to simmer and make some lunch."

The Behindkind creature, still howling, straightened itself. I don't know what it saw this time, but it wasn't smirking when it leapt for me, its tarry arms outstretched and its claws deadly sharp.

I yelped again and ducked, and something swift and grey collided with the Behind creature above my head, knocking it out of Between and into the human world. I got up and hastily trotted myself right back into the human world after them. I'm capable of getting myself from the Between world and into the human world when I'm not being stopped, but I can't say I enjoy being Between by myself.

By the time I got back, the Behind creature was in a mangled pile on the kitchen floor, and the entire kitchen was spattered with tar, or blood, or whatever it was that constituted its insides. Jin Yeong, puffing a breath up at the single lock that had fallen from his perfectly coiffed hair, narrowed his eyes at me, then looked down pointedly at the length of his body. His grey suit was now a black-spotted grey suit, and none of the spots were tidy, either. Even Jin Yeong's pouty little mouth wasn't red anymore; tarry mess coated it, spilling down his chin and throat to make a complete wreck of the white shirt below that.

I started grinning. "Oh, what a shame! Your suit's all mucky!"

Jin Yeong's teeth showed just slightly, stained with black. "*Yah.*"

"Hey, if you can't stop biting everything, don't blame me! You could have chopped off its head, but no, you had to go all psycho vampire on it. I mean, is that even blood?"

Jin Yeong shrugged. "*Bisutae.*"

I didn't know what that meant, but it was obvious that whatever had been inside the Behind creature, it was similar enough to blood to appeal to Jin Yeong. I looked around at the mess on the kitchen walls—and worse, on the food I had just been preparing—and made a face.

"You wrecked dinner," I said.

"*Nega? Nega otteokae? Niga!*"

"Hey, I didn't kill the thing," I pointed out. "That was all you. Look, you've spread bits of him all over the bench. It's gonna take me ages to clean it off, and I'll have to bin every bit of food I'd got ready. That was the last of the kimchi, too."

"*Aish*," muttered JinYeong, glaring at me. He turned on his heel and stalked into the bathroom. I heard the shower start up a minute or two later; JinYeong hadn't closed the door, which probably meant he was standing beneath the shower fully clothed. I'd seen him do that once or twice. If there's anything I've learned about vampires in the last couple of months, it's that they are neat and finicky to the point of OCD when it comes to clothes and house. Well, JinYeong is, anyway. Maybe it's rude to generalise about vampires.

Around the bathroom door, I called, "How come you're back before the others, anyway?"

I don't know why I bother to ask him stuff. It's not like I understand more than a couple of the things he says on any given day, and it's not like he's going to talk to me in English, either.

I heard him say something in Korean, and caught the words *busy* and *stupid*. From that he probably meant me to infer that Zero and Athelas were busy, but had expected me to be an idiot and so had sent him ahead.

"Hah!" I said, poking my head around the door. "Says you!"

Unfortunately, JinYeong's dripping jacket was in a soggy pile on the bathroom floor and his shirt was just about to join it when I did so.

I slapped a hand over my eyes and howled, "Yuck! Close the flamin' door when you're going to do that!"

"*Kohjjoh!*" snarled JinYeong, and a wet, tarry business shirt hit me in the face.

I knew what that word meant, too; but even if I hadn't, the shirt in the face would have been pretty clear.

"Yuck!" I complained again, feeling for the door knob. I pulled the door shut and yelled through it, "Normal people close the door!"

He yelled something back, and I heard the word for person in there, followed by a negative, so I suppose he was saying that he wasn't a normal person. Yeah. 'S'if I don't know that.

I turned back toward the kitchen, peeling wet shirt and tar from my face, and grumbled under my breath. This was going to take *ages* to clean up. And how the heck were Behind creatures getting into the house, anyway?

Hang on. You don't know about Behind—or Between. I'm gunna assume you know about the human world, though, so let's start there. There's the human world, and the world of the Fae—amongst others. You might think it'd be called Faery or Fairyland, but that just shows how much *you* know. The Fae world is the world Behind the human world. Still connected to us, still insanely, dangerously close, but sorta behind our world. And then there's the space between, where it *could* be here, or *could* be there, just depending on how it feels. The sort of place where an umbrella might sometimes be a sword, and a stone gargoyle might suddenly become a bit more lifelike. The sort of place where you can die really quickly if you don't notice the shadowy changes creeping along the street toward you.

And speaking of death creeping up on people—through the front window, I could see two very familiar figures walking up the street. "Ha!" I said gloomily, toward the closed bathroom door. "Looks like they didn't trust you not to be stupid, either, Mr Slim-line suit!"

My other owners were coming home.

In the lead was Zero, my half-human, half-fae owner. Huge and almost blindingly white, with shoulders as wide as the front door, Zero has a look of pure blue ice that can freeze the sun, and a certain way of saying *Pet* that does much the same. If I stay behind him, he doesn't let anyone kill me, though, so that's pretty nice.

A step behind him was Athelas, fae steward and tea drinker. If Zero's roar could shake you to your bones with fear, Athelas could seep a chill into your bones with the softness of his voice. He *seems* harmless enough, all soft smile, laugh lines, and brown curls, with milk-coffee skin that makes him look sorta warm, you know? But he's not harmless. I know that because he's killed me about six times now.

Yeah, I'm still alive. You'll get used to that.

I watched them come up the street while the jug boiled away merrily in the background, giving off the faint stench of tar from a few spots that had splashed on it. They'd probably want tea and coffee when they got in—I could see the blood on Zero from here, and Athelas always wants tea, whether or not he's bloody. It wasn't like I could give them lunch with the kitchen in this state.

Funnily enough, they used the front door today. Usually, they don't worry about stuff like doors—or walls or, you know, natural laws of nature and that—they just slip Between and pass right through the walls.

Of course, now that you know about Behind and Between and all that weird stuff, maybe we should go back a bit. Back to this morning, maybe.

This morning was when something big and magic twitched the whole house sideways and maybe tried to turn it inside out. I grabbed the umbrella, and maybe that seems like an odd thing to be grabbing, but this umbrella isn't always an umbrella. Sometimes it's a sword—and right then it was definitely a sword, which meant that whatever was coming through Between was something that shouldn't be getting into the house.

Slender fingers pinched my right ear, tugging me away from the sword, but my fingers were already wrapped around the umbrella handle that felt like a sword grip, and I staggered sideways, pulling it out of the stand.

"*Manjiji ma*," said Jin Yeong, tugging lightly on my ear again.

"Look, the sword told me to pick it up, so who am I supposed to listen to?"

"Nae *mal dulo*," he said, threateningly.

"Yeah, but if I listen to you, what about the sword?"

Jin Yeong sighed, then reached over me and grabbed the umbrella sword. To my disappointment, it let him take it. I mean, I dunno what it would have done to stop him, but it would have been nice to see him get the magical equivalent of an electric shock again.

"*Darrawa, Petteu,*" he said, and pulled me back toward the living room by one wrist.

"I can walk by myself," I said, and as I said it, there was a knock at the door.

Nobody went to answer the front door for two reasons: First, if anyone went to the door, it should have been me, because I was the pet; second, the knock didn't come from the front door. Nope. It came from the linen closet door, which was already a sign that it was someone we didn't want in the house.

If I'd had any say in it, I would have said not to open the door. I didn't, of course. You don't ask the pet whether or not you can open the door, and by the time I realised what was happening, our uninvited guests were already inside.

So I shut my mouth. I might also have scooted just a *smidge* back behind Jin Yeong, whose fingers tightened around my wrist. It was the golden fae again; the emissary of the Enforcers, who Zero used to work for, and who were still hoping that he'd come back and join them. And this time, he'd brought a couple more friends with him.

Around Jin Yeong's arm, I saw the tightening of the golden fae's mouth as he saw Jin Yeong holding the umbrella. "Why does *that thing* have the Heirling Sword?"

Seriously. The bloke has been in the house *twice* and he's comfortable enough to insult everyone? I couldn't help feeling that he'd gotten far too confident for someone who had brought an offer to Zero and had been turned down pretty firmly.

How come Zero wasn't kicking him out?

I opened my mouth to say something rude, but I thought better of it a split second before Jin Yeong's fingers crushed my wrist. I kicked the back of his shiny shoes, then poked him in the ribs for good measure. I heard him mutter a complaint beneath his breath, but when I looked up at him, his cheeks were sharp in a dangerous smile directed at the golden fae.

"Oi. Ask him if he wants anything to eat," I muttered, tugging at a pinch of his suitcoat.

JinYeong's cheeks sharpened just a touch more, and his lips parted.

"Hello," he said in Korean that was layered through Between and very carefully understandable to the golden fae. "Would you care for something to eat?"

I was a bit disappointed when Zero, with a rumble that nearly shook the house, interrupted to demand of the golden fae, "What business is it of yours who I allow to bear my sword?"

The golden fae's female lieutenant went just the tiniest bit pale, which I took as sign of good sense, and exchanged looks with the other two fae behind the golden one.

The golden fae didn't seem to be as wise; he just kept on going. "My lord, I really must protest! The Heirling Sword is not a weapon that should be borne by such things as *that*!"

He was speaking about JinYeong, but toward Zero, which broke the glaring match between him and JinYeong and took the threat level in the room down by a decent amount.

I heard the faintest of sighs from JinYeong. "*Ashipda*!"

Stroppy blood-sucker. He just wanted to fight. Usually it was Zero he was trying to fight. I much preferred him having a go at the golden fae—I thought the fae could do with a good lesson, too, and I was about as clueless to why Zero wouldn't allow it as JinYeong apparently was. Maybe it was the big brother in Zero that came out with me, too. He wouldn't let other people fight me, either—though in my case, that was probably just as well until I got really good at fighting by myself. I mean, I *was* learning. Trying. When I wasn't dying and stuff. But there's a difference between a fully trained Behindkind and a fully trained human.

Heck, I was pretty sure there was a difference between a new-born Behindkind and a fully trained human, and I was betting the advantage wasn't going to be on the human side.

"JinYeong bears the sword when I wish him to bear it," said Zero, with finality.

That was a stretch to the truth if ever there was one: JinYeong was only bearing it because I'd been bearing it a minute or two ago, and it was even less proper for me to be doing it. Mind you, I'd rather bear the sword than bear with JinYeong, so there's that.

"Your father will be displeased."

I coughed a bit of a laugh into the shoulder of JinYeong's suit jacket, and murmured just loud enough for him to hear, "He just pull the *I'm telling your dad on you* thing on Zero?"

"Mm," JinYeong murmured back down at me, and then: "*Jaemi isseo.*"

Oh well. At least he was having fun.

"What my father thinks of it is very little to the point, is it?" said Zero, ice and fire at once. "He is not here, and I am certainly not there. I'm a member of the Enforcers, not the Family."

"But my lord, we come with an offer from the Enforcers!" protested one of the fae I hadn't seen before.

Good for him. He was probably sick of the golden fae making a huge mess of their offers. I approved. Despite the fact that I didn't like or trust the golden fae, I wanted Zero to take what he'd been offered, and the golden fae wasn't helping his own case.

What was the offer? Glad you asked. It was an offer to make sure no one bothered Zero while he made sure the humans around here were kept safe. Sounds like a job for the police, right? Well, the Enforcers kinda *are* the police—the fae version, anyway. There's no human version of what they are, either, which means that fae mostly get away with hurting humans with no one to help. Zero can help...but whether he will help or not is another question.

Zero said flatly, "I gave an answer to your proposition last time my dwelling was invaded. Why are you bothering us again?"

"A new situation has arisen," said the golden fae, scowling back at the other fae. "It has nothing to do with that previous offer, though if you're willing to think that over again—"

"I imagine that's why you've brought a few friends with you?" suggested Athelas, gently swinging his foot. There was no reason for the movement but to show the assembled fae that he was whole and hearty—which was worrying.

Because if Athelas was trying to make sure that people thought he was whole and hearty, he was probably still feeling pretty awful. It made sense: we'd only just rescued him from a torture chamber the other day. He wasn't supposed to be up and fighting when his insides were still healing.

Athelas' eyes met mine for one moment, then went back to the golden fae, faintly enquiring.

"They are here as representatives," said the fae.

"Representatives of whom?" Zero asked him, voice hard. "And what situation has arisen?"

One of the questions must have embarrassed the fae, because he went slightly more bronzy about the cheeks and chin. I reckon I could have guessed which question it was that embarrassed him, too, though I wasn't exactly sure why. It was the question he answered first.

"As always, I represent the Enforcers and Behind Law."

Jin Yeong sniffed a laugh. "*Cogitmal.*"

Lie.

I flicked a look up at him, and saw that he had his hunting look on again, though it was more glittery and amused than usual. More like when he was threatening to fight me instead of Zero.

"How interesting," said Athelas, and his voice held a layer of amusement, too. "I was under the impression that your branch of the Enforcers is very, er...*family* oriented."

"Do not tempt me," said the fae, through his teeth, "to teach you otherwise."

"I am singularly good at instruction myself," Athelas replied, with a faint smile.

"The *situation*," Zero reminded them both, the words icy cold.

I shivered a bit, and so did the hand that still clung to JinYeong's suit jacket, pressed between my chest and his arm. I let go, and maybe he thought I was going to move further into the room, because he tilted his head to glare down at me, one incisor a warning not to move.

I would have stuck out my tongue at him, but the female lieutenant was watching me, so I shoved my hands in my pockets instead and grinned at her.

"You lot want tea and coffee?" I asked.

"*No!*" said the golden fae.

"Yes," said Zero.

I saw the way his eyes met JinYeong's eyes, and the *very* slight tip of his head toward the kitchen, so I wasn't surprised when JinYeong tugged me away into the kitchen by the cuff of my sleeve. He brought the umbrella sword with us as well, which meant that while I was getting tea and coffee, I could jerk my chin at it and ask, "What's he mean, *Heirling Sword?*"

JinYeong raised both eyebrows at me and pursed his lips. That was his *not going to tell you* and *what are you going to do about it?* look.

Since the jug was still boiling, I thought about it for a bit, then said, "Heirling Sword *musen dusiya?*"

He gave a short, incredulous laugh. "*Yah, banmal?*"

"Dunno what you mean," I said. Technically, it was true. I mean, I was pretty sure he was having a go at me for not being polite enough, but I didn't actually know the word he was using. "Maybe if you spoke in English I could understand you."

His teeth showed in a snarl. "*Yah, Petteu; choshimhae.*"

I pulled a face at him. "*Wae?*"

"*Hangukmal hajima!*"

That made me grin as I filled a tray with tea and coffee and good things to eat. No way I was going to stop speaking Korean.

I'm gunna tell you something you probably don't already know. Learning Korean is *hard*. It's backward—and I mean almost literally backward—from English. And what with learning Korean and how to fight, plus how to not die when it comes to Between, my brain is just as floppy and tired as my body is, these days.

So why learn it? Well, because it annoys the heck out of the vampire.

Petty? Yeah, but then, I *am* a Pet.

What? I already told you I'm a pet. You didn't think Pet was actually my name, did you? Nah. I've got a name, but right now, everyone just calls me Pet. It's better that way. If I'm a good pet— cook the dinner, stay behind Zero, stay alive, that sort of thing— I'll get my house back to myself. For good, this time. I've got a fae agreement and everything.

I was too busy being smug about annoying JinYeong; I didn't see the way he had his head tilted—like he was listening to something—until the jug stopped boiling and I realised I couldn't hear the others talking in the living room. I took one step toward the doorway, and JinYeong also stepped swiftly forward, incisors showing.

"*Petteu*," he said, in a purr. "*Hajima*."

"Wasn't doing anything," I said, but I stepped back behind the kitchen bench. When he spoke all silky like that, with the glint of danger in his eyes, I didn't know whether or not I'd end up getting bitten.

Flamin' rude, I thought, narrowing my eyes at the doorway. It wasn't just the fact that JinYeong had unmistakeably told me I was to stay in the kitchen—it was the fact that I couldn't hear anything from the other room.

Nothing. Zilch.

Which meant Zero was doing something to make sure I couldn't hear.

Well, that wasn't on. I mean, there probably wasn't much I could do about it, but beggar me if I wasn't going to *try*. I might be the pet, but there was no reason for them to be keeping me out of the conversation again.

I spooned tea into Athelas' strainer, focused on stealing even the smallest peep of noise from the other room, and there was a clear chime of metal against metal as the spoon tapped the strainer.

As the chime lingered on the air, far longer than it should have done, I heard Athelas' voice say, very clearly, "How unusual! I was under the impression that the higher-level Family members in the human world were much better guarded than that! However did they manage to lose their hearts?"

Okay, so he could have been talking about fae falling in love, but I was gunna bet—

"That is precisely what we wish to know!" snapped the golden fae. "It is unprecedented for fae to have their hearts torn out, even those living in the human world!"

Yep. There we go.

Athelas' voice, fading with the chime on the air, said, "Dear me! A novel method for dispatching fae."

There was a professional kind of interest to his voice—like he was curious to know how the perpetrator had done it, or how he might replicate it. Maybe a faint sort of approval.

It was the kind of tone that made me shiver, reminding me that Athelas was about as deadly as Zero when it came to dealing out death and destruction. Just a bit more polite about it, maybe.

The chime was gone, but I thought I might just be able to keep hearing their voices. If I listened in *just* the right way, with a bit of Between to the hearing...

"I see no reason to help the Family," said Zero, very faint and scratchy. Whatever he was doing, it was *really hard* to get around, even now that I was using a bit of Between to make things more clear. "Our interests...not aligned."

Flaming heck. I was losing him.

I saw a bit of Between edging Zero's coffee cup, and touched a finger to that instead of concentrating on Athelas' tea strainer. The cup could also have been an ornament—well, *was* an ornament if you saw it the right way Between. Even now, I could see the filigree and jet edges to it. That was probably because it was the cup Zero used all the time, and Between seems to attach itself to stuff and places so that Behind can seep through into the human world. Like a disease or something.

And maybe I could use that connection to Between to give me a bit of an opening into the living room. I turned around with the coffee mug as if I was just going to fetch the coffee tin from the upper cupboard and spoon some in. Like Zero drank instant coffee instead of the drip pots I usually made.

"In addition, there is...information. The Family will release that...to you...culprit is apprehended."

Just a bit more, and I had it. Just a *little* bit more.

"*Petteu*," said JinYeong in my ear, with an unmistakeable edge to his voice. He spoke in Korean, but the meaning came through Between, loud and clear when he said, "If your ears become too big, I will bite them."

He had that look again where I wasn't sure if he was going to bite me or not when I turned around, so I shut down what I was doing pretty quickly. Reckon I've already had enough vampire spit running around my system to last me a lifetime.

I got some of it in worse ways than others, too.

"That reminds me," I said. Zero's always trying to teach me that I need to use surprise in my attacks. "You *kissed* me the other night! It's bad enough that I have to be drugged up because you bit me! Why've I gotta be kissed as well?"

And yeah, I know he kissed me because he was dosing me up on vampire spit, but he could have—

Well. To be fair, I didn't like it when he licked his finger and shoved it in my mouth that one time, either. If it came to that, I didn't much like being bitten. There isn't a good way to get vampire spit. No one should have to ingest vampire spit.

JinYeong shrugged, and this time when he spoke, it was pure Korean without any edge of Between to translate it. "*Nae maum-daelo hae.*"

He spoke in a swift, self-satisfied mumble that made it hard to separate the words, even if I had recognised them.

I retorted, "Speak in English!"

"*Shilloh.*"

Don't wanna.

Well, wasn't *that* flaming typical?

"Yeah, well if you try it again, I'll flamin' bite you," I grumbled.

One of JinYeong's brows went up. "*Haebwa, Petteu,*" he said, and sauntered away toward the living room.

I followed him out there, and trotted around between the fae like the good little pet I was, grinning at the female lieutenant as I pushed the tray at her. Her lips curved just the smallest bit, and I saw a gleam of white.

Heck yeah. On the Zero scale of emotion, that was a definite grin.

I sidled around behind them once my tray was empty, trying to make my footsteps as light as possible. If I could *just* edge around behind them, there was a good chance I could stay and listen and...

"Pet," said Zero. "Kitchen."

Oh well, there went *that* plan.

CHAPTER TWO

I DIDN'T GET TO HEAR A SINGLE WORD MORE, AND BY THE TIME I could get back into the living room, the fae were gone. The three psychos went out straight after, too, even though the time was going on for three in the morning by then. Zero wouldn't tell me where they were going, which was flamin' annoying, and Jin Yeong smirked at me on the way out, which was even more annoying.

And now they were all back home, after spending all the morning and early afternoon out without a single word of explanation.

Flamin' typical.

I chucked the rag I'd been wiping the kitchen down with onto the bench, giving up on cleaning the tar for a little while. I came out into the hall just in time to meet Zero and Athelas at the door like a good pet should. Zero had a tiny tear in the shoulder of his leather jacket as well as the blood I'd already seen on his jeans through the window, and Athelas' usually mildly untidy curls were dishevelled.

Behind me, the bathroom door opened, wafting a cloud of

scent that heralded JinYeong's re-emergence. Zero took in JinYeong, his hair still wet from his shower, and his blue eyes flicked to the small splattering of black blood that extended from the kitchen and into the living room. Then those eyes came back to rest on me.

"Don't blame me!" I said. "JinYeong's the one who messed up the kitchen. I'm cleaning it."

"Clean your face first," said Zero.

"Don't tell me I'm gunna turn into a tar beastie or something, now," I grumbled.

"I think not," said Athelas. "But that fluid tends to bleach the skin when left too long."

"That's JinYeong's fault, too," I called, ducking back into the kitchen to use the sink there. I'd be gassed if I went into the bathroom. "He threw his shirt at me."

In the living room, JinYeong protested in a stream of injured Korean that was too fast for me to follow.

"Dear me," Athelas' voice said, as I heard them entering the kitchen behind me. "How novel!"

I snorted a mix of water and black blood through the streaming tap. "If that's what you want to call it. Who have you two been fighting this time, anyway?"

"No one."

"What, you just rolled in some blood you were passing or something?" I turned my head to look at them, dripping blackened water into the silvery sink. "*And* there's a tear in Zero's jacket."

"When my lord says he has not been fighting, he refers only to fighting to bloodshed," said Athelas. "The blood and the tear are two separate incidents, nor was the blood pursuant to the fighting."

"Busy morning, then."

"Indeed."

I came away from the sink wet-faced but clean, and dabbed at my face with my t-shirt. "Oi. If you lot want lunch, it's gunna have to wait. I gotta finish cleaning the kitchen first, and then find something else for dinner. I can do tea and coffee, though."

If they were having tea and coffee, there was a good chance they were going to discuss what they were up to. I didn't like fae popping in and out of the house at random times, but I liked Zero and Athelas disappearing without telling me what they were up to even less. When they didn't tell me what was going on, surrounding humans tended to get hurt. If I wasn't there, there was no one to remind them to be careful with the humans.

But Zero said, "No coffee."

"Is there any necessity to be quite so severe?" protested Athelas.

Zero's eyes met mine again. "Oh, I think so. There have been a few too many vibrations around the house since last night."

"If you're trying to tell me something, you're gunna have to be more clear about it," I said. He might be hinting that he'd noticed me eavesdropping last night, but if he wasn't and I was just feeling guilty, I didn't want to give the game away. "Do you lot take lessons in being obscure?"

"Something like that," agreed Athelas.

"I suppose JinYeong takes lessons in being an annoying shower-hog, too."

"*Yah*," said JinYeong through his teeth, stepping up into the kitchen.

Ignoring him, I started wiping down the kitchen bench, and said to Zero, "You lot were gone for a while."

"We took as long as we needed to take."

"Yeah? And what takes about twelve hours to do, then?"

Zero's eyes went a shade bluer. "Typically, working a curse-breaking enchantment into a sword."

"Draining a fully armoured fae of blood," mentioned Athelas.

Jin Yeong said a short, mocking sentence that made no sense to me, but I understood the dark amusement in his eyes.

I blinked. Opened and shut my mouth. They were *teasing* me? "Oi!" I said at last. "You can't do that!"

"If one knows the right people, one can certainly do so," Athelas said. "Or perhaps you're referring to the armoured fae, in which case I'm happy to inform you that you're still incorrect."

"Hang on," I said, side-tracked. "How come you said a fully armoured fae? Does it take less time if they're unarmoured?"

"Certainly," said Athelas. "Fae tend to wear armour that enhances their physical aptitudes—among them, blood flow. There's a reserve contained in the armour."

"Your armour has *veins*? That's disgusting."

"Perhaps," Zero said. "But it gives fae a prospective five minutes longer to survive if things go wrong."

"Yeah, it's still gross. Anyway, *talking* about blood, how'd you get that blood on your jeans?"

"I fell into some blood."

"What, someone just left it out for you to fall into?"

"Pet," said Zero. "If you've finished cleaning the kitchen, maybe you could start on dinner?"

"Yeah, maybe," I said. So he wasn't gunna talk, huh? "But I reckon I'll need some more groceries, now that someone spilled tar all over the stuff I was making. Anyway, I'm not finished cleaning it, not by a long shot. You lot sure you don't want tea and coffee now that the bench is clean?"

Athelas looked at Zero, who looked away.

"Don't ask me," he said, though I wasn't sure if he was talking to me or Athelas. "I'm going out again. Do as you please. Just don't leave the Pet without supervision again when the house has recently been opened to Behind."

"Hey, I'm not the one who made a mess on the kitchen floor," I pointed out.

Jin Yeong hissed in annoyance and made a grab at me, but I darted behind Zero.

"You splatter the kitchen with my blood, and you'll just have more to clean up," I told him, from behind Zero's arm. "*And* there'll be no one to clean it for you."

"You're so energetic these days!" said Athelas to Jin Yeong. It sounded like an off-hand remark, but there was a sarcastic look to his eyes that I was pretty sure meant something.

Jin Yeong was pretty sure, too. He threw Athelas a stormy, sulky look, but couldn't seem to decide what part of the remark he could take exception to, so he went back into the living room.

"Clean the rest of the kitchen before you make tea," said Zero, and followed Jin Yeong.

That left me with Athelas, who said, smiling gently, "China does reverberate so strongly, doesn't it?" and joined the other two.

I was about as unsure as Jin Yeong had been earlier, if he was mocking me or trying to tell me something. Heck, with Athelas, it could be both. So I cleaned the rest of the kitchen without trying to listen to what was happening in the next room, and only started making tea and coffee after I heard Zero going out into the back yard.

Athelas was sitting in his usual chair when I bought the tray out. I put the biscuits down next to him and poured the tea. He usually does it for himself, but what the heck? I'd been working on my tea making skills, and this was the *good* stuff. I wanted him to smell the scent of it on the air.

Athelas' eyes dwelt on the curling steam for a moment, then rose to meet mine, faintly amused. "Well, Pet?"

As I put the teapot back down, I asked, "What's going on with all the armoury fae and stuff, anyway?"

"Believe it or not, Pet, there are some things which I, too, believe it best for you not to know."

"Yeah, but that doesn't stop you telling me when you want to."

Athelas shrugged one shoulder. "That entirely depends upon the reason for which it is best not to tell you, don't you think?"

"Maybe if I think about that for another ten years it'll make sense," I muttered. "What's the current rate of exchange, anyway?"

"I'm not sure I know what you mean, Pet."

I grinned at him. "Yeah? I'm pretty sure you do."

"Stop trying to bribe my steward, Pet," said Zero.

I jumped. Flaming heck! I hadn't even heard him come in. "Wasn't bribing him," I said. "I was just um, keeping up with fae economics."

"You said you had some groceries to buy," he said, pointedly.

"Yeah, but—"

"We'll take dinner at the usual time."

Usual time, yeah *right*. There was no usual time—just things like tar beasties breaking into the place and murderers to catch and stuff that meant we ate whenever I cooked.

I huffed, and got up. "Fine," I said, heading for the door. "Talk secrets. I'm taking money for the groceries."

I had my *own* stuff to do. I needed to go check up on Daniel, anyway. If they wanted to be secretive about their investigations, I would just use that secrecy to nip off and do what I needed to do.

And then, I thought, stuffing my hands in my pockets with a good shove that stretched the stitches in the lining, *then* I would figure out a way to find out what they were up to. I'd just make sure Daniel was okay first.

When I first met Daniel, I didn't know he was a lycanthrope. I thought he was just a stroppy teenager. These days, I knew he was a stroppy lycanthrope—one who'd been injured while helping defend me, so I felt obliged to make sure he was all right. Which would have been much easier if Zero hadn't secreted him away somewhere to stay safe and heal.

And of course, because Zero didn't want me finding Daniel, I had to do it quietly. I'd found him a little while ago—even had a good place where I could keep an eye on him—but the problem was, I'd had to tell someone I was a cop to be able to do it.

Well, I didn't exactly tell her I was a cop; I just didn't correct her when she made the assumption that I was one. She was so pleased with herself for figuring it out, and who was I to pop her bubble? Especially not when her room was the perfect place to scope out where Daniel was staying without anybody seeing me. I was betting Zero had spies there.

I took my time walking there, partly because I wanted to go by a roundabout way so that Athelas and Zero wouldn't notice if they happened to be looking out the window, and partly because I was wearing sandals instead of my sneakers. I wasn't used to them, and I'd already started with blisters by the time I got to the end of a couple blocks.

After that, I took my time because I caught sight of someone in the shop windows across the street—someone who was taking every turning I was taking, and holding back just far enough for me not to be able to tell who it was in the reflections.

Flaming heck. There was someone following me again.

Hopefully it was just the old mad bloke who used to live across the road. He was pretty harmless, but he liked to follow me around and pinch food off me. Sometimes I left it out for him on purpose. Which reminded me—I'd have to leave out a bit of food where he could get at it, now that Zero had started warding the house against unexpected visitors.

I didn't want the old bloke to think he could get away with following me without me noticing it, though. And if it was Upper Management instead of him, I reckoned I wanted *them* to know it, too, so I turned left when I got to Palfreyman's Arcade and nipped past the fountain to hide behind the edge of the toilet block there.

At least I knew it wasn't one of the more dangerous Behind beasties; those ones were pretty easy to spot, even through a store window reflection. If I hadn't been able to see them, I would have felt the edge of Between that they carried with them, too. Sorta like the stink of Faeryland or something. If I'd sensed that, no way I'd be hiding behind the loos, waiting to jump out at—

Detective Tuatu. It was Detective Tuatu who appeared around the edge of brickwork.

"Flaming heck!" I said, and came out. "It was you!"

"What was me?" said the Detective, trying to look like he hadn't just jumped a mile.

"Following me. Thought I saw someone."

"I wasn't following you," said Detective Tuatu. He sounded a bit miffed. "I just walked up behind you. I wanted to check on you, but you were walking too fast to catch up with. I was just about to call you."

"Oh. I'm alive."

"I see that. You didn't answer my text messages."

"Did you message me?" I made a grab for my phone and fetched it out of my back pocket. The screen lit with messages as soon as I tipped it up, and I grimaced. "Oh. Sorry 'bout that. I was busy dying and cutting through moonlight."

"What?"

"Nothing. I was a bit busy the last couple of days, that's all. How's things, anyway? Someone still trying to frame you?"

"No one's thrown another body at me, if that's what you mean. But one of your..."

"Psychos?" I suggested, by way of helping him out. I knew why he didn't want to say *owners*. Tuatu didn't like the fact that I was someone's pet. I mean, it wasn't me in particular—he would have been upset at any nearly-eighteen-year-old being owned by fae. He was still pretty stressed about the existence of fae, if it came to that.

"Yes, one of *them*," he said, without gratitude. "One of them, the quiet one in tweed, called me the other night. They want help with one of their cases."

I nearly said, "*They* want help?" but it occurred to me at the same time that this was a very good opportunity to learn what they were up to. There was no way Zero would agree to helping the golden fae do anything unless he'd been offered something very important in return.

"You find out anything?" I asked, instead. "Come down to the café. I'll buy you a cuppa."

I could still catch up with Daniel afterward. There were a couple things I wanted to ask Detective Tuatu about.

He looked a bit unsure at that. "Shouldn't I be buying your cuppa? Have you got any money?"

"A bit," I said. I had the shopping money, and as far as I was concerned, a cup of coffee that I didn't have to make was a fair repayment for doing the shopping. A sorta tax, you know?

Maybe I'd been living with fae for too long already.

"Is that what you were messaging me for, then?" I asked, leading the way out of the arcade. There was a coffee shop across the street and up the road a bit; I'd never been in there, but it always looked warm and wooden and leathery, with booths further back in if you didn't want your voice to carry too far.

"Yes—I had some follow up questions, and neither of them were answering their phones."

"All right," I said, hauling open the coffee shop door. "Quick, get the last booth at the back!"

Tuatu just shot me a look, so it was left to me to slide into the booth before another eager customer took it. It was a pretty busy coffee shop—well, maybe it was a café. I could smell food cooking, even if the primary scent was coffee.

Tuatu slid into the other side of the booth and rejected the menu the waiter tried to give him. "Just tea," he said. "Earl grey, no sugar."

"Coffee, black, no sugar," I said, and the waiter left us alone. "What'd you find out?"

"My boss think it's a once-off," he said.

Someone in the living room had said *hearts* in the plural, I was pretty sure. And it had been fae hearts. Mind you, would the human cops know fae if they saw them, even if they *were* dead? Their blood was blue, so it should be obvious, but I had a feeling that we humans didn't always see what was actually there.

"You reckon there's more?"

"*They* do," said Tuatu.

"My psychos?"

"Yes. And I've been digging through digital case files since they left—someone has been hiding similar cases and funnelling them to the same two detectives. There have been more on the mainland, too, being sent to specific detectives in each main city. The detectives here weren't happy about me nosing around, so I thought one of those three could come and have a word with him."

"That's weird. I thought the psychos were gunna sort that stuff."

"You and me both. They said there was some extra muscle behind all this. Something about family business and more access than usual."

I hadn't thought there was much more access to be had than Zero and Athelas usually got.

"Maybe it's Upper Management again."

The detective looked uneasy. "I certainly hope not."

"You said you had some questions. Not just about my psychos helping you get some information, I s'pose."

"Yeah." He hesitated. "I need to know what it was that tore out that heart—well, all of them, since I suppose they were all done by the same...person."

"How come? Isn't that something my lot's going to be looking for?"

"Yes, but the way the case files have been hidden makes it easier to look for them if I have keywords. And even if we don't know about fae and Behind and all that, we're still capable of looking for a murder weapon if we know what we're looking for, you know."

"Didn't you get any CCTV footage or anything?"

"We got it," said Detective Tuatu grimly. "The footage wasn't...exactly clear."

"Right," I said, as though I knew what he was talking about.

Tuatu sipped his tea, and frowned. "Didn't they tell you? They asked me to make some copies for them so they could have a look at it, too."

"Oi. You see the fight?" I asked, by way of changing the subject.

Tuatu grinned. "I wouldn't call it a fight. More of a dusting. One of the crime scene boys was getting a bit too bossy for his own good and tried to stop the big one from getting in. If he'd spoken before he acted, it might have been all right, but he just tried to haul him back by the jacket as he passed."

"Reckon he wishes he hadn't, now."

"Probably. No bones were broken—and you can thank him for me, if you want. I thought Phillips was going to come out of it with worse than a decent winding."

"Zero musta been in a good mood," I said. "How'd he get blood on him, anyway? He wouldn't tell me."

Detective Tuatu frowned, fiddling with his necklace pendant. "That's what I've been trying to figure out. I don't seem to be able to remember it properly, and I don't like that."

"One of those things, was it?" I said knowingly. "Reckon there were a few other um, people there, then."

"Yes!" he said, pointing the pendant at me. "That was it! There were a few others—they were annoyed about a sword, as far as I could make out."

I couldn't help the way my brows went up. "You saw a sword?"

"No, they were just arguing about it. Then one of them made a leap for...for Zero. That right! That's what happened with the blood. Zero chucked him across the crime scene and messed with the blood evidence, and the bloke came after him again. They both got a bit of blood on them. The female one dragged him off, but Zero must have thought she was coming after him instead."

Shame. I liked her. "She get hurt?"

"Not her!" he said, with a bit more enthusiasm. "By the end of it, he had a knife to her throat, but she had one at his stomach. They weighed up for a bit and separated without talking."

I grinned. That was pretty normal for both of them. At least I knew what had happened now—and what they'd been doing this morning. The thought of it made me grin a bit more, but while I was congratulating myself and deciding what else I should ask, Detective Tuatu's phone bingled.

The screen lit up, and I was pretty sure it said *Message from: Thing One*. I hid a grimace behind my coffee mug, because I was pretty sure there was only one person Tuatu would put in his phone like that—mostly because he probably couldn't bring himself to label Zero as *The Fae, Pet's Owner*, or *Lord Sero*.

Hopefully I was wrong, but...

Tuatu looked down at his phone, and closed his eyes for a brief, exasperated moment.

Oh yeah, it was definitely Zero who had texted him.

He said, "You didn't know about any of this, did you?"

"Define *didn't know*—" I began.

"They didn't tell you anything about it. *I* wasn't supposed to tell you about it."

I hedged, "Define *wasn't supp*—"

"As in, I was just threatened with dismemberment if I tell you anything."

"Whoops. Sorry 'bout that."

"Really? Because you're grinning, and I don't think you are."

"If you don't tell 'em, I won't," I suggested cheerfully. "No need for dismemberment. Just sorta...keep me in the loop."

"I'm not telling you anything else!"

"Spoil sport. All right, so long as you don't tell 'em you told me anything, you're golden. I'm not gunna rat."

"That makes me feel *much* better!" Tuatu looked down at his mostly finished cup of tea, and said in a voice of horror, "This was a bribe, wasn't it!"

"Nah. It's only a bribe if you know about it," I told him. "It was more of a distraction."

"Great!" he said. "Now I've got to go and tell them what I found out without looking guilty!"

"You should practise!" I called after him, as he got up and headed for the door. "Tell me about it first!"

He didn't take me up on it, of course. I grinned a bit and finished my coffee, then trotted back along my way to Morgana's place with a warm, sunny feeling even though the days had started to chill off. The coffee was *good*. I'd have to go back to that café more often. Maybe I could come back on the way home and get coffee for the others. Now that I knew a bit about what they were investigating, I felt more kindly toward them. Hopefully, Tuatu would be sensible enough not to tell them I knew.

I WAS FEELING THE CHILL OF EVENING ON MY TOES BY THE TIME I got to the old three-story place where Morgana lived. It was a relief to step inside, though it wasn't much warmer in there. At least there wasn't a cool, sneaky breeze. The place was as quiet as it always was, the wooden stairs echoing beneath my feet without any other sound to soften it. One of these days, I'd probably meet with the other kids that lived here, but Morgana said they were shy, and I'd never seen 'em.

I let myself into the room on the left-hand side of the third story hallway, and walked into a shiny nest that could have belonged to a bower bird that liked reflective bits and bobs instead of the blue stuff that bower birds usually collect. Mirrors and other shiny patches covered most of the walls, tilted in odd directions to give the perfect view out of all the windows if you sat on the bed.

On the bed, pale and panda-eyed as always, was Morgana, far too cheerful for her gothic appearance.

"You're just in time!" she said. "I got a card game in the mail!"

"I'm not supposed to play games," I said, but that was only for appearances' sake. Actually, I didn't know how to play most card games, and I'd learned that Morgana was terrifyingly good at poker.

"You're just saying that 'cos I whopped you last time," Morgana said, undeceived. "It's not poker, anyway. Want a coffee?"

"Nah, just had one. You?"

"Please."

I went and made coffee in Morgana's tiny kitchen. And if you're thinking it's rude for her to offer coffee and make me get one for her, you're dead wrong. Morgana can't walk—well, not most of the time, anyway. She's got stuff to help her start again, but I've never seen her use it. I haven't seen her out of her bed, if it comes to that, though I s'pose she must get out of it for the loo and to get her dinner. Maybe her parents help her with that stuff, though—but I haven't met them, even though they live across the hall.

I passed her the coffee and plopped down on the bed, shuffling backwards until my shoulders hit the wall. There was a good spot there where I could see nearly everything from the windows without being seen myself.

That put my sandaled feet in view, and Morgana tilted her chin at my toes. "What happened to your sneakers? They were really cool."

"Yeah," I said gloomily. They'd been flaming comfortable, too. "I know. I was at a crime scene and they got bloody. The v—my um, partner cleaned 'em for me, but they haven't come out right."

Morgana made a face at the tv. "I probably wouldn't want them after that, anyway. That's gross."

I couldn't help grinning, and she must have caught it in the reflection of the telly.

"What?"

"Dunno. You just look all goth and hardcore, so I didn't expect you to be worried about blood."

"Me either!" she said. "The concept's okay, but it turns out I faint at the sight of blood, so…"

"That's pretty inconvenient, isn't it?"

Morgana looked surprised. "Why? It's not like I see blood every day. I can go for years without seeing blood."

"What, so period blood's okay?"

She shrugged. "I don't get periods. Don't ask me why."

"That's weird."

"Yeah," said Morgana, grinning. "But pretty convenient!"

"What about when you cut yourself on stuff?"

"I don't cut myself. I mostly stay in this room, too—where am I gunna get hurt?"

"Yeah, but still—"

"Wouldn't it be weirder if I was seeing blood every day?"

I opened my mouth to disagree, but I remembered just in time that my life was hardly the yardstick by which to measure normal. "I s'pose."

"Even in your job, you wouldn't see blood every day."

I thought about Jin Yeong's blood bags in the fridge, and grinned. "Yeah. 'Course not. That would be weird. Oi. He been moving much?"

"Daniel? Yeah. He saw me last night when I was looking out the window."

"What'd he do?"

To my surprise, Morgana chuckled. "Flipped the bird, what else?"

"Yeah, he's a pretty rude bloke," I said, more careful than usual when I peeked out the window. I didn't want Daniel—or, worse, his handlers—to catch sight of me.

I saw the top of his head: he was sitting backward in his bed, with his feet on his pillow and his back to his handler. Either he didn't want to look at the bloke, or he was still annoyed with him for not letting him out of the room.

"He's stopped throwing his food at 'em, though," added Morgana. "I think he was getting too hungry. He's had a visitor today, too."

"Really? They let someone in to see him?"

"Nah, but I reckon the bloke was there after him. He stayed out on the street, but I'm pretty sure he was looking up at Daniel's window. He a cop, too?"

"Nope," I said sharply. "What'd he look like?"

"I thought you might ask," Morgana said, sounding pleased with herself. "I got a couple pictures for you."

"Beauty!" I said, forgetting that I was supposed to be a cool policewoman and not a soon-to-be-eighteen year old. "Nice work! He didn't see you, did he?"

"'Course not!" she said, with a bit of indignation to her voice. "I'm good at not being seen!"

"Then how come Daniel flipped you the bird?"

She grinned. "I wasn't trying not to be seen, then. This is the bloke. Recognise him?"

I looked at her phone, and felt a chill. There was a big, slightly balding bloke wearing a jeans-and-jean-jacket combo that didn't hide his muscles, and beside him was a tall, thin figure I recognised very well. I asked with a tight throat, "What about the other bloke next to him?"

"What other bloke?" She took the phone back, and tilted it. "You must need glasses. That's not a bloke, that's a shadow on the house."

"Yeah, my bad," I said, grabbing the phone again. It wasn't a shadow on the building—it was the same kind of mothman type Behind creature I'd met once before. The sorta creature where you look at it and forget that you're looking at it straight away.

The sorta creature that has another face underneath the face it wears on top—all feelers and twittering antennae and huge, unblinking black eyes that burn themselves into your soul. "I don't recognise the human. The bloke, I mean. I don't recognise him."

Morgana made a disappointed face, but said, "I'll send it to you anyway. What's your number?"

I gave it to her, and when the photo came through, I looked at it again, more closely. Yeah, the mothman was definitely there. I would have to figure out a way to ask Athelas, without making him suspicious, why some Behind creatures didn't show up on film to humans. Well, to *normal* humans, anyway: obviously I wasn't a normal one. Or maybe it was just that I'd seen one of the Sandmen's real faces. They're kinda hard to forget.

I only stayed for a couple of hours; long enough to be talked into being trounced in poker and drink another mug of coffee, long enough to make sure Daniel was starting to eat, and that he looked pretty much as happy as I could expect to see him. I still had to make dinner for the psychos, after all.

I headed home, nipping into the grocery store to buy a few token groceries to prove I'd been doing what I said I'd been doing, and make sure we had dinner tonight. I also stopped briefly at the specialty tea store in the Wellington Court. There was a good selection of teas there, and I'd had my eye on a Tassie-produced lavender earl grey that I thought might come in handy to soften up Athelas a bit every now and then.

Athelas and Jin Yeong were in the living room when I got back home, but Zero wasn't in the house. I made a bee-line for the kitchen to put away the few groceries I'd bought and make tea and coffee. It was more likely that Athelas or Jin Yeong would talk to me than it was that Zero would. Moreover, both of them were much more likely to talk when they were fed up with tea-and-biscuits and blood respectively. I didn't want them to know that I'd met Detective Tuatu, but I did want to know what else I could find out. It might be fae dying that they were interested in, but it was never *just* fae dying. I had to make sure that the humans were looked after, too; and that was very hard to do when they wouldn't include me.

I didn't even know why they wouldn't include me. It wasn't like they took me with them everywhere, but lately they'd started to include me more and more in their investigations: like a sort of useful beast of burden, yeah, but at least I was there with them.

So why hadn't I been allowed to go to this crime scene, or even know what was happening? Was it because of what it was, or the people who had brought it to the psychos' attention?

Whatever it was, I was going to find out. So I put a blood bag in my pocket to warm it up for JinYeong as the jug boiled, and carefully made Athelas' tea.

The scent of lavender wafted gently after me as I stepped down into the living room and plopped JinYeong's bag of blood gently down beside him instead of just chucking it at him. I saw the way that Athelas' eyes almost closed before resting, curiously, on me.

"Allow me to congratulate you upon your interrogation skills, Pet," he said.

JinYeong, looking up from his blood bag with eyes half-lidded in contentment, sent me a mocking look. "The blood is good," he said in Korean. "Am I grateful, I wonder?"

I stuck my tongue out at both of them. I hadn't thought I was *that* obvious, but here we were. They were both letting me know they knew what I was up to, and that I wasn't going to get anything out of them.

"Shove over," I said to JinYeong, who was lounging over my side of the couch as well as his own. I reinforced the demand by pushing his shoulder away from my side of the backrest. "Let me guess—Zero said I'm not allowed to know what's going on?"

"*Maja*," said JinYeong, nudging his shoulder back to where it had been, which meant it was touching me.

I glared at him and nearly said *"Look, blood breath,"* but I remembered just in time that I was meant to be winkling information out of them both, and said instead, "This is *my* side."

"Don't care," he murmured around the blood-bag, the meaning crystal clear with a Between edge. "This side is *warm*. I'm sitting here."

"It's warm because a human is sitting here," I complained. "You can't just sit on my side 'cos it's warm—yours will always be cold because you're flaming cold."

"Pet," said JinYeong, tilting his head back to gaze up at me, eyes as liquid as the blood he drank. "Was I not warm when I held you close and murmured in your ear?"

"Dear me," said Athelas, his voice lightly amused.

"Don't say it like that!" I protested, shoving JinYeong's head away this time. "It makes it sound weird! Are you drunk?"

"*Maja*," he said again, and chuckled a bloody chuckle against my shoulder.

"You're quite invested in our work these days, JinYeong," Athelas said, breathing out a whisp of steam. "How singularly pleasant to see you intent on ah, pleasing my lord!"

JinYeong made a soft *tch*! of a laugh and purred a short stream of Korean at Athelas that began with something very like *invested? What investment?* and ended with *food is good, that's all*.

It was obvious that he hadn't meant me to understand it, because there was no touch of Between to aid my understanding. I wasn't sure if he was talking about my cooking or my blood, so I said, "You better not be talking about me," just to startle him, and added, "You know what I think?"

JinYeong's eyes flicked up to my face, as startled as I would have liked, but Athelas only sipped his tea. "I am positively agog, Pet."

"Yeah, I bet. I think this murder of yours is—"

"I don't believe," said Athelas lightly, "that any of us mentioned a murder."

"Yeah, but Zero came back with blood on him that *you* said wasn't from him half killing someone, so I reckon it's a pretty good bet. Is Zero keeping me out of it 'cos of the murder, or 'cos of who asked him to investigate it?"

"*Yokshi, Petteu!*" said Jin Yeong, laughing softly.

"If you think that the application of this *very* delightful tea will cause me to become in any way more open-mouthed, I fear you are doomed to disappointment."

"Reckon that means it's because of who asked you," I said.

"At any other time, I would be fascinated to discover exactly how you arrived at that conclusion, but since I fear you'll only interpret that as something else wholly unintended, I think it safer not to do so."

"Oh, is that why?" I said, unconvinced. Athelas was *technically* harder to read than the other two, but there was a kind of twisted logic to him that made him easier to read than Zero, in general—and even than Jin Yeong, on occasion. I was pretty sure I was right. "Anyway, I've been helping you lot with your investigations for the last couple of months, so I reckon there's something different about this one. Those fae asked you to investigate, too, so I reckon they've offered you something in exchange. Reckon it's something I'm not supposed to know about."

"Good heavens, Pet!" Athelas said placidly. "Don't overtax yourself, will you?"

Jin Yeong, wedging his shoulder against mine even more firmly, tilted his head and said in Korean, "Annoying Pets shouldn't *yap yap yap.*"

I elbowed him, and yelped when he bit my shoulder. "Oi! You can't do that! He can't do that, can he?"

"It's certainly inadvisable," said Athelas, as Jin Yeong threw his empty blood bag on the coffee table.

I had the feeling he was talking to Jin Yeong rather than

answering me, but I said anyway, "Great. Am I gunna go to sleep again?"

"Did not bite so much as that," murmured Jin Yeong. Oh, so *now* he wanted to be understood?

"I think not," said Athelas; but even if he hadn't said it, I would have been able to guess.

I was still a little bit faster and stronger than usual with the last bit of vampire spit I'd had running through my system, and instead of the lethargy I'd felt spread through my body the first couple times it happened, only my shoulder and arm grew numb. The rest of me, though—the rest of me felt sparkling and alive and very slightly inclined to bite back.

"*Hajima*," said Jin Yeong warningly, catching my eye.

"Wasn't doing anything!" I shot back. "Stop biting me, you flamin' blood sucker!"

He grinned, and lounged back to take up even more of the couch.

"I *reckon*," I said again, stubbornly going back to my point because I was pretty sure Jin Yeong had only bitten me to distract me from it, "I reckon that they offered you something. Maybe some information. And I reckon—"

"I think not, Pet," said Athelas, with finality in his soft voice. "I'm of the same mind as Zero when it comes to this particular matter."

"You mean you lot are gunna keep ducking in and out and not telling me *anything*?" I demanded.

"*Maja*," said Jin Yeong, far too cheerfully.

"'S'pose that means it has something to do with Zero, then," I muttered. Even Jin Yeong told me stuff sometimes. He told it to me in Korean so that there was only a thirty percent chance I'd understand him, but at least he *talked*. And Athelas liked to tell me stuff without really *telling* me—probably for the fun of watching to see if I'd get it or not—but again, at least he talked.

And that—that made me realise exactly what it must be that

was stopping Zero from talking. Or at least, a part of it, because there had to be more to it than that.

I said, "Someone's been murdering people like my parents again, haven't they?" without surprise. Of course the murderer was back. The psychos were just waiting around here until someone else was murdered like that again, after all. If the fae had bargained with them to take a case, they would have had to offer something big enough to tempt Zero. Information on the murderer might just be enough to interest him, but I was betting it wasn't all he'd been offered.

"Who has been talking to the Pet?" demanded Zero, striding into the room. "I told *both* of you—"

Jin Yeong spluttered a laugh into the corner of the room, and crinkles appeared by the corners of Athelas' eyes. Zero breathed out the faintest sigh of annoyance.

"I see," he said.

Athelas sipped his tea, and said to me, "My lord evidently prefers that you refrain from polluting the atmosphere with your suppositions."

"Pretty sure he just wishes I hadn't caught on," I remarked, catching Zero's eye. If his face had been expressionless before, now it was pretty much stone. "What else did they offer you? 'Cos I reckon they had to offer you more than that."

"Whether or not they did is not your concern," Zero said.

"Reckon that means yes," I said, catching a brief flicker of surprise from him. I grinned. "Anyway, who's gunna save Athelas if I'm not there to help you lot?"

There was a very small, tea-soaked cough from Athelas' side of the room, but his voice said easily enough, "I suppose I will simply have to do the best I can, Pet."

"What am I supposed to do while you're all gone?" I asked. Oh, there was no way I wasn't getting in on the investigation. They were *my* psychos, and if the golden fae had offered something important enough to make Zero change his mind on something he'd been so much against, I was going to make sure he got that information.

"Behave yourself," said Zero. Maybe he saw the determined expression on my face.

"Oh. Well, wouldn't it be better if—"

"No."

"Yeah, but—"

"No."

I sighed. "You're no fun, you know that? The bloke killed my parents, you know—I should be allowed to know what's going on."

Zero's mouth opened, but he didn't speak. Just as I was about to prompt him, there was a hurried *bang bang bang!* from the front door. Like someone had decided to knock and then done it in a hurry because they were scared.

"Flaming heck!" I said, jumping. "We're getting pretty popular these days, aren't we?"

Zero strode across to the window, carefully twitched one of the curtains aside, and then shut it again. "Don't open the door," he said, as I was getting up.

"Yeah, but it's the *front* door!" I protested. "They're not trying to get in through the linen closet, at least!"

"We don't have time for visitors," he said.

"Why? What are we doing?"

Something metallic flickered in the air, and I caught at the black part of it without thinking. There in my hand was one of my practice knives, point facing out as if I'd meant to do it.

"Come upstairs, Pet," said Zero.

"What, we're doing practice again? Beaut!"

"I was under the impression that you were finding your training more irksome lately."

"Yeah, well, being killed six times changes a person's mind."

Zero's eyes lightened with amusement. "No matter how well I teach you, you'll never best Athelas."

"Yeah, yeah," I said. "Anyway, I've got a handicap because Jin Yeong bit me, so you gotta go easy on me."

At least I was a bit more hopped up on vampire spit at the moment; that was bound to help a bit, even if my arm still felt dead. Maybe I'd even get a chance to score a hit against Zero if he'd take it easy on me.

———

CHAPTER THREE

———

GET IN A HIT? TAKE IT EASY? FAT CHANCE! ALL I GOT WERE bruises, all up and down my legs and a toe that might have been broken or might just have been me being a wuss.

"Next time, wear your boots," said Zero, when I was a sweaty, pulpy mess of welts, already colourful bruises, and new carpet burn. Upstairs is *not* my favourite place to train.

"Can't we practise outside next time?" I complained, rotating my shoulder. At least the numbness had worn off, but that just meant it hurt more. "Oi. Where have Athelas and JinYeong gone?"

There was an emptiness to the lower house that I could feel seeping up the stairs. Now that I was used to people being here with me all the time, the lack of them was like a physical sensation.

"They had things to do," Zero said.

"Right. S'pose you're not going to tell me what they're doing, either?"

"Athelas is visiting the police station and JinYeong is kidnapping someone," said Zero, his eyes just a touch lighter in colour.

He was laughing at me. "Oh, *very* helpful," I said, sarcastically. "Do I have to cook for the person he kidnaps, as well?"

Zero considered that. "It won't hurt," he said. "If Jin Yeong tells them to eat, I'm sure they will."

And that reminded me. I'd been meaning to ask him for a while now, because I'd already asked Jin Yeong, and Jin Yeong didn't know.

"How come Jin Yeong's persuasion doesn't work on me, anyway?"

"We're not sure," he said, and stopped short. His face had gone blank, and I was pretty sure that meant he was annoyed with himself for giving away even as little as that. Flamin' fae. Always worried about giving away too much information. It wasn't like it was gunna hurt them to tell me, after all. They just didn't like ignorant humans getting less ignorant. Flamin' hypocritical, if you ask me. They obviously just liked feeling superior.

"What about yours?" I asked, but he was ready for that one.

"What makes you think it doesn't? Humans don't remember fae coercion."

I sniffed, just to let him know I didn't believe him, and headed off to the kitchen to cook dinner. Now that the kitchen was clean again, it was just a matter of cooking something that would take a bit less time than the chilli con carne that was meant to have been simmering on the stove for the last five hours.

That *would* have been simmering on the stove for the last five hours if it wasn't for the tar beastie that attacked me.

Oh yeah. The tar beastie.

"Oi," I said through the doorway, the tray of steak I'd taken out of the fridge still in my hands. Good thing I'd stopped at the grocery store long enough to get it; there wasn't much else the psychos would have thought of as dinner in the fridge.

"Yes, Pet?" said Zero. He'd settled on the couch with a book spread open on the coffee table, and he was poring over it with a frown between his brows.

"How'd that thing that attacked me get into the house?"

Zero actually laughed. It was more of a short chuckle, and it cut off before I was certain I'd heard it, but it was a laugh. "Your questioning lacks focus, not to mention prioritisation," he said, without looking up. "Next time, lead with the questions that are most important."

"I did," I said. "Whatever it was, however it got in, I figured you blokes were already working on it. I was just curious."

"I can think of many questions that should be important enough to be asked first," said Zero. "None of which involve any investigation we're working on, or the reasons pertaining to doing so."

"If I could understand *half* of those words," I began, in an injured tone, "then I'd be—"

"Don't pretend ignorance with me, Pet."

I nearly asked if he was calling me a liar, but I already knew the answer to that. "Yeah, but you're not me," I said. "And you lot keep saying that fae aren't good at emotions and stuff, so—"

Zero turned a page. "We're not good at feeling emotions. We're very good at reading and manipulating them."

"Yeah," I said again. "But that means you're not good at empathy, too. So I don't reckon you'd know what's important to me anyway."

"Your family is important to you," said Zero. "Your house. Looking after people weaker than you. Curiosity. Surviving."

"My family's dead," I said flatly.

"You," said Zero, turning another page far too soon, "have a habit of making family with people you shouldn't make family with."

"All right, all right," I grumbled. "So you know some stuff. You know, for an emotionally constipated half-human, you're pretty flamin' keyed into feelings."

Zero looked up from his book, wholly startled. "*What* did you call me?"

"Nothing," I said. "You want steak? 'Cos that's a priority we've all got pretty straight, I reckon."

A faint smile came and went on Zero's face. "It would be much more healthy for you if you reversed your list of priorities," he said, and went back to his book. "And got rid of the soft heart that's always taking you into trouble."

"Trouble, yeah," I said, to the top of his head, "but I helped you lot to solve a few problems, didn't I?"

I think he muttered something beneath his breath, but since I was pretty sure he'd only deny it if I asked him what it was, I just turned back to the kitchen. By the time the steak had sat for a while, and the veggies were done, hopefully Jin Yeong would be back with whoever he was kidnapping, and Athelas would be back from his assignment—which, I strongly suspected, was helping Detective Tuatu talk to another detective.

I was still chopping the veggies when someone knocked at the door.

"Leave it," said Zero, before I had a chance to move.

"The lights are on," I pointed out, without bothering to speak more softly. "They've gotta know we're at home."

"It is not," he said, very pointedly, "a priority. Kindly lower your voice."

"Yeah, but it might be for the person who's knocking," I called, tipping my chopped veggies into a saucepan. "You lot got alcohol in the house?"

"Not for you."

"Rude!" I said. "I'll be old enough to drink in a few days, you know. And it's not for me, it's for the sauce I was gunna make to go with the steak."

Zero considered that, then said, "Athelas has half a bottle of wine hidden somewhere."

"What, does he reckon I'm an alcoholic, too?" I said indignantly, rummaging around in the cupboards.

"I think he prefers that Jin Yeong should not know about it. Pet?"

"Yeah?" I wanted to ask why Athelas didn't want Jin Yeong to know about the wine, but there was an undercurrent to Zero's voice that made me wary. "I didn't do anything."

"I beg to differ," he said. "Tomorrow morning, I'd like you to practise what you were doing last night."

"What, cooking? I'm already pretty good at that, so—"

"The listening," said Zero, cutting through my voice. "You were trying to listen to what we were talking about last night."

Beggar me. Did he notice, or did Jin Yeong rat me out? Either way, it was no use protesting ignorance to that impassive face.

I blew out a breath, and then it occurred to me what he'd actually said. "Hang on, really?"

Physical training, I could understand. That gave me an edge if I was attacked again. Teaching me how to covertly listen to people, on the other hand, gave me an edge I could use against my three psychos, and Zero must know it.

"I prefer you not to give yourself away if we've got visitors."

"Hang on—are we likely to have more of that kind of visitors?"

"Now and then, until I sort out a few things."

"Until you solve your murder, you mean."

"And if we see how you work, it will make it easier for us to tell if you're trying to listen to us," Zero added, ignoring my aside.

"Right," I said. That made sense. "Thought you were gunna tell me that I couldn't be doing it or something."

"You can't," said Zero. "It's not possible. But if you're doing it, you should be doing it under supervision. Athelas will help you."

"So long as he isn't going to bash me in the shins every time I don't grab something sharp and pointy quickly enough," I muttered. I was still sore, in more ways than one.

Zero didn't reply to that, so I turned on the stovetop for the veggies and went back to looking for Athelas' secret wine.

The steak was just finished cooking when Jin Yeong, looking particularly fine and pleased with himself, sauntered through the front door. That was weird, for a start, because like the other two psychos, he usually came into the house by way of Between.

There was someone with him, though, which explained using the front door. Hang on—there were *two* people with him. A woman, her chic, untidy bun perched a little askew and her Doctor Who t-shirt just long enough to cover the waistband of her high-waist jeans, and a bloke, scruffy and bearded, carrying enough boxes to build a fort. The boxes had a logo on them, but I was too busy stickybeaking at the two visitors—kidnappees?—to see what it was.

Jin Yeong led the two humans upstairs, a very well dressed pied piper, then came down again to look expectantly at me until I dished out his dinner.

"Zero only said you were kidnapping one person," I said to him. "I don't have enough steak."

Jin Yeong shrugged one shoulder at me. Words filtered through Between that said, "If I eat, that's all that matters."

"What are they doing up there, anyway?"

"*Pemil*," he said, grinning at me over his plate.

"How come it's a secret?" I demanded. "I could just walk upstairs and look!"

"Later, Pet," said Athelas, just a little before it registered in my distracted mind that the wall had become a bit less wall-ish beside me. I don't know what place he was coming from, but wherever it was, it made the soft patch of kitchen he'd walked through all pink and gold around the edges. "First, dinner. I believe I smell a familiar bouquet...?"

I MEANT TO SEE THE TWO HUMANS SAFELY OUT OF THE HOUSE again, but I fell asleep on the couch after dinner instead. Very pet-like of me, but really the only reason it happens so often is that my psychos are up at all hours and none of them need more than a few hours' sleep each day.

And then there was the time when I was dying over and over in my sleep, which tends to disrupt your sleep patterns a bit...

I woke up to the sound of someone knocking on the front door, long and loud and desperate.

"I think not," said Athelas, as I sat up.

"What? I wasn't doing anything."

"Don't answer the door. It's nothing. My lord tells me we're to practise your hearing. In my room, I have left a certain recording on a loop. I would like you to attempt to hear what it says."

"What, we're starting before breakfast?" I protested, edging toward the kitchen. "I haven't even had a cuppa, and Zero will want—"

"I assure you that my lord is content," said Athelas. "Moreover, Pet, trying to see who is at the door from that window is a useless exercise; Zero enchanted it last night to show nothing."

"That doesn't make any sense," I protested. "I mean, yeah, I can understand enchanting it so no one can see *in*, but why enchant it so that no one can see out? What's the use of that?"

"I wonder?" murmured JinYeong to himself, in Korean. He was sitting elegantly on the stairs, goodness knows why.

"No one asked you," I told him.

"The recording, Pet," Athelas reminded me. "Kindly concentrate. What do you hear?"

"Beggar all," I said. It was true. I couldn't hear a thing from Athelas' room. Even if I strained my ears, all I could hear was the faint noise of Athelas' trousers as his foot tapped in mid-air, one leg crossed over the other.

"That's a shame," said Athelas. "Since that recording has to do with our investigation. I arranged it particularly for your benefit."

Interest flared in me, but there was nothing to grab onto; no immediate sound to pursue. How had I done it the other night?

Something moved upstairs, a shiver of the house resettling

part of itself into Between space, and I heard the squeak of leather as Zero left through the upstairs living room wall. When that sound faded, and the house shook itself back into normality, I still couldn't hear a thing.

"There's nothing," I muttered. "I can't hear it."

"Perhaps we should have begun with you in your room as we did at first," said Athelas thoughtfully. "I did not anticipate needing to help you on with something you seemed to have grasped all by yourself."

He gazed at me for a long time, his eyes very faintly amused, and it occurred to me suddenly what he was wondering.

"You think I'm pretending not to know something," I said.

"The thought crossed my mind."

"You're a one to talk," I said gloomily. "You're just distracting me so that Zero can sneak out and do dodgy stuff without me knowing."

"Dear me!" said Athelas. "Can you tell when we leave the house as well, Pet?"

"Yeah. Didn't you know?"

Jin Yeong chuckled in a sarcastic sort way, and said something that sounded very like, "Worried?"

"I've yet to decide," Athelas said. "Try again, Pet."

"Hang on, that's it? That's your teaching? *Try again?*"

"What else did you expect me to say, Pet?"

"Well," I said uncertainly. "You're not gunna tell me *how* I'm supposed to hear it?"

"Unhappily, it is not a particular skill in which I excel."

"How come you're teaching me, then?"

"Well, as you so aptly pointed out a moment ago, Zero has left the house on his own business—"

"Murder business, more likely," I muttered.

"—and since I am marginally more useful than Jin Yeong when it comes to this sort of thing—"

"*Hotsori,*" muttered Jin Yeong.

"—my lord asked me to supervise you."

"Yeah, well I can't hear anything," I said. I might have sounded a bit sulky, because I was half-convinced that there was no recording in his room, and the whole thing was just an elaborate ruse.

"You managed well enough trying to hear us the night before last," Athelas said.

"Yeah, but you're people, and I know you."

"Very well. We shall begin again with you in your room while Jin Yeong and I converse in this room."

"Nah," I said. "That's too easy."

"Easy in what way, Pet?"

"Well, that's just acoustics," I said in surprise. "That beam that runs up through the roof goes through my bedroom. I can hear everything people say in the living room from there. That'd be cheating."

Athelas laughed softly. "I assure you, it's nothing of the kind."

"Yeah, but it is," I said, but I could hear the uncertainty in my own voice. "That's how it works. That's how it's always worked. Even when—even when my parents were here, I could listen in on their conversations if I wanted to."

"If that is so, Pet, perhaps you'll explain how you're able to get any sleep in this house?"

"I mean, I'm not concentrating on the noise all the time," I protested. "Just when I go over there on purpose to hear something."

"Exactly so."

"You saying it's got something to do with Between?"

"If that's the way you'd prefer to think of it, by all means."

"Well, it's not like it's *me* doing it!"

"Is it not? I'm sure you know best about your skill set."

"Yeah? Then why do you sound so flamin' sarcastic?"

"Very well," said Athelas, smiling faintly. "Perhaps we'll play a game. For the next few minutes, I will speak with Jin Yeong about the case we're working on. If you're able to hear, you'll satisfy your curiosity a great deal."

"What?" I said, startled. "Wait! I gotta prepare!"

But I could already see his lips moving, and no sound came out. Mongrel! Jin Yeong, silent and mocking, winked at me as I tried to scramble some thoughts together.

I'd heard something first, last time. I'd heard a little bit of conversation coming through Between, and I'd sort of *grabbed onto* it. But I couldn't hear anything from Athelas, so—

Oh. Athelas.

Last time, I'd had Athelas' tea strainer, and that's how I'd heard Athelas' voice—through the faint sound of a spoon against the metal. After that, it had been Zero's coffee mug. Maybe I needed another connection?

What connection could I use? Not Athelas; I couldn't fetch his teacup without giving it away.

Vampire spit, though, I thought, looking directly at Jin Yeong. There was a connection, right?

Jin Yeong's brows went up, and his mouth pursed. *What are you looking at?* that look said.

I grinned at him. Just you wait, you flaming blood sucker.

His eyes narrowed at me, and his lips formed the word, "*Mwoh?*"

I saw it, and I heard it.

"Jin Yeong, do not bait the pet," said Athelas mildly. "Allow her to concentrate."

"*Nae maum daelo hae,*" Jin Yeong told him.

And Between translated it for me without me even having to think about it.

"I do what I want."

I frowned and looked down just before Athelas' eyes turned from Jin Yeong and to me, my heart skipping a beat. Careful. I was pretty sure that as soon as he knew I could hear, Athelas would stop talking about the case. The fun, for him, was talking about it when he *knew* I couldn't hear. There was no fun in the Pet actually being able to hear, and there was a lot of trouble from Zero.

Jin Yeong said, "Are we really to discuss the issue in front of her?"

"For now. Did your people install everything we needed?"

"They said so. They couldn't lie to me."

I tilted my head a bit, still frowning, and let my eyes flick from Jin Yeong to Athelas. I heard Jin Yeong's soft sniff of laughter.

He said, slow and amused, "*Yah*. She's trying so hard, isn't she?"

"Indeed," said Athelas, watching me very carefully in return. "Now; the latest body was found in the bath house of a private club in Salamanca—the sort of place that you can't get into without being known by the concierge."

"So then how did our murderer get in and out without the concierge's knowledge?"

"Exactly what I would like to know. And then there's the unique distribution of bodies—three high level fae, one human, and then another fae. So very interesting! The detective seems to think—Ah, Pet! I see you're with us at last."

"Flaming heck," I said in annoyance. I'd twitched when he mentioned a human victim; hadn't been able to stop myself.

"*Ashipda*," murmured Jin Yeong, and there was still a touch of Between to the words when he said, "Not. Clever. Enough. *Petteu*."

I stuck my tongue out at him, which made one of his eyebrows lift briefly.

"*Pal oddae?*" he asked; a smooth threat.

"The arm's fine," I answered. "You threatening me?"

"*Tangyeonhaji*," Jin Yeong said mockingly.

Flaming rude, that.

"Anyway," I said, making the best of things, "what's all this about a murder victim at a club in Salamanca?"

"I have no idea to what you're alluding," said Athelas. "For the very good reason that Zero forbade us discussing the matter with you."

"Yeah, but—"

"And I have not," he added, "discussed the matter with you."

"Okay, that's true. So why don't you just keep discussing it with each other?"

"*Hae bolkka?*" said Jin Yeong, with a sparkling look at me, then Athelas.

"Certainly not," Athelas said, to both of us. "Jin Yeong, do not encourage the pet!"

"That's rich!" I said. "You're the one always telling me stuff!"

"As I said!" Jin Yeong said triumphantly, crystal clear. "Good Pet. I will have coffee. I deserve biscuits."

"I wouldn't go that far," I said. "You're not telling me stuff, so you don't deserve biscuits."

"Biscuits!" said Jin Yeong, and left his guard to wander into the kitchen.

I would have gone after him, because I could hear him rummaging in the drawers for biscuits, but Zero arrived home just as I was about to go, so I dropped down on the arm of the nearest lounge chair and grinned at him.

"Busy visiting crime scenes again? You should get Detective Tuatu to do that for you. Thought you lot were working together sometimes these days."

For a minute, I thought I might have gone a bit far and given myself away, but there was a soft laugh from Athelas, and Zero's eyes softened a touch.

"I was not visiting a crime scene."

"Yeah? Bet that's nice for a change. Where'd you go?"

I didn't actually expect him to answer, so it was a surprise when he said, "I revisited the former human quarters of Upper Management. I was curious to see if it was still there."

"Was it?" I asked, though I was pretty sure if he was talking about it in front of me, it didn't have anything to do with what he was working on. Talking was still talking, when it came to Zero.

"Technically, I suppose it was still there. There's still a seventh floor to the police station, but it's no longer...occupied. No doubt the normal humans will become aware of it again once the enchantments on the stairwell and elevator dissolve."

"Curious, but not entirely unexpected," said Athelas. "It was merely a branch, after all. After my...rescue, it would be foolish for them to come back. We did leave rather a mess."

"How'd you get captured, anyway?" I'd been wondering that for a little while now. Athelas wasn't careless, and he definitely wasn't stupid. "I mean, they were all humans."

"That is a question to which I would also like to know the answer," said Zero, but there was an edge to his voice that suggested he already knew the answer to the question, and didn't like it much.

"Think of it as forcing their hand," Athelas said, smiling faintly.

"I thought as much," muttered Zero, his mouth grim.

I said, "You got yourself captured *on purpose?*"

"It is sometimes necessary to sacrifice a pawn in order to take a knight."

"Yeah, but you're not a pawn!"

"Thank you so much, Pet!" said Athelas. "I had no idea you thought so well of me! I'm gratified."

"Yeah? I reckon you're being sarcastic again, but whatever. So you really weren't kidding when you told me that time that you were exactly where you wanted to be?"

"It wasn't too far from the truth," agreed Athelas. "Though I must admit, if I'd realised how well prepared they were to encounter fae, I might have rethought my decision."

"I reckon!" I said, with a shudder of remembrance for the condition in which I'd found him—pierced through with moonlight and helpless. "You ever wonder if you're too clever for your own good?"

"I feel like I might just as well turn that question back on you," Athelas said, and although there was no coldness in his voice, I reckoned it was better to shut my mouth.

I couldn't help grinning, though. "Want a cuppa?" I asked him.

"Not right at this moment, I think," said Athelas, and I saw the way his eyes very carefully didn't go to Zero.

"Tea and coffee, Pet," said Zero, with that unmistakeable edge of command.

"Sorry," I told Athelas. "You're on your own."

This time, I wasn't the one in trouble. I joined Jin Yeong in the kitchen just in time to see him waltz out with the last pack of shortbreads, and was too late to say more than "Oi!" at him in passing, which he ignored.

By the time I got back to the living room, there was still a chill to the air, but Zero had left the house again and Athelas was calmly contemplating the ceiling.

"There you are, Pet," he said. "I was just wondering how much longer you would be."

"Sorry 'bout that," I said, pinching Zero's coffee. His loss, my gain. "Didn't mean to get you in trouble."

"Trouble is an inescapable fact of life," said Athelas. "Now, what were we discussing before my lord came down?"

"You were telling me about heirlings," I said.

Athelas' spoon made the smallest *chink*! as he put it in the saucer. "I really don't think I was."

"Well, maybe not. But if you're not gunna tell me about the case you're working on, I wanna know about heirlings and why that sword is called the Heirling Sword, and why Jin Yeong's not supposed to touch it."

"The fae do not object so much to Jin Yeong's touching the sword as the fact that he exists."

I was about to say that I didn't love the fact of Jin Yeong's existence much, either, when it occurred to me, mouth open, that he was saying it wasn't Jin Yeong's personality that offended the golden fae so much as Jin Yeong's *kind*.

"You lot are pretty flaming xenophobic, you know that?"

"I'd prefer not to be lumped in with the fae who were here earlier, thank you, Pet," said Athelas mildly. For all the mildness of it, I felt the chill of his displeasure. "I object to Jin Yeong upon the grounds of his personality and his general inconvenience, not his birth."

"Oh," I said. I felt much the same, so it wasn't like I could object. "Hang on, though," I said. "You're still pretty flaming toffy-nosed when it comes to humans!"

"Humans," said Athelas, and there was a ghostly gentleness to his voice that made me blink and sit back, "are such soft, delicate creatures. So very likely to die. So full of weaknesses and exploitability. Inferior in nearly every way."

"Oh, just *nearly* every way?" I asked crabbily. "Flamin' broad-minded of you!"

I should have put a laxative in his tea.

"Pet," said Athelas, and there were crinkles beside his eyes again. "I really advise against interfering with my tea."

"We were talking about heirlings," I said, trying not to clear my throat. "You said a while ago that they're some kind of humans."

Athelas sipped his tea, and although his lips didn't smile, his eyes glowed with amusement. "Not necessarily."

"Well, that they're *part* human, anyway."

This time, Athelas nodded. "Indeed. It is a peculiarity of the requirements that any heirling must have human blood in some part."

I might have snorted a bit.

"Yes, I thought that would amuse you. The irony of it is not lost on me, I assure you."

"Hang on," I said. "I thought Zero said that heirlings are fae, or a mix of fae and another race who have the right fae blood. Doesn't that mean someone without human blood can be an heirling?"

"Fae don't like to admit to mixed blood," said Athelas. "But I do assure you that even the purest of the royal lines have had a drop of human blood."

I grinned. "Bet *that* flaming rankles!"

"A little. Ah, Pet, as enlivening as this conversation is, I have a job for you."

"Really? What is it?"

"This," he said, bringing out a tiny flash drive from his pocket.

I took it from him gingerly. "What is it?"

"Video surveillance. I'd like you to watch it through."

"Yeah? You bring that home from the cop shop? Thought I wasn't supposed to know what you're working on."

"There are some things we will not discuss. Others are more flexible."

"Right." It must not be anything important, then. I waved the flash drive at him and asked, "How am I supposed to watch this? I can't do it on my phone."

"Perhaps you noticed that Jin Yeong brought home friends last night," suggested Athelas.

"Kidnapped a couple of people, you mean? Yeah. What about them?"

"My lord seems to have decided that certain accoutrements are necessary if we're to stay here any longer."

"What's that supposed to mean?" I asked suspiciously, but Athelas only flicked his eyes toward the staircase and sipped his tea.

I took my coffee upstairs into the living room there, and found a computer set up, bright, shiny black screen and silver accessories and everything. I didn't even have to turn it on: Jin Yeong's kidnapped techs had set it up and left it on, just waiting to be used. I plugged the flash drive into the back of the computer and it opened automatically, a drive with five folders. I double-clicked on the first, which seamlessly brought up a media player, and smiled a satisfied smile at the setup. I even had *wifi* now! The techs must have been here all night setting up the stuff. No more searching things on my mobile phone—or sneaking to the library.

Mind you, when Zero and Athelas learned how to search browser history, I'd have to start being a lot more clever about hiding the sort of things I searched for.

But for now—now it was pretty close to perfect.

I was still smiling happily when a coloured room interior showed up on the media player. Pink and gold, it was obviously an expensive room in an expensive house, and I was pretty sure I was watching security footage. High class security footage, but definitely security footage.

The room was open and wide, with a couple of desks around it and a lot of bookshelves—maybe a library of some sort. Long windows opened out onto what must have been a balcony, judging by the bit of pot and foliage I could see poking in. A man worked at one of the desks, his polo shirt as blue as the room was pink, and his hair gelled neatly in place; probably a business man who made more in a month than most people made in a year. Was it the club they'd been talking about? I remembered the pink and gold that had brought Athelas home the other night, and decided that yes, it must be.

As I watched, the lights flickered a couple of times, and died. It must have been daylight, because I could still see pretty well, but it was harder to see the bloke's face, and the colour faded around the room. The man stood up from his desk, head twitching around, and went for the door. I saw him test the handle once, twice—then three times. When it didn't open, he pounded on it a couple of times, too. Then he started back across the room, the light from the windows showing up his face.

He was halfway across the room before another figure came

through the long windows from the balcony, his face obscured by the lack of light in the room and a dark cap. The first man stopped, then started forward again, and I squinted at the screen. What, he recognised the other bloke? What was happening now? I couldn't see a weapon, and if this was about what I'd heard the other night, someone should be losing a heart at some—

Window bloke shoved a fist at polo shirt bloke—like he was punching him, but straight out, at his chest. I expected the dude to stagger back, or move away, or *something*.

And I mean, yeah, he staggered all right, because window bloke's fist went *right through his chest*.

Blood blotted light material in the shadowed room, and polo shirt bloke swayed, transfixed by a human looking arm and fist that shouldn't have been able to punch right through his chest. The window bloke moved his shoulder a bit, like he was, I dunno, feeling around for something. Then he wrenched his fist back out, slimy and dark and glistening, and something big and wet pulsated between his fingers, dripping blood.

"*Athelas!*" I howled.

"Yes, Pet?" said Athelas' voice mildly, right by my ear. What the heck? How did he get there so quickly?

I didn't ask either of those questions. Instead, I wailed, "He *pulled out* the other bloke's *heart*! He shoved his hand in there and pulled it out! You could have warned me!"

"I was curious to know what you would see," he said, leaning against the computer desk with one hand.

"I saw a bloke pulling out another bloke's heart! What the flaming heck else would I have seen? It's a surveillance camera—it doesn't change!"

"Humans are often mistaken about that. What else did you see?"

"I didn't finish it, if that's what you mean. Got kinda distracted by the bloke who was *reefing out someone's heart!*"

"I see," said Athelas. "I thought it was rather neatly done, myself. I do apologise. If you can bring yourself to look again, perhaps you would be good enough to tell me what else you see?"

"Blood," I muttered, wincing and looking back at the screen. Window bloke was still where I'd seen him last, though polo shirt had dropped onto the floor, and the heart was still where it had been, too, though it wasn't dripping as much as I would have expected. "And how come it's not blue?"

"Should it be blue?"

"You tell me," I said. "If they're fae, yeah. Zero's blood is blue, and so's yours."

"I don't believe I said the victim was fae."

"Yeah you did," I told him. I would have grinned if I wasn't still feeling a bit sick. "You said fae were having their hearts torn out."

"You heard rather a lot, didn't you, Pet?"

"So why isn't it blue?"

"Those fae who are based in the human world and do most of their work here have built in safety protocols to keep the humans from discovering them. Blood is one of those things that is taken care of."

"What, so if someone tears out their hearts, the police won't be freaked out?"

"It's a little less sensational than that," Athelas demurred. "But if a fae should happen to die unexpectedly, we prefer that they not inform unwary humanity of our existence."

"Tearing hearts out is pretty sensational," I pointed out. "Pretty flamin' bloody, too."

"And yet, for the injury, there is remarkably little blood, would it not seem?"

"Maybe his hand is really hot," I said.

"Cauterisation? I think not. There were no such marks on the body, and there's too much blood for that method. There's little enough of it, but not that little."

"Doesn't look like he's drinking it, either." It wasn't too bad now that I wasn't surprised. Athelas was right—there wasn't much blood, and the slightly unreal surveillance footage made the floppiness of the body not quite as horrible as it might have been if I'd been seeing it in real life. It also gave the murder itself a more surreal feel, which was kinda nice if you can call anything about a murder nice.

And whatever Athelas or Zero said, I knew that this was the case they were working on. I'd heard enough of what the fae were talking about the other night to know that much. So this bloke had been a high level fae?

On impulse, I asked, "Where is this, anyway?"

"That is not important," he said.

"Yeah, yeah," I said, but I wasn't really cranky because I was still pretty sure I knew exactly where it was. "Not important to know where it is, or if it's the case you're working on, or if the bloke's human."

"You surprise me, Pet!" said Athelas, with a feathering of amusement to his voice. "Following our conversation earlier, I really didn't think you would discriminate against a person based on his lineage!"

I grinned. "You shouldn't stick your tongue out at the pet," I said. "It's beneath you."

"How many of the files have you watched?"

"Just the one," I said, feeling a bit grumpy again. "I s'pose the others are just as gory?"

"This camera had the best angle," said Athelas. "Alas, the others are nothing like as clear."

"Yeah, I'm devastated. Is this the only camera in the room? We can't see his face like this."

"It was the only one. People in that place have an…expectation of privacy."

"Woulda thought they had an expectation not to be killed, too," I said. "Oi. How come he turned off the lights first?"

"To make it more difficult to see his face, one assumes," said Athelas.

"Yeah, but the other bloke already recognised him. He walked toward him, and he wasn't scared or anything. And we can't see his face from this angle, anyway, *plus* he has a cap on."

"It is not unknown for a murderer to want to take more care than necessary, Pet."

"Yeah." I mean, Athelas was the expert, after all. I was just the pet.

"And yet," he mused to himself, "there could be a purpose in it, after all. He always has his back to the camera, so he evidently knows where they are. Do look at the others, Pet. Let me know what you think."

"All right," I said. There were still a couple of moments left of the footage, but not much was happening. The murderer just stood there with a heart in his hand, the floor dark with shadow and blood. Maybe he was waiting until it stopped dripping, I dunno.

When he finally moved again, backing toward the windows and turning away from the camera as he did so, the shadows and blood seemed to trail after him, huge and swiftly moving; a bird of prey following the carrion. I blinked at it, but when he moved through the window and into the light, there was only a human shadow following after all.

I sat staring at the screen for a few seconds longer before it occurred to me that it had stopped moving altogether not because no one was moving, but because the footage was at an end. I closed it down with a sigh, and looked glumly at the folder.

One down, four to go.

――――――

CHAPTER FOUR

――――――

ATHELAS AND JINYEONG MUST HAVE BOTH LEFT THE HOUSE again while I was too busy watching gory surveillance footage upstairs to notice them going.

"Flamin' typical!" I muttered, when I went back downstairs for more coffee. Out investigating while I had to sit at home and watch creepy videos. They weren't even useful creepy videos—just more of the same thing the first one had been. A bloke, getting punched in the chest and then having his heart pulled out. One woman, too. No good angle of the murderer's face, his cap pulled low, and a good knowledge of where the cameras were.

I tapped the on button to start the jug boiling, and leaned against the kitchen island, fishing out my phone.

Oi, I texted Detective Tuatu.

I'm busy and I'm not helping you. I need my limbs.

I made a face at my phone. Talk about ungrateful! I'd saved his life a couple times now; risking a few limbs was the least he could do. I texted back, *They've given me the surveillance footage to watch. I got a question.*

A minute or two passed while I waited for my phone to ping with a message, and I hunched my shoulders. I must still be creeped out from watching that footage, because I could swear I heard someone breathing too heavily nearby. Not weird breathing, just like someone was a bit drunk or a bit out of shape.

I shook myself, and jumped when my phone pinged.

Are you lying to me?

Even more rude. *Nope. Just watched four blokes and one woman get their hearts torn out. How's your day going?*

Why did they give that to you!

Dunno, for the fun of it, I s'pose. I got a question. The one with the balcony, did the murderer climb up?

The phone bingled with a call instead of a text tone.

"Don't watch the footage, Pet!" said the detective's voice. He sounded annoyed, but I was pretty sure he wasn't annoyed with me.

"Too late," I said. "You got an answer to my question?"

Detective Tuatu sighed. "All right; he didn't climb up. No one did—the outside cameras show nothing at all from the lower floors. The balcony runs across two rooms, and the last person the cameras caught entering that room next door kept his face from the cameras the entire way through the club. He was identified by the concierge, though."

"He sounds kinda dumb," I said.

"I don't know," said Tuatu. "We're not sure the concierge's testimony can be trusted—we're thinking he's been drinking a lot. He insisted that the murderer never came down again, and he refused to believe us that the murdered man was dead, too. We've got him in the drunk tank at the moment, but I'm not sure it's going to get a whole lot better. He's got a wild look to him."

"Probably saw a bit much," I muttered. Between and Behind stuff had a tendency to do that. Even the old mad bloke was only the way he was because of all the Behind stuff that happened around him. Heck, I could be the next one to go mad if I wasn't careful. "All right, that's all I wanted to know."

"Are you all right?"

"Yeah, apart from having the feeling that someone's breathing down my neck," I said.

"I know the feeling," he said, with heartfelt agreement. "Call me if you need anything. Not information, just...anything else."

"Catch ya," I said, and hung up. Detective Tuatu had enough of his own worries; I didn't want him to worry about me, too.

I took my coffee into the living room, still fighting the urge to hunch my shoulders. There was definitely something bugging me, and until I knew what it was, I wasn't going to get any peace and quiet to enjoy my cuppa.

I put my mug down on the coffee table and settled myself down to listen, or feel, or whatever it was I did with Between that somehow made me able to sense stuff I wouldn't have otherwise sensed. Nothing Between or Behind was stalking the house, and all of the walls and places were still just house, so at least I didn't have to worry about another tar beastie.

What then?

I still felt that sense of someone breathing over my shoulder. Or maybe not over my shoulder so much as toward the front of the house. The front door, maybe?

All of a sudden, I remembered the knocking at the door over the past two days. What if someone was there again? What if they'd given up knocking because they were unconscious, or dead? I stood up uncertainly, and took a step toward the door.

Zero had told me not to answer the knock at the door.

On the other hand, there was currently nobody knocking. Just...a creepy sort of silence that breathed. And if it was a human rather than a Between or Behindkind type thing, there was nothing to worry about, right?

What if I just *listened*? They couldn't object to that.

I left my coffee where it was and went softly to the door, using Between to soften my steps as I went, and put my ear up against the wooden surface.

Oh yeah.

There was definitely someone leaning against the other side of the door. I shouldn't have been able to feel the weight of him leaning against it, or hear him breathing. There was a flaming *door* between us. But of course, I'd been getting some practise at listening lately—the kind of listening that isn't done just with your ears—and I could definitely hear it.

I mean, I had to go out eventually, right? I had to do the rest of the shopping, right? Zero wouldn't be happy if there wasn't a meal on the table tonight.

And okay, yeah—I could always climb out through the window in the back, but I wanted to know who was at the door. I wanted to know who Zero and the others had avoided by leaving by way of Between—because they *must* have known he was there if I'd figured it out. And it wasn't like the world and his dog knew who and what my psychos were, so it probably wasn't dangerous to open the door, either.

Not really.

It wasn't like Zero had told me I *couldn't* leave the house. If he'd wanted me to stay home, he would have said. And if it was the same person who had knocked on the door yesterday, it must be something pretty important they wanted to talk about. Maybe even the murders Zero was trying to solve.

I mean, it was practically my *duty* to see who it was. Or at least go outside, you know?

So I opened the door.

I didn't expect someone to fall through the door when I opened it. He was definitely leaning against the door, and he must have been leaning there for a while, because when I opened the door he just sorta plopped down in a spineless pile next to the umbrella stand in a strong draught of alcohol-scented air.

He was an older bloke—maybe fifty-ish, but looking good for it—all fancy watch and business suit that was too expensive to be wearing while sitting on someone's verandah. His round, gold glasses looked expensive, too, but he definitely smelled like he'd been at the pub for a bit too long.

He climbed to his feet without staggering, despite that smell, and said, "*Finally*. I've been waiting for some time and there's no chair out there."

I blinked a bit, but didn't tell him there *was* a chair out there because I was pretty sure someone from inside had hidden it from him to make him less likely to hang around.

"Who are you after?" I asked, instead.

"I was told someone at this address could help me with my... problem. I'm Preston."

He said it like I should have known the name, or maybe like I should have been impressed.

"Yeah, pleased to meet you," I said. "They sometimes help people, but more often they don't."

"They have to help me," he said. His face a had a pinched, unpleasant look to it, but I was pretty sure there was as much fear as arrogance in the unpleasantness. "I was told the Troika would help."

"The what?"

For the first time, Mr. Preston looked unsure. "I was told— they said there were three...people here who could help someone like me. And a girl who helps the Troika."

I looked at him doubtfully. He was talking about the psychos, obviously. They had an actual name?

"I don't know how much I can do. My owne—bosses are the ones who do most of the um, useful stuff, and they're not here right now. I just help out."

"The detective said I should speak to you because they probably wouldn't talk to me."

"Right, yeah." Funny, that. I hadn't thought he would send anyone to me like this; much like the psychos, he didn't like me getting involved in stuff. *And* he hadn't mentioned it on the phone, which was just rude. "Detective Tuatu sent you?"

"Yes. Detective Tuatu," he said. "He said to talk to you first."

"Okay, but I'm gunna have to talk to them, too."

"That's fine."

"So what's the go? What's worrying you?" Heck, maybe it was just something small, something I could do without talking to the psychos about—

"Someone is trying to kill me," said Mr. Preston.

Or maybe not.

"Someone? Shouldn't you go to the police about that? They're the ones who deal with threats and stuff." Weird that Detective Tuatu had sent him here.

Mr. Preston's eyes flickered around the room, as if he expected someone to point and laugh. "That's the thing," he said. "It's not —it's not exactly *someone*. It's some*thing*."

That sounded more like our sort of thing. "What sort of something?"

"I don't know."

"You don't know, or it's not a believable thing?" I asked, grinning. I was betting on it being the last one.

"It's not...*I* don't even believe it."

"What sort of thing is it? An animal sort of thing or a person sort of thing?"

"It's...I don't know." He fiddled with his tie for a few moments, and then burst out, "It's like fingers and claws in the bath and tentacles in the shower. But I can't see it before it gets me, and by the time I can see the tentacles or the claws, the *thing* is always behind me. I nearly drowned in the shower last night!"

I shivered. I'd only known about Behind and Between for a little while, but I'd already met a lot of things I'd rather not meet again. Whatever Mr. Preston was being bothered by was definitely one for that list.

"You thought about going in for oil cleansing?"

"I haven't had a drop to drink that wasn't alcohol since last night."

Well, that explained why he smelled like a brewery, even if he wasn't drunk.

"Want me to get you some water?" I asked.

"No!"

"Might be safe if I'm the one getting it," I said, pushing a bit. Even if the bloke lived through this, his liver wasn't going to last long.

"Please," he said, for the first time. It nearly choked him, but he said it. "Don't!"

"Okay." I put up my hands placatingly. There wasn't much else I could offer him, apart from milk; I'd used up Athelas' half bottle of wine in the sauce last night, and I didn't think Mr. Preston would want Jin Yeong's blood, either. "You want milk?"

He pushed his hands along his suit trousers, as if wiping away the sweat. "Yes."

I thought he looked a bit too desperate to be there to sticky-beak through Zero's book collection, or anything, but I still kept him in sight through the kitchen opening as I fetched milk for him.

From the fridge, I called out, "Who wants to kill you, anyway?"

Mr. Preston shrugged unhappily, and his pinched face got a bit more pinched around the mouth. "There are a lot of people who could want me dead. No one's tried before, though."

I came back with his milk and gave it to him. "You a taxman or something?"

Again, that look of arrogance, as if I should have known who he was. Mr. Preston settled his shoulders and said, "I'm a lawyer."

Okay, that explained a lot. The question was, was he the sort of lawyer who'd be helping out with Behind cases, or was he just someone who was caught up in something well over his paygrade?

Cautiously, I asked, "You ever help out on...weird cases?"

"I do what I'm paid to do," he said, and there was a defensive-ness to his tone that suggested he'd had this discussion once or twice before. "If they can pay, I do the work. Nobody explains *everything* to me, even if I ask them to do it. Everyone has a right to be defended in court."

"All right, what's your latest job, then?" I asked, filing away for later the thought that he had *definitely* been engaged on some weird cases. He probably didn't want to think about them. The fact that he was even here talking to me meant that he took the threat seriously. He didn't think he was mad, even if he was afraid that other people might think he was.

"I'm defending an um, *person* who has been charged with kidnapping and murder. She's not very good with people, so she's been putting everyone at loggerheads with her—not to mention the people who don't want her found innocent. She's—"

He stopped and took a swig of the milk.

"You think she couldn't have done it?"

"Oh no, she could have done it," he said, so frankly that I knew that whoever his client was, he was scared of her, too. "But I don't think she did. I got a warning in the mail the day before I took the case."

"So why'd you take it?"

Mr. Preston's nose twitched a bit. "They're paying me two million to do it."

"Yeah, but now someone's trying to kill you."

"That's what I've got you for," he said sharply. "You have to make sure I don't get killed."

"So what is it you want my bosses to do for you?"

"Protection until the police catch whoever's doing it. They need to at least come and look at my flat, but I'll stay here if it's not safe enough there."

"I don't think you will," I told him. Mr. Preston might be talking in fear, but he was also still talking in arrogance, and that wouldn't fly with Zero.

"I'll talk about that with your owners," he said, and that had me frowning.

Mr. Preston might not know a lot, but he knew a bit more than I was comfortable with. And the question was, how was I going to talk to Zero about this? He was very unwilling to help humans, despite being half human himself, and even if I thought that was because he was unwilling to endanger humans by bringing Between and Behind too close to them, I couldn't get him to admit that. It would be a hard sell to get him to help someone, let alone someone like Mr. Preston. But someone had to help the bloke, and there was no one else to do it. I couldn't let a bloke die just because it was too hard to persuade Zero to help him.

On the other hand, since this case obviously already involved Behindkind, it might be a bit easier to convince Zero. I mean, he'd always helped out in the end, even though he'd refused at first. He'd stopped a cohort of changelings from feeding off human bodies and deceiving their loved ones. He'd also found the Behindkind who had been killing humans and lycanthropes, and stopped me from turning into a lycanthrope.

He'd definitely help this time, too. I just needed to keep... pushing it. There was no way that Mr. Preston was the only human being harassed by this Behindkind creature, whatever it was.

I looked uneasily at Mr. Preston. Zero would help, though. He had to help. Athelas and JinYeong, I wasn't sure of, but if I had Zero on my side, it'd be fine.

I'd been thinking for too long. Mr. Preston had sunk in on himself, clutching his milk and looking nervously around the room. The only trace of the arrogance remaining was there in the unpleasant lines around his mouth.

I took pity on him and asked, "How'd you meet Detective Tuatu, anyway?"

He jumped. "What? Oh, I've called him as a witness from time to time."

Pretty tenuous connection for Tuatu to be sending him over

to us, I thought, frowning. Still, if the bloke was in danger of his life, he probably thought it was necessary. I just wished Tuatu had come over with Mr. Preston himself.

It would have made it easier to bring up with Zero, too. And speaking of Zero, it was probably a good idea to get rid of Mr. Preston until I could talk about him with my three psychos. If he didn't want to go home, there was always a coffee shop nearby—just so long as Zero didn't see him straight up.

"You'd better go now," I said. "Gimme your card or something, and I'll call you when I've talked to the psy—"

"The Troika?"

"Yeah, them. What do you know about them, anyway?"

"Just their name and that they have a reputation for solving problems permanently. And that they're not...affiliated with anyone."

I didn't like the way he said *permanently*, but I wasn't sure if it was because I didn't care for his tone, or because there was always a disturbing amount of blood and death in the psychos' methods.

"Okay, well, you have to come back—"

"I'm not coming back. I'm waiting here."

"If you wait here, it'll be much harder to persuade them to help you," I said.

"If I wait anywhere else, it'll be much harder to stay alive long enough to be helped," he said sharply. "No thank you. I'm staying here."

"Yeah, but—"

A stirring of Between around the front door tripped my heartbeat up a notch, and the faintest thread of JinYeong's voice murmuring through the softness of it sent chills across my neck.

Ah heck. I was too late.

"Sit down," I said to Mr. Preston, who had stood in his emphatic refusal to leave, and was now staring at the less-than-solid front hall. "And for pity's sake keep it polite when they come in."

I stood in front of him to block his view, but he just leaned around me anyway, and I reckon that's what Zero must have seen when he walked through the door.

"*Pet*," he said, in a voice of ice. "What are you doing?"

"Had an accident," I gabbled. "Went out to get some groceries and tripped over a bloke. He sorta just fell in through the door so I gave him some milk."

"He just *fell into* the house."

Close enough. "Yeah."

"No one answered when I knocked," said Mr. Preston. "I came back two times, and this time I waited all night. You need to help me."

I mean, it wasn't like he was a nice bloke or anything, but he did need our help. S'pose we'd been lucky so far that the people who actually needed our help were nice ones, but even horrible people need their lives saved sometimes. *Especially* horrible people need their lives saved sometimes.

I pointed at Zero and said, "He'll help you. Zero, Mr. Preston. Mr. Preston, Zero."

"Pet," said Zero, through his teeth. "Coffee."

"Don't be scared," I told Mr. Preston. "He just growls sometimes. He doesn't bite."

"*Pet.*"

"Coffee. Got it."

I hurried off to the kitchen, eager to be there and back before too much conversation could happen without me, but I didn't realise Athelas had followed me until I turned around from the cupboard to see him leaning on the kitchen island where Jin Yeong usually leans.

"Pet," he said amiably. "I'm certain there has already been some conversation on your lamentable desire to bring home other pets with you."

"Didn't bring him home," I pointed out. "He was already here.

Reckon he must have followed one of you blokes home last night, so..."

"I suppose that's a fair enough point," Athelas conceded. "Still, he doesn't seem the most...sensible sort. Was he very rude to you?"

"Yeah, a bit," I said. I found that I was grinning a bit.

Athelas' eyebrows went up the tiniest bit, and I saw an upturn to the corners of his mouth that had been very straight until now. "Then I take it he also didn't threaten you."

"Nah, he's just a condescending git who doesn't know how to speak to people." I mean, I had a lot of experience with people like that.

"Very well," he said. "Kindly don't give me that sarcastic look, Pet."

There were creases beside his eyes as he said it, though, and I couldn't help laughing. "You want biscuits?"

"Naturally. I shouldn't bother to make tea or coffee for your Mr. Preston, however."

"Nah, he wouldn't drink it anyway," I said. "He's afraid of water."

"That's not exactly what I meant," said Athelas.

Of course it wasn't. I hurriedly gathered up all the tea and coffee things onto a tray and dodged around him back into the living room, just in time to hear Zero say, with finality, "We do not take on outside cases. We have our own area of interest."

"You'll regret it!" Mr. Preston said, his face pinched in a rictus of anger, disdain, and fear. None of those emotions covered the fact that I could see him shaking.

"C'mmon, mate," I said, leaving the tray on the coffee table. "That's not the way to get people to help you."

"I *said* I'd pay you well!" he shot at Zero.

Oh man. He needed help, because he definitely wasn't helping himself.

"I don't care about money," said Zero. "I've got enough."

"What about them?" Mr. Preston pointed rather wildly around at Jin Yeong and Athelas.

"*Quanshimi obseo*," said Jin Yeong, shrugging. He didn't say it to be understood, but I knew enough Korean to understand when he added, "Ah, *hyeong*, he's so noisy. Throw him out."

"No!" I protested. "He needs help!"

"You told me you'd talk to them!" Mr. Preston said furiously to me. "All you've done is make coffee!"

"You can thank the Pet that your limbs were not removed immediately when we arrived," Athelas said, smiling pleasantly at him. "Jin Yeong smelt you long before we got in, and the Pet was kind enough to mention that you hadn't...damaged anything."

That wasn't exactly what I'd said, but whatever. "I told you I can only do so much," I told Mr. Preston. "You're not really helping yourself, mate."

"I should have known not to go to you first," he said bitterly. "I should have gone straight to the fae."

Athelas' eyebrows went up, and I reckon I must have been a mirror image of him.

"You know a bit more than you told me you knew," I said.

"Leave now," Zero said.

"The people who employ me will not be happy!" snapped Mr. Preston.

"*Out*," said Zero, in such a commanding voice that it didn't surprise me to see Mr. Preston wheel about, his face furious and frightened, and march himself to the front door.

"Pet. The door."

I didn't feel the same kind of compulsion as I could see around Mr. Preston, but you can bet I flaming jumped for the door. I was already in enough trouble. I got there before he did and pulled it open just in time to prevent him bloodying his nose on it. He glared at me on the way through, but I said softly, "I'll talk to them. Just—try not to die in the meantime, okay?"

He didn't answer me, but I wasn't sure if that was because

Zero was doing something, or because he didn't want to answer. I shut the door behind him and went slowly, reluctantly back down the hall to the living room. My coffee was waiting for me, so I took it, avoiding Zero's eyes, and flopped down into my seat with my fingers wrapped around the porcelain warmth.

Zero said, "Are you tired of living in this house, Pet?"

A sick warmth of fear sank deep into my stomach. I was so close to having my house back. I just...needed to be more careful. Quietly, into the steam of my coffee, I said, "He needs help."

"He needs some lessons in manners," murmured Athelas, helping himself to tea from the tray. "Something with which I would be more than happy to provide him."

I huffed a breath. "Yeah, he's a galah. But he still needs help."

"He knows more than a human should know," JinYeong said, making himself plain. He dropped down beside me on the couch, reaching around me for his own coffee and making a brief, welcome shield from Zero's icy blue eyes as he gathered biscuits.

"Yes," said Zero. "JinYeong, you *have enough biscuits*."

I saw the edge of JinYeong's dark, sharp grin. "*Hyeongeun ssaugo shipeoyo? Kuraeyo. Ssauja!*"

"What are you fighting about *now*?" I demanded, whacking his arm. "Stop picking fights!"

"*Wae?*" complained JinYeong, looking across reproachfully at me. "*Yah, Petteu—*"

"I'll make you some blood snacks instead," I told him.

JinYeong's eyebrows flew up, and after a still moment, he sat back against the couch cushions with his coffee.

"This is more important," I explained. "Mr. Preston is a galah and a twit, but someone's trying to kill him. He's scared. He obviously knows a bit too much about *something*, but we're exactly the right people to help him."

"We are not a unit to assist humans," Zero said. "I've told you that, Pet. I won't tell you again. And if you invite another human into the house without my express permission, I will consider our agreement reneged upon, and throw you out of the house."

There was a bitterness at the back of my throat, but I tried to push it down. I remembered times Zero had helped me—had helped other humans, even though he said he wouldn't. As much as Athelas couldn't be listened to only by his words, was Zero more communicative through his actions than his words.

I wanted to trust him. I could trust him. He wouldn't kick me out—he would help Mr. Preston.

So I said, "He said it's something in the water. Something he can't see until the water's running, and then it comes up behind him."

Athelas looked distinctly interested, but Zero's eyes went a shade cooler. "Mr. Preston told me that himself," he said.

"So what is it?" I asked. "The thing that does something like that?"

"There's no need for you to be knowing about such creatures."

"There is if they're doing stuff to humans!" I protested. "Maybe we could have told him how to keep safe until—"

"There is no *until*," Zero said impatiently; and without so much as an *I'm going out*, he turned and stepped into a sudden dissipation of Between.

I sat staring at the space where he'd been, my mouth open, caught between fury and helplessness. He didn't even *argue*—didn't even engage. He just *left*. How was I supposed to fight against that?

Eventually it occurred to me that both JinYeong and Athelas were watching me—Athelas, faintly amused as always and JinYeong smirking—and I shut my mouth.

"Thus the charm of authority," said Athelas.

"Is that what it is?" I said sourly, sipping my coffee. "I thought it was—"

"Careful, Pet," Athelas said softly. "I would not like to have to prove my loyalties."

"What, you'll kick me out of the house on Zero's behalf? Thanks."

"I think not," he murmured. "You've such a convincing way about you. I'm sure you'll manage to find another way to discuss the matter with my lord."

"That won't do any good if he just walks away while I'm still talking."

"But then, you *are* the pet," he gently reminded me.

I was surprised at how much the poniard point of that soft remark hurt. "I know that!" I snapped. "He could have at least told me what's bothering Mr. Preston, though! I could have warned him. The bloke's just trying not to die."

"Rudely."

"Yeah, but just because he's rude, doesn't mean he deserves to die! And what if something like that happens to me? I wanna know what to look out for!"

"I believe I've mentioned it before, but your education is sadly lacking."

I grumbled, "We don't get taught about Between and Behind in school, you know."

"Perhaps it would pay you to read more, Pet."

"Yeah, like there's a library of Between and Behind stuff I can go look at."

Athelas' eyes rested briefly on Zero's shelf of books; fat, tall things, all of them.

"I can't read those," I protested. "They aren't even in English!"

"*Nado mothae*," said JinYeong, leaning forward for more biscuits.

"Nobody asked for your two cents!" I told him, but he only grinned. That was annoying. It meant that my instinctive feeling for Athelas' meaning was probably right. "Let me guess—the books are like Between. You have to see 'em the right way to be able to read them."

"You managed to arrange them in order," Athelas reminded me, rising from his chair to prowl in front of the bookcase.

Yeah, but only because I hadn't realised they were in a different language until I'd started arranging. I didn't think I could do the *pretend not to look at it until it forgets about you* kind of thing that worked with birds at the park and titles in fae script for as long as it would take to read a whole book.

"*Moggo*," JinYeong said, throwing one of his biscuits at me. Maybe he was tired of the conversation.

I stuck out my tongue at him, but I caught the biscuit, too. My coffee was starting to get cold, and I was *hungry*. I'd forgotten while I was annoyed.

"Fine, I'll study," I said. "But if this is just you trying to tell me stuff without telling me stuff, I'm gunna start doing that with your flamin' video surveillance."

"How dreadful," said Athelas complacently. "Start with these, Pet."

I took the books he gave me, aware of JinYeong's smirk, and accidentally-on-purpose swung my elbow a bit too close to his nose as I turned back around.

"I do suggest that you confine your studying to those times when all your other chores are done," Athelas said, returning to his chair. "And I suggest that despite your reservations, you prepare yourself to be...appropriately forthcoming about the surveillance footage when Zero asks you about it."

JinYeong threw another biscuit at me, and this one bounced off my head. I threw it back at him, but I must have been weak from lack of sufficient coffee or something, because he only caught it in his mouth and smirked at me yet again.

"Fine," I said. "But I'm not gunna like it."

"Oh, there's no expectation of that," said Athelas, smiling into his tea.

CHAPTER FIVE

JinYeong mustn't have had anything to do, because he spent the rest of the afternoon sitting on the couch beside me, alternately throwing biscuits at me and putting his feet up on the coffee table right where they'd be the biggest annoyance. And yeah, it would always have been annoying, but while I was trying to pay attention but not *too* much attention to my book, it was even more annoying.

As soon as I got up to make dinner, though, JinYeong sprang to his feet and followed me into the kitchen, which made me think he was just making sure I followed through on my promise to make him blood snacks.

"All right," I said. "But I'm getting dinner ready first."

"*Ne*," said JinYeong, and leaned against the kitchen bench.

"You don't have to watch me," I protested, but he must have thought he did, because he didn't go anywhere.

Zero, the big, sulky fae, didn't come home for dinner at all. I put aside his dinner in the fridge, twitching it out from under the hands of JinYeong, who tried to eat it himself. There wasn't enough food in the house to make another dinner for Zero if he came home hungry.

Jin Yeong glared at me, but he didn't try to take the plate out of the fridge; just came and sat down on the couch with his fresh blood snacks to annoy me again. I ignored him and tried to read the books without scaring the meaning out of them by too much attention, but it was hard to balance the proper amount of attention with Jin Yeong flicking crumbs at me.

"Gunna put something nasty in your room again," I said, below my breath.

I didn't think Athelas heard what I said, but he smiled, anyway. Maybe he caught the tone of voice I used. Maybe he was just smiling at whatever was in his book.

Jin Yeong looked smug and sat back against the cushions, though I wasn't sure what he was being smug about. I was trying so hard to ignore him and pay just enough attention to the book that I didn't notice when my head began to drop toward the coffee table. I didn't notice when I curled back up on the couch, either, bare feet making dusty patches on Jin Yeong's trousers, and fell asleep.

They were all talking when I woke up the next morning, probably about their case. Unfortunately, the first thing I heard properly when I woke up was Zero's voice saying, "It's awake. Breakfast, Pet."

I groaned, my eyes still closed, and sat up. "Yeah. Breakfast. Got it."

"*Aish*," muttered Jin Yeong, and I heard the light slapping of someone dusting themselves off. "Dirty Pet."

I rubbed my eyes and looked blearily at him to find that he was brushing off his trousers where my feet had been. Wearing sandals meant I gathered a lot more grime on my feet than usual.

"Sorry," I yawned, tottering on my feet. "Put it on a hanger later and I'll brush it off."

I staggered off to the kitchen to make toast, but I must have needed coffee a bit more than usual, because I forgot to put the drip pot on. I left the psychos to the toast and wandered back into the kitchen, still yawning, and felt a sudden buzzing in my pocket.

My phone was vibrating. I pulled it out of my pocket and squinted down at it, confused. Somehow during the night I must have turned the sound off; I could see the tint of orange on the off/on switch.

In my peripheral, I saw Athelas look up, and climbed up the two steps to the kitchen as I unlocked my phone. Nice and casual, that's it. There hadn't been a sound, after all; I was just…I dunno, messing with a game or something. Just so long as I didn't pause, or look guilty, I'd be fine.

Because the message that had flashed up on the screen as I tilted my phone, was, *It's me, Morgana.*

I grinned. I still had the pictures she'd sent; they were sitting in the chat above her message. I knew who it was.

What's up? I replied, then poured my coffee.

We got a problem. That bloke came back and they let him in.

Ah heck. I didn't dare look in Athelas' direction to see if he was watching me through the doorway, but I caught a reflection of him in the screen when I turned it a bit, and he was talking with Zero. I slipped my phone back into my pocket, and made up another tray for the tea and coffee.

Looked like I wasn't getting any coffee this morning. I trotted back down into the living room to put the tea and coffee beside the toast pile, and went for the front door.

"I'm off to get some groceries!" I called.

"Don't take long," said Zero. "You have training, and I want a report on the surveillance footage."

"Yay," I said gloomily, and left the house, my sandals rubbing against the raw patches they'd already made. I waited until I had crossed the road toward the Brooker Highway and gone down one of the sideroads before I pulled my phone out again.

Morgana picked up before the first ring sounded all the way through.

I asked tersely, "Did they get Daniel?"

"Um, not exactly."

"What does *not exactly* mean?"

"I mean they didn't get him; he jumped out the window."

I took in a breath. "Is he okay?"

"Yeah. He didn't—he didn't jump down to the ground."

"I'm guessing he didn't fly, so where'd he go?"

"The building next door. I couldn't see him for a while, but that dog was back. Pet, I reckon it must be his dog, because it was fighting off the bloke who came after him."

"Where's Daniel now?"

"Um."

"It's okay if you don't know. We can find him." It was gunna be a pain, but at least I knew he was on the mend and not under surveillance of any kind anymore.

"No, I know. I tried to get over to the window so he could see me calling the cops—figured if I was really loud about talking on the phone with the window open, the bloke might get scared and run off. But I couldn't get my legs to work, and while I was still trying to get up off the floor again, someone burst into my room."

"It was Daniel, right? Not the blokes—I mean the bloke who was after him?"

"Yeah. But he took my doona off the bed and he won't come out from under it so I don't know what to do."

I tried not to grin. Mostly it was relief, but it was kinda funny, too. It was a good thing Morgana was so oblivious to the way her world was edging into Between around her. She was already burdened enough; bringing Behindkind into the mix wasn't a good idea.

"I'll be there as soon as I can," I said. I slipped my phone back into my pocket and started out at a jog-trot, aware that somewhere behind me, someone was following. This time, though, I knew it was just the old mad bloke—probably looking for a feed, or a drink—and I didn't let it worry me. His figure was a pretty familiar sight all through my childhood, after all, and he'd never done me any harm, apart from pinching a few drinks from me.

Morgana's house was quiet when I got there. That was pretty normal, though the quietness around the outside of the house worried me a bit. I couldn't *see* the Sandman or the big bloke in the jeans-on-jeans combo, but I was uneasily aware that it was possible they saw me. With the hair standing up on the back of my neck, I took the stairs two at a time and entered Morgana's room.

I didn't expect to see her still on the floor, which was a bit dumb of me, since it wasn't like she could easily pick herself up, after all. She wouldn't want to drag herself over to her bed while there was a lycanthrope under there glaring at her, either.

"You okay?" I asked, automatically grabbing the arm she held out to me.

"Yeah. Just—can you help me up and put me on the seat here?"

She was *light*. I nearly asked her why, but that wasn't the most important question right now. I manoeuvred her onto the seat of the exercise machine she'd pointed me toward instead, then went to crouch next to the bed.

Daniel's face, flushed and sweaty, glared at me from a mass of doona.

"You coming out?"

"I can't," he snapped.

"You can't stay there. You gotta come out eventually."

"I *can't*," he said again, angrily wrenching at the doona. It slipped slightly off one shoulder, and it occurred to me with a sudden spurt of amused relief, that Daniel wasn't hurt. He was naked.

Morgana craned her head down to one side, risking a fall. "Is he…is he okay? He wouldn't talk to me and he wouldn't come out."

I grinned. "He's fine. He's just um, naked."

"He's what?"

"Shut up, Pet!"

"What? You gunna stay in there all day? She's not gunna leave —it's her room, and she can't walk out."

There was the sound of mumbled swearing from beneath the bed before he said, "Just cover me, all right?"

"You're already covered," I pointed out, but I took the top sheet off the bed anyway and held it up. "All right, we're looking away."

"I'm not," said Morgana. "I can't see anything anyway. You're hiding behind half my bedding."

"Your dad got anything he can loan?" I asked, while shuffling and exasperated breathing caused the sheet to billow slightly.

"He can borrow my pyjamas," said Morgana. "It's no use looking for Dad's stuff—he's the wrong size. My pyjamas are all extra large anyway. There's a pile next to the bed, I think."

"Oi, coming through," I said, giving Daniel a chance to rearrange the doona again. "Here, use this stuff. The pyjama pants and t-shirt'll fit you."

"I don't have any jocks for you, though," Morgana said apologetically.

"I'll manage," muttered Daniel, snatching the pyjamas, and hurried away toward the bathroom.

I tried not to grin, but it was funny seeing him so concerned about being naked when it hadn't bothered him while he was fighting for the rights to his pack. Mind you, he'd come back from fighting for his life, then. Maybe being naked matters more when you're under a girl's bed, who knows?

I glanced over at Morgana, and saw her looking out the window, her pale face bright with a bit of colour high on the cheeks. "Dude, he is *gorgeous*!" she said.

"Who?"

"The Chinese bloke out there now."

That wiped the grin from my face, all right. "What Chinese bloke?" I demanded, leaning over her, but I already had a sinking feeling that I knew what I was going to see. I looked out the window, and sure enough, there was JinYeong looking up at the window. He saw me as soon as I saw him, so it was no use ducking back in and pretending I hadn't seen him.

Beggar me. Why was he following me? I was sure I'd gotten out of the house without the lingering smell of cologne drifting after me.

I said slowly, "Korean. Yeah, he's my um, partner. He was meant to be doing something else."

"Is he coming in too?"

"Maybe," I said gloomily. Morgana was far too excited about JinYeong; she was already too pale, and a vampire wasn't likely to do anything good when it came to people who were too pale. "Just...don't get too close to him if he does."

Morgana looked disappointed, then interested. "Are you dating?"

"What? Yuck! Definitely not. He's just...trouble—and you're not even fourteen!"

"I am too! I'm sixteen this year!"

"Oh. Sorry."

"Don't worry about it," she said, grinning. "I haven't grown for the last couple of years. Most people think I'm still twelve. You going to bring him up?"

I looked out again, and JinYeong, very deliberately, pointed one slender finger at me. *I know you're there*, that finger said. *Come down.*

What a pain in the neck! I was going to have to convince JinYeong not to tell Zero about this. He would definitely know that Daniel had been kept in the house across the street—at least until today.

There had to be some sort of leverage I could use. Bright side was, he hadn't already run off to tell Zero what I was up to, so there must be a reason for that. If I could find out what it was, maybe I could use it.

I stopped at that thought, blinking a bit. Maybe it was bad for me to be around fae so often—I seemed to be thinking like them more these days. How to manipulate here—how to sneak around there. Using people's weaknesses against them.

"It'll be mostly us, though, won't it?" said Morgana. "The other cop was by himself, too. Said this sort of stuff was usually just a one person job."

She didn't sound disappointed at that, despite her obvious interest in JinYeong, and I felt a stab of guilt. Speaking of manipulating people...

"Yeah, just us," I said. "He doesn't need to come up here."

"Who doesn't need to come up here?" demanded Daniel, emerging from the bathroom. In Morgana's pyjamas, he looked slender and young and far too defenceless to have been chased around by a stiff breeze without falling over, let alone a Sandman.

"Stay away from the window," I warned him. "It's JinYeong."

It was Daniel's turn to grin at my discomfort. "What? Didn't tell those three what you're up to, huh?"

"What three?" asked Morgana.

"My bosses."

Sotto voce, Daniel said, "Is that what you're calling 'em? Pft."

"My two bosses and my partner," I said, glaring at him. "I didn't tell any of them about this, so..."

Morgana frowned. "Are you going to be in trouble? The other bloke said he was going to be in trouble, and then he never came back."

"Nah," I said. "Well, maybe. We'll see. I'd better go down and talk to my partner before he goes back to our bosses."

JinYeong was waiting for me downstairs, just outside the door. When I started out into the garden, looking around for him, he detached himself from the wall and said agreeably, "*Mwoh hae, Petteu?*"

"None of your business," I said. "Why are you following me?"

He leaned close, and sniffed from my shoulder to my ear. "*Petteu*," he said, showing a bit too much tooth, "you smell like dog."

"Look who wants to be understood all of a sudden," I complained. "And it's pretty flaming rich for you to be complaining about how people smell, with the amount of perfume you're wearing."

Jin Yeong narrowed his eyes at me. "It is not perfume."

"Could have fooled me. Anyway, I smell like d—like Daniel because that Sandman thing tried to get to him and he had to escape."

"You helped him?"

I grinned. "Well, sorta." I mean, I got him clothes. No need to tell Jin Yeong that he was upstairs with Morgana if I didn't need to.

He tipped his head at the building. "*Kogiso wae?*"

"I was up there because I was visiting a friend of mine."

"Pft," Jin Yeong said dismissively. "Spying."

"You gunna tell Zero about this?"

"*Molla*," he said, shrugging one shoulder. "Maybe, maybe not,"

Yeah right. His mouth was already pressed together smugly, and his eyes glittered. He was enjoying this.

"'F'you tell him, I'll get chucked out."

"*Ne*," Jin Yeong said, lips curving. "What will you do, Pet?"

"Which means no more homemade kimchi, no more dinners, and no blood snacks. *And* you'll have to go hunting when you'd rather just sit down and be lazy with a blood bag."

"Pft," he said again, but he looked thoughtful. "If the dog is no longer at that place, Zero can have no objections."

"Yeah, he's definitely not there anymore," I said. I was going to have to warn Daniel against changing into his wolf form anywhere in Morgana's place; Jin Yeong would definitely smell him on me again if he did. And maybe get him to have a bath or something. It wasn't like he could stay there or anything, but for the meantime, there were very dangerous Behindkind nearby looking for him.

"*Uri jib caja*," he said, tilting his head toward the gate out.

"Why are you following me, anyway?" I asked, even though he'd stopped layering his words with Between. Obviously he was finished with everything he wanted understood, which was all right for *him*, but I still had questions. "And it's no good just speaking in Korean, you know. In a couple of years I'll be able to understand everything you say, anyway."

He sauntered ahead of me out the gate, and shrugged. "*Sankwani obseo.*"

"Yeah? You'll care a lot when you're being rude about those two and I tell 'em what you say. Oi! Where are you going?"

Jin Yeong stopped. "*Uri jib.*"

"Yeah, but I gotta do the shopping first," I told him. "Unless you don't want dinner tonight."

I started off down the opposite way, toward the Brooker, even though it would have been quicker to go the way Jin Yeong was going. I wanted the time to text, *Keep him away from the window. Call me if you need me*, to Morgana.

I'd just slipped my phone back into my pocket when Jin Yeong caught up with me and slowed his step to a saunter. If he'd been walking properly instead of like a wannabe model, maybe it wouldn't have been so annoying, but I couldn't help the scowl that rose naturally to my face.

Jin Yeong gave me an offended look and demanded, "*Wae?*"

"Dunno. You're just annoying."

He considered that, and grew smug. "*Ne.*"

"S'pose you think that's a compliment," I muttered.

He shrugged, but he was still smiling to himself when we got to the grocery store.

"You stay out here," I told him. Shopping with JinYeong was even more annoying than walking with JinYeong was—all the female staff tended to converge on the place he was in, whether or not he expressed any need for help. I still wasn't sure if that was something his Behindkind vampire nature brought out, or if he deliberately lured them in just to annoy the people around him, but either way, it was irritating. This shop was worse than most, too, because we'd both worked in it briefly while undercover.

Luckily for me, he didn't object to waiting outside. Usually, JinYeong prefers to do whatever will annoy me the most. Today, he seemed happy to let his eyes roam Campbell Street as the traffic swept past the pedestrians, his hands in his pockets and his shoulders fashionably curved. Like he was shooting a commercial for the casual businessman outside the local grocery store or something.

I nipped around the aisles as quickly as I could, snatching up a pack of noodles here, flour and salt there, biscuits from the international foods section to give Athelas something to smile about and more maple syrup for Zero's pancakes. He still hasn't told me he loves them, but I've seen his face when he eats them. It's a sort of rebellion of mine—giving him stuff he loves to eat when he refuses to tell me he loves it. Sorta make things harder for him.

I was in the frozen food aisle when I saw the bloke. It was probably a good thing that I saw him in the reflections first, because I'm pretty sure my mouth was open for a good five seconds.

It was one of the dead blokes. Last I'd seen him, he'd been sitting on a couch in a private sitting room of the Orient in Hobart, looking up with a smile to greet his murderer. After that, it had just been shock, and blood, and dead eyes staring up at the camera.

Now, he was looking at frozen fish with those eyes, and

dressed in a trakkie-dak and hoodie combo that was a pretty far cry from the brand name track suit I'd last seen him in.

What. The. Heck.

His eyes flicked up from the package of fish, and I made a slow blink and let my eyes travel on to the stuff in the freezer in front of me, closing my mouth. If he caught me staring at him— especially staring at him in the reflection of the window—I would completely give myself away. And I wasn't even sure what I'd be giving away, apart from the fact that I recognised his face. I mean, if either of us should be worried about giving themselves away, it was him—he was meant to be flaming *dead*.

I grabbed the icypoles I'd come for and headed down toward the back of the store while he headed for the front of the store. I didn't want to be seen following him, but I sure as heck was *gunna* be following him. So I passed along the back of the store and came up the tea aisle again as his figure flickered past the end of the aisle to join the queue for the self-serve registers. I stood at the end of the fifteen-or-less lane instead, where I could keep an eye on him without having to scan my own groceries. I could always give Jin Yeong the nod to follow him if I needed to.

The murdered bloke came past me as I paid, and stood at the cigarette counter to ask for a pack of smokes, which was handy. It was handy because he looked pretty young, and if the employee did the right thing—yep. He was asking him for ID.

Bonza!

I stepped softly behind him and leaned casually on the glass of the service desk, my eyes flicking to the name on the ID.

Cameron Michaels.

Right. I was gunna have to call the detective again and hope that he felt compromised enough from helping me last time, to help me again. I had no idea if Cameron Michaels was actually the name of one of the murdered blokes. I mean, unless he had an identical twin brother, it *had* to be him, but I'd seen enough weird stuff to make me check and double check everything.

I gave his profile another once-over while he waited for his cigarettes, and maybe he felt the interest, because Mr. Michaels' head turned toward me. I let my eyes slip past him, and past the ID just as he would have met my eyes, looking down at the phones beneath the glass counter instead.

"That one," I said to the bloke who was coming back with the cigarettes. "Can I look at it?"

"Yeah, sure," he said. "I'll just finish up here first."

"Too late," I said, as JinYeong's suited shoulder moved sightly into sight through the front window. "I gotta go. Thanks anyway!"

I mean, the bloke was dead, and I was only going off security footage, but it really looked like him. Maybe it was Behindkind doing weird things with bodies again. Mind you, if it was a fae body, could they do the same things with them? From what Athelas had said, changelings could only do their work with human bodies. Whichever way I looked at it, it was weird.

And that made me wonder about the one human body Athelas had spoken of. Which one was the human? Why had a human made it into a list of dead, high-level fae? Was Cameron Michaels the human one?

I gave him one more, furtive look as he passed me on his way out of the grocery store, trotting casually behind him so it didn't look like I was too interested in him. I was pretty sure I wasn't the only one who used reflections to watch the people around me.

I was still frowning when I got outside, but JinYeong must have thought I was frowning at him, because he didn't ask what was up. He was still gazing out on the street. Trying to look cool and suave, maybe, I don't know.

"Oi!" I shoved a couple of bags at him. "Did you see him?"

JinYeong's brows rose. "*Nuga?*"

"That bloke—he looked like one of the murdered men, didn't he?"

He shrugged, unconcerned, and a bit more of my surety faded. If JinYeong had been watching the parking lot as closely as he seemed to be doing, there's no way he wouldn't have seen and recognised the man.

"Never mind," I said. It might really be that I'd seen someone who looked enough like a security footage version of a murdered man to be confused. It might be a good idea just to look at the footage by myself again. I was probably wrong, but I wanted to know for sure.

Jin Yeong was about as talkative on the way home as he usually was, but his eyes flickered back and forth along the street, and I was pretty sure I saw him keeping an eye on the windows and shadows as we passed, too. I began to wonder if I hadn't been wrong, and if he *had* seen the man, and just wasn't telling me.

Annoying, but very possible.

Fine. I would talk to Detective Tuatu instead.

CHAPTER SIX

There wasn't much of a chance to call the detective when we got home, because Zero first demanded lunch, and then sent me out into the back yard to warm up before practice. They probably just wanted to talk together without me hearing them, I thought grumpily, and refused to feel bad about not telling Zero about Mr. Michaels. If he *was* one of the murdered blokes, JinYeong would be telling him about the man right now, anyway, and they sure as heck wouldn't be planning on telling me.

"Find a weapon, Pet," called Zero, striding from the house.

I scrambled to find something useful, knowing from experience that there was no stopping that massive stride, and that he would seize anything—a sapling from the ground, a board from the fence—and come for me regardless of whether or not I managed to get a weapon.

The first thing I snatched up, a stick I'd already had my eye on, didn't seem to have a Behind form. It stayed a stick in my hand, and I abandoned it, diving as Zero's swords scythed toward me, swift and deadly. I collided painfully with the shed, old, rusted tools scattering around me, and grabbed the first one to hand without thinking about it.

A rusted, wonky-handled pair of shears faced toward Zero as I rolled to my feet, and I reefed them apart. Rust scattered from them in a brown cloud, and then there were twin knives in my hands.

"Ah, beauty!" I said, and crouched lower in the stance Zero had taught me.

I mean, it didn't make my defeat any less ignominious or swift, but it was the quickest I'd brought something through Between, and I hadn't had to think about what it could be or should be somewhere else. I'd just known I needed it, I'd grabbed it, and it was exactly what I needed.

Afterward, bruised and sweaty, sitting beneath one of the trees in the backyard, I asked Zero, "How come the stick didn't change to anything?"

"Some things have a form Between and Behind different from their form here. Others don't. Still others are very determined about what they are. Those without another form can't be changed by humans into another form."

"What about if the stick's just, um...determined about being a stick?"

"Then you have to convince it otherwise. You need to be more certain that it's not a stick, than it is that it *is* a stick."

"Makes perfect sense," I said, and I was only half-sarcastic, because it kinda did make sense. Not human sense, but a weird Between-sense. A kind of logic midway between Human logic and Behind logic. "How can you tell the difference between something that doesn't have another form, and something that doesn't *want* another form?"

"I have had," said Zero, very deliberately, "a great deal of experience in discerning stubbornness from lack of aptitude. Lately in particular."

"Yeah?" I said. "I mean, Jin Yeong's pretty annoying, but I would have thought he's been annoying you for longer than that."

"My lord," said Athelas' voice from the back door, subtly

amused. "If you're finished er, exercising the pet, there is something that requires your attention."

"What is it?"

"We've had another...visitor."

I scrambled to my feet. "Not Mr. Preston again? Did you get him to stay?"

"Not a human visitor," Athelas said. "In fact, it's more of an interloper than a visitor. We would appear to have an infestation of sorts."

"Something else came through?"

"Indeed. A small cohort of banshees has begun to wail in the rafters, and you know how irritating Jin Yeong finds them. For my part, I confess that I find Jin Yeong's irritation more inconducive to a comfortable afternoon's rest than the banshees, but no doubt that's a personal failing of my own. Perhaps you would be good enough to ward the house once again, now that the constant in and out of the Enforcers is making weak spots in our defences?"

Zero's eyes went slightly bluer, a sure sign of amusement. "Where is Jin Yeong?"

"The last I saw of him, he was searching for matches with a cannister of some pressurised, perfumed spray."

"He'll burn the house down!" I said in protest, darting for the back door. There was no way I was going to let Jin Yeong burn down my house because he couldn't put up with a few—what did Athelas say they were? Banshees? Well, they couldn't be worse than Jin Yeong, anyway.

When I skidded into the living room, Jin Yeong was already stalking the further recesses of it, a glittery look to his narrow eyes and the gas lighter in his left hand. In his right, was a can of body spray.

"Oi!" I said indignantly. "Put that down! If you burn a hole in my ceiling, I'm gunna put holy water in your coffee!"

"Go away, *Petteu*," said Jin Yeong, in Korean.

I wasn't sure if he said it with some edge of Between, or if I just understood it anyway.

"Not while you're threatening to burn down my house!"

"The house is not yours!"

"It flaming well—What the *heck*?"

Spine-tingling, hair-raising, and right on the dissonant edge of harmony, something was wailing in the ceiling. Not just one something, but several somethings, their voices high and wild and carrying.

Jin Yeong's eyes shut for a fraught, exasperated moment, then opened in a glittering slit. There was murder in those eyes. He strode toward the source of the wailing, the gas lighter clicking into life, and leaped onto the old phone table-and-chair along the back wall.

I saw them, maybe. A shifting, hairy mass of movement with eyes and feral teeth, snarling at Jin Yeong as he brought the body spray cannister up to the lighter.

I yelled and leapt for the arm with the cannister, pulling down with all my weight, my feet slipping on the slick leather of the seat.

"Stop pointing that at them!"

"*Shilloh*!" snapped Jin Yeong, turning sideways to leave me with less space.

Mongrel! He was trying to edge me off the seat and knock me to the ground. I wrapped my right hand around his wrist instead, then leaned across him to grab for the lighter with my left. The chair rocked beneath us and Jin Yeong steadied himself against the rafters with the hand that held the lighter, glaring down at me.

"*Petteu*," he said, through his teeth, "*mwoh hae?*"

"I'm stopping you burning down the house!" I panted. "Stop clicking the lighter! It'll explode!"

"*Anin ko kata.*"

I made another grab for the lighter, but Jin Yeong hissed a laugh and moved the hand with the can further away, unbalancing me. I grabbed for that wrist with both hands again, teetering at the edge of the seat, and saw Athelas sit down in his chair with the air of a man who's given up on worrying about the oddities of his household.

"Oi!" I said indignantly. "A bit of help?"

"Oh, I think not," he said, crossing one leg over the other. "Do make tea whenever you've a minute, Pet."

"*Petteu*," said JinYeong, looking down at me with a worrying gleam to his dark eyes. "I think you will regret it if you don't release my wrist."

"Yeah? What are you gunna do? Bite me? I'll just get faster again, and then what?"

JinYeong jerked his arm inward, which sent me tumbling against his chest and his back against the wall with a thump. He mustn't have been expecting it, because he exhaled pretty suddenly.

"Serves you right," I said sourly, to a background of Athelas' gentle laughter. "Zero, JinYeong's trying to burn the house down!"

"JinYeong, stop playing with the Pet," said Zero, a growl deep in his voice.

JinYeong tilted his head at me, eyes liquid and dangerous. "I do as I wish," he said very clearly. Silkily, he added, "*Petteu*, you should let go now."

I opened my mouth to tell him my own version of *I do as I wish*, but sudden movement behind his head caught my eye. A single something had separated itself from the horde of other somethings. It was very small, very hairy, and wearing a rag of tartan below the hair. I wasn't sure if the hair was a hat or a beard, it was so matted, and it didn't seem polite to ask.

"Oi," I said to it. "What do you want?"

JinYeong, startled, said something in Korean that I couldn't pay attention to because I was trying to apply my Behind hearing to the sing-song voice of the hairy tartan thing.

They wanted, said the meaning that came through Between, to *sing*.

"You can't sing in here," I said. "If you wanna live here, you can't sing. The vampire doesn't like it."

"I hate them very much," said JinYeong clearly. "They cannot live here. No singing. No living. *Hyeong*! They cannot live here!"

"You better put that down," I told him, threateningly, tipping my chin at the lighter.

He cocked a brow at me, but the flame flickered out on the lighter. I saw it drop from his hand; heard it hit the leather of the seat and then the ground. A moment later the spray can made a metallic *ting* as it hit the carpet, circular edge first.

Steadying himself with his right hand, JinYeong let the other hand drop from the rafters. Attached to that wrist and too short to steady myself on the rafters, I teetered backward and grabbed him around the waist to stop myself falling.

"Oi!"

JinYeong grinned down at me and opened his mouth to say something, but before he could say it, one huge arm wrapped around me from behind, plucking me away from him. Zero dropped me on my couch after the swift passage of a few steps, making me squeak, and crossed back to the other side of the room.

I turned and stuck out my tongue at JinYeong, who dropped down from the chair silently, with a resentful look at Zero.

"I will deal with the banshees," Zero said to him. To me, he said, "Pet, make tea and coffee. I have something for you to do."

I brightened. "Really? What?"

"Tea and coffee first," he said.

I leapt to my feet and went for the kitchen with a lightness to my steps, darting around to fetch all the things on a tray as the kettle boiled. I bounced while I waited for the kettle to finish boiling, then bounced back out to see what there was to do.

Zero, turning over JinYeong's can of body spray in one hand, accepted his tea with the other. The can moved through a few frames of reality Between, changing colour and shape as it came, and I frowned at it.

"Is it determined to be a can of perfume, or what?"

"I'm not telling it to be something, I'm building a spell around it," said Zero.

"Oh. What's this job you've got for me?"

"I need you to pick up something for me."

"Where?"

"Salamanca—this is the address. All you have to say to the man at the front desk is "pile-driver". He'll give you an envelope. Bring it home."

"I'm supposed to just say "pile-driver" at the bloke?"

"Zero did a little...preprograming," said Athelas. "You'll find him perfectly amenable, Pet."

"Who says *pile-driver* in everyday conversation?" I asked indignantly. "I'm gunna look a right galah, walking up to the bloke and saying *pile-driver* at him!"

"The unusual character of the word is in a great measure why we chose that word," Athelas said mildly. "An ignition word is very little use if someone else activates it, after all."

"You're not to talk to anybody else there," Zero said, flipping the can again. "No witnesses, no normal people, no staff."

Heck yes! I was going to one of the crime scenes? They were letting me help? "Yeah, but what's in the envelope?"

"And no poking your nose where it's got no business being."

"I never poke my nose where it's got no business being," I said piously.

Zero's chilly blue eyes rested on me for more than ten seconds, but I held my pious face. At last, his eyes lightening, he said, "Be back within the hour."

I went before it could occur to him that he hadn't told me I couldn't talk to the bloke who had the envelope. I mean, he *couldn't* have told me that, because I needed to talk to the bloke to do what I was supposed to do. But Zero didn't qualify the instructions, either, which meant I could ask the bloke other stuff as well. My guess was that he wasn't important enough to know anything crucial, and that's why Zero hadn't taken the trouble, but that wasn't going to stop me finding out for sure.

The bloke at the desk looked pretty bright and awake for someone I was supposed to be getting pre-programmed service from, so it took a bit of brass face to saunter up to the desk, lean on it, and say, "Oi. Pile-driver."

It didn't make him look any less wide-awake, but it did make him say, "I've got your mail here."

"Thanks," I said. I folded the envelope in half and slid it into my back pocket. "You see anything the other day, when the bloke was murdered?"

"I wasn't here," he said. "And I'm not supposed to tell you anything about the murder, or let you upstairs."

"Fair enough," I said. "What about the other concierge, then? You allowed to tell me anything about him?"

"I don't have instructions about that, just the murder."

"Right. So how come everyone thinks he was drunk?"

"He's either drunk or going crazy," said the concierge bluntly. "He keeps seeing dead people."

"Yeah? I've seen a few dead people myself," I told him, with a sparkle of excitement to my stomach. "What dead people did he see? I thought it was just the one."

"It was just the one until yesterday," the concierge said. "He swore black and blue that he saw the murdered bloke come downstairs after he was murdered, so the boss put me on the front desk and the cops took Sammy with them."

"What was the next dead person he saw?"

"It wasn't next exactly. The cops came back because they found another one of our members dead. They reckoned he'd been dead for at least two days, but Sammy reckons that was the member he saw going upstairs."

"Only members allowed upstairs?"

He thought about that for a while, which was weird until I realised why.

"I'm asking about club rules, not about the murder," I told him.

"Yeah, that's right," he agreed, his face clearing. "You're right: we know all the members by face, and no one who isn't a member is allowed past the desk."

"Was that all the dead people he saw?"

"As far as I know," he said.

I don't know how much of Jin Yeong's or Zero's persuasion had gone into the bloke, but it had certainly made him willing to talk if I asked the right questions. It left me regretful that I would have to go away without asking all I could, because I didn't think he'd be as easy to question if I came back without an errand from Zero. Unfortunately, I couldn't think of any other questions to ask, and I was on a time limit, so I gave him a nod, took my envelope, and said, "Catch ya later."

When I got back out on the street, feeling pleasantly guilty, it didn't take long to realise that I was being followed again. This time, it was easy to spot the person; he didn't trouble to make himself invisible. I saw the birds-nest beard and the wild gleam to the old bloke's eyes, even in the glass reflection of the café I was passing.

I grinned to myself. It'd been a while since I'd seen him properly, which probably meant he wanted me to see him. Maybe he wanted a coffee. He'd be pretty hungry these days, too; I'd been meaning to leave something out for him, and I still hadn't done it. On impulse, I turned right down Salamanca Lane instead of left, and went down the street to Wooby's Lane. I could have stopped at the café down the corner, but there was a churro shop just beyond the brass cat and dog in the square, and I was pretty sure the old mad bloke would enjoy a churro or two. I knew he liked doughnuts, anyway.

It wasn't like I was going to be gone long, so Zero couldn't complain—so long as I got back within the hour.

I ordered and sat in the outdoor section at the corner. There was a little alleyway between cafes behind and slightly to the side of me—just close enough for someone to sneak around and grab a cup of coffee and a few churros from someone's table, if they felt like it.

He must have felt like it, because I'd only been sitting there for a little while when a strong whiff of unwashed person drifted around me, and the coffee cup was gone, along with two of my churros. I gave it a few seconds before I turned my head again— long enough for him to sneak away, giggling, like he always used to —and then looked around. Where the coffee had been, there was a flower, pink and perky, its petals fluttering in the slight breeze.

I grinned a bit at the flower as I finished my churros. It was nice to know that the old bloke was safe. I hadn't seen him properly since we'd been separated on an unexpected jaunt Between, and although I'd known he would be safe, it was nice to *know* it.

I took the last churro with me as I started to head homeward, wending my way slowly up the hill toward Macquarie street. The shadows rippled softly over me, sunlight speckling through the leaves, and as I passed one of the blue ticket boxes, a tall, suited figure stepped out in front of me.

"What the—" I said, startled, and looked up.

Huge eyes looked down at me unblinkingly below two feathery, twitching antennae, and a crawling panic tried to come up my throat.

Ah heck. It was a Sandman, its face chillingly here and there, human world and Between, at the same time.

I opened my mouth to choke out a call for Zero, and one soft, slender hand reached out to rest on my shoulder. It felt like it sank into me instead of touching me, like dough sticking to an unfloured benchtop, and a curiously muffled voice said, "Where are you going?"

That was weird, because it didn't have a mouth.

"Get off!" I said, jerking my shoulder away, and my voice sounded muffled, too. That should have shrugged off the hand, but instead, it came with me, soft and sticky and viscous.

A muffledness sank into my limbs, beginning at my ears and shoulder and meeting somewhere in the middle to spread out again. Distantly, I heard a dog snarling. White fur sprang up between me and the Sandman, disconnecting the hand on my shoulder, while a terrible growling filled the air between us, clear and loud.

Daniel. It was Daniel.

I nearly said his name aloud in my relief at being able to hear and feel properly again, but I shut my mouth on it just in time. Whoever or whatever the Sandman was, Zero hadn't been happy about it knowing about me. The less it knew about what *I* knew, the better.

"You should sleep," said the Sandman, in its odd, multilayered voice, and tried to lay its hand on Daniel's head instead of my arm.

He snarled and bit its wrist, shaking his huge head to snap the bone, and the Sandman gave a sighing gasp that made me feel sick. I didn't understand why he didn't try to pull away until I saw the way that hand was shaping and growing around Daniel's teeth, filling his mouth with pliable whiteness while Daniel shook his head, eyes rolling.

Ah heck. What was I supposed to do against something even a lycanthrope couldn't beat?

I looked around wildly for something, *anything* that looked like it could change into another form, but we were well and truly in the human world. There was a glimmer of Between to the pillars that made a doorway into St. David's Park beside us, and I took off for that sliver of hope.

The Sandman's voice rippled through the air behind me, giving chase, and the flicker of Between around the park entrance bled toward me as I ran. A couple of steps before the park itself, the world dropped down half a foot—or maybe it just went a bit sideways. Whatever it was, it jarred my teeth and set the world into shades of grey around me. I wasn't quite Between, but there was a shade of it over everything I was looking at.

And the Sandman, dragging Daniel behind it on an elastic, swiftly lengthening hand, flickered between the trees along the edge of the park as it grimly made its way toward the entrance.

Flaming heck. I still needed a weapon.

But now the world around me was full of possibilities—grimy, leafy, spray-painted possibilities—and I felt the stirring of hope. I knew how to work here. I still couldn't beat Zero, probably never would, but all I needed to do was put the Sandman off its game for long enough to run away.

I was good at hitting stuff, and running, and hiding.

I flicked a glance around me, and there were sticks everywhere. Sticks that might not be sticks if I could be persuasive enough. I picked up the closest, a thin, long one that was almost impossibly straight, and said to it, "You're a golf club."

Maybe it already was a golf club. Maybe it had always wanted to be one. When I picked it up, there was no doubt about it—it was a golf club.

I sprinted back toward the entrance of the park, and as the Sandman turned the corner, I let it have it around the head with the golf club, hard and fast. It impacted like I'd hit a piece of well-rested dough, sinking into the plastic-y face the Sandman wore on the outside, and somehow closed *around* the haft of the club.

The Sandman staggered, its elongated arm shuddering, and tried to reform. Daniel collapsed to the grass on four tangled legs, but scrambled to his feet in a moment, lurching at me. I grabbed his scruff and turned to run for it, unsure if I was pulling him along or if he was pulling me.

Gotta get to the end of the park, I said savagely to myself. *Just to the end of the park.*

I could see the exit as we ran; a distant, not-quite-right version of itself from the inside of the world, brightly coloured with a patch of the human world between its pillars.

Something gibbered at us from the trees as we ran, but I didn't dare look up. I knew that there were still some doll parts hanging from the trees further up, an art display from far too long ago, and I didn't want to see what they looked like here. Mostly I was just afraid that they'd still be doll parts.

We tumbled into the buzzing colour of the human world and legged it up the hill toward Davy Street without stopping until we got to the construction site at the top. Then we stopped, panting, and Daniel nipped in past the fluttering plastic, me following his tail. It wasn't until he started changing back that I remembered he'd be coming back without much to cover him, and hastily turned around.

I heard scrabbling, then shuffling, and Daniel's voice said, "It's all right; you're pack."

"Might be all right for you, but there's stuff I don't wanna see," I said.

There was a bit of a snort from behind me, but he said, "Don't worry. We've got dead-drops around the city." He came into view, feet bare and hair rumpled, but at least he had on a wrinkled t-shirt and jeans.

"Thanks for the help," I said. "How come you were following me, anyway?"

"I wasn't following you, I was following *it*," said Daniel. "I'm trying to trace it back to somewhere useful."

"Yeah? How useful is that gunna be to you when you're dead?"

"I'm not going to attack them or anything," he said impatiently. "I'd call my pack in."

"Yeah, and get all *them* killed."

"I'm not trying to get anyone killed," Daniel said, even more testily. "I'll talk to the Troika once I've got a location. They're pretty keen to know where Upper Management keeps themselves these days."

"Make sure you tell me, too," I said.

"Of course," he said. "I told you: you're pack."

"They'll tell you not to tell me."

He shrugged. "They're not pack. They don't control me."

I felt a warmth of friendship with him that even being part lycanthrope hadn't bought about. "Thanks," I said.

"Don't be stupid," he said uncomfortably. "What else would I do? I'll walk you home, okay?"

"Better not," I said. "I'm already gunna have to run for it to get home on time, and if they see you with me as well, I'm going to be in for it."

"All right. I'll go with you as far as the mall, then."

I was very nearly late home, after all that. I managed to catch a bus that was heading up into North Hobart along Elizabeth Street in the nick of time, and caught a glimpse of Athelas strolling up the path to the house as the bus passed just beyond my street to the next stop.

The flaming sneaky so-and-sos! I thought indignantly. What was the bet that they'd sent me off to do something errandy while Athelas was sent off to do the Real Thing.

Scowling, I came down the bus steps and hurried toward the house. Annoyed or not, I had the feeling I'd better not be late, especially today. I was already going to have to find some way of telling Zero that I'd been attacked by the Sandman again, without mentioning the appearance of Daniel. Whether or not Zero already knew about Daniel's attack and escape, I didn't want to let him know I'd been seeing Daniel.

There wasn't a sound of wailing to the house when I let myself in, and the air was heavy with JinYeong's body spray, so I was betting Zero was done with whatever he'd been doing to the can earlier. Maybe he'd turned the cologne into anti-banshee spray or something.

I trotted into the living room to hand him the envelope and tried not to look like I was dying to know what was inside it. Now, I thought, sitting down on my side of the couch, all I had to do was figure out a way to bring up the Sandman. I puffed a sigh into the living room to disperse a bit of the perfume, and considered my options while Jin Yeong said something sniffy to Athelas.

"Pet," said Athelas, in such a ruminative sort of way that it took me by surprise when he said softly and unexpectedly, "You seem to have picked up an admirer."

I looked up to find his eyes on me, and tried not to swallow. Beggar me. Had he seen the old mad bloke following me lately? "Yeah? What d'you mean?"

"Jin Yeong says you smell like...*dog*."

I glared accusingly at Jin Yeong, but he just raised a brow at me, mouth pursed. Like *he* was miffed at *me*. What the heck did he have to be complaining about? He was the one who'd just ratted on me!

"Ran into a wer—lycanthrope. That's all."

"I told you not to go looking for the lycanthrope," said Zero briefly.

"*Nan mariya,*" Jin Yeong said. "*Ah, nemsae!*"

"Look who's talking," I shot back at him. "The whole house smells like you! It's a flaming *pong*!"

While he was muttering, "Pong*i mwohji?*" I said to Zero, very carefully truthful, "I wasn't looking for Daniel. I was minding my own business, walking along the street to get home after running my errand, and that mothman thing—"

"It is in fact, a Sandman," Athelas reminded me. Like I'd really forget that fa—well, that was kinda the idea of a Sandman. You did forget their faces. Or couldn't see them. Or something.

Anyway, I'd seen its real face, and I wasn't gunna forget it in a hurry, even if humans usually did.

"Yeah, the Sandman," I said. "I was minding my own business, and it tried to grab me. Daniel must have been following me like you said, 'cos he came out of nowhere and went for its arm."

"Interesting, wouldn't you say?" Athelas said, to Zero. "That's the second time it's taken an interest in our Pet."

"Hang on, *it*? It's the same one? How do you know?"

"There are very few Sandmen in the world at any one time," said Zero. "It would be unlikely for there to be another in the whole of Australia, not to mention Tasmania. And I would like to know why it has an interest in my pet."

"Yeah, me too," I said approvingly.

Zero, looking as annoyed as I had seen him, said, "This... complicates matters."

"Indeed," said Athelas, but his eyes were more amused than annoyed. "Quite the conundrum. Then shall we bring the Pet with us, or leave her?"

"She gets into too much trouble when we leave her alone."

"Oi!" I said indignantly. "I'm right here, you know."

"I told you," Zero said, leaning forward across the coffee table, "not to visit that werewolf."

"I didn't go to visit him," I said, nose to nose with Zero and unblinking. "And actually, they're *lycanthropes*."

Zero coughed. "Don't push things too far, Pet," he said threateningly, but there wasn't the coldness that's usually in his eyes when he gives orders. "Put on your coat."

"Beauty!" I said, and went and grabbed my hoodie from my bedroom.

Zero came down into the living room as I was leaping down the last couple of stairs, and looked frowningly at my sandals.

"You can't wear those if you're coming with us," he said. "Put on your sneakers."

"Can't," I said. "They got ruined while we were getting Athelas out of that place."

Across the room, JinYeong's brow went up, and I shot him a

narrow-eyed look. He sniffed and looked away. The shoes weren't exactly ruined, they'd just been soaked in so much blood that despite Jin Yeong's cleaning, they'd kept a rusty-red shade to them. It wasn't just that—they'd gone all stiff and weird from the soaking, and no matter how often I tried to tell myself they were clean, it was hard to think of them as clean when I knew they'd been soaked with so much blood.

"Fine," said Zero. "But you're not coming Between with your toes uncovered. You can go the long way around with Jin Yeong."

"Don't see why you can't piggy-back me," I muttered, but since I didn't really fancy the idea of going Between with my toes out there for any passing goblin to spear with their little needles, I only muttered it.

Maybe Zero heard anyway. I saw the edge of one eyebrow up as he turned to go with Athelas, and there was that lighter blue shade to his eyes that meant he was trying not to show that he was laughing.

Jin Yeong sniffed and said the Korean equivalent of "as if!" but he got up, too. With Between edging the words into my understanding, he asked, "Where do we go?"

Zero looked at me. "Where is the closest sea?"

If I'd been under the impression that we were going to the sea for any reason that had to do with the murders, I was wrong. We went so that Zero and Athelas could recharge their fae batteries or whatever.

Oh well. I didn't much fancy being left alone in the house if the Sandman worked out where to find me, after all, and Kingston Beach was nice if you knew where to go. Jin Yeong talked someone into driving us there, then stared out the window the whole time without looking at me.

He was still looking pretty sulky when we got to the beach and found the other two, so I sat next to Zero, nudging myself against his side to avoid the rocks he used as a prop, and watched Athelas watch the sea with half-closed eyes. After a while, even JinYeong sat down near Athelas to glare at me; and after a while, that glare turned into a more mellow expression, his eyes half-lidded against the golden evening sunshine.

I wriggled a bit to dig my sandaled feet into the sand, and leaned my head against Zero. He wasn't very warm, but he was comfortable to lean against, and the sunshine was warm enough, anyway. I stuck out my tongue at JinYeong, who was now watching me with more of a smouldering resentment than an active dislike, and shut my eyes.

CHAPTER SEVEN

WE PETS TAKE OUR SLEEP WHERE WE CAN GET IT. YOU NEVER know when you're going to have to go out in the middle of the night, or when you're going to be staying up until all hours. So it could have been the prosaic wisdom of sleeping when I could, or even extreme tiredness that made me fall asleep on the beach. But I was inclined to think it was mostly because it was nice to be sitting in sun-warmed sand with the huge, slow in-and-out of breathing that was Zero relaxed and recharging, behind me.

I woke up once to a feeling of steady, running footsteps, then the sensation of flying, my feet tucked safely away in Zero's leather jacket and my arms folded against his chest. Brickwork fluttered past my eyeline briefly, and I came to the conclusion that Zero had sprinted up a construction ramp and leapt into space that grew green and feathery around us.

We landed lightly in something that was much softer than the concrete I expected, and I fell asleep again, secure in my safety. There was no Sandman who could catch me now.

I dreamt of flying and woke at about noon on the couch, my sandaled feet hanging over the edge of the cushions and still sandy. I yawned up at the ceiling, then lifted my head to see all of the psychos around me. Jin Yeong hovered by the kitchen, as if he didn't care to be seen paying attention, but Athelas was wearing one of his more amused looks.

I sat up, about to demand, "What?" when something boxy hit me in the stomach. I caught it instinctively, and said "Oi!"

"Open it, then make lunch," said Zero.

"What is it?"

"Open it," he said briefly.

"Yeah, but it's a *shoe* box."

"One inevitably finds shoes in a shoe box," remarked Athelas. "Thus the mystery ends."

"No, one flaming doesn't," I said. "Sometimes one finds a dead pet."

But there were shoes in this one: boots, to be exact. They were black and leather, with buckles around the ankle. They weren't light like my sneakers had been, but they looked like they might be comfortable once I'd worn them in. And they had enough sole to them that I wouldn't have to worry about blood soaking in.

"Ugh," I said, grimacing.

"If you don't like them, I can take them back," Zero said stiffly.

"What? No, I was just thinking that I live a life where I have to think about what kind of shoe is best to stop blood getting into 'em," I explained. "These are perfect."

"*Nae malun,*" said Jin Yeong smugly.

"What, *you* picked 'em out? Rubbish. Athelas did it, didn't you, Athelas?"

"Jin Yeong picked them out," Zero said. "I was going to get you the same sneakers again. Athelas wasn't there."

I gave the offended Jin Yeong a slightly approving nod. "All right, your taste isn't so bad."

Jin Yeong said coldly and clearly, "My taste is always perfect."

"When did you get them, anyway?" I asked. It had been well

past Tasmanian shop hours when we were at the beach, even if I could have seen any of the three psychos striding into a shoe shop to purchase shoes. "And how did you get the right size?"

"Play with them later," Zero said briefly, apparently at the end of his capacity for answering questions. "Lunch first. What of the surveillance footage you watched, Pet?"

"Pretty much what you saw," I said. "Blokes getting their hearts torn out by someone who knew where the cameras were. Oh. And one woman copping it as well."

"Was there anything odd about any of them?"

"Apart from the fact that a bloke was punching people in the chest and pulling out their hearts? Not really. Did you ask Detective Tuatu if he figured out how the murderer knew where all the cameras were? S'pose you got the footage from him, so I bet he's been looking at a bit more than that."

"Take another look at them after lunch. I want to be sure there's nothing more there."

That was all well and good, I thought gloomily, as I went into the kitchen to make pancakes; but if Zero wasn't looking at the footage himself, it was because he didn't think there was much there. And that meant it was a distraction. Still, I already had a few questions for Detective Tuatu, and this was just one more. If the murderer knew where all the cameras were, he must have been scoping out the place earlier. Maybe he'd been picked up on the cameras while he was learning where they were.

When I came back into the living room after washing the lunch dishes, there was a general stirring about the room; Zero slipping knives into his cross-chest sheaths, Athelas shrugging himself into his houndstooth jacket. Only Jin Yeong stayed where he was.

"You're just trying to keep me busy with the footage so I don't try to sneak after you all when you go out, aren't you?" I said suspiciously.

"That was the general idea," said Zero, without cracking a smile.

Flaming condescending of them, I thought indignantly. Still, it was something to do that was at least slightly helpful, and it would be nice to see their faces if I turned up anything interesting or important.

"Fine then," I said. "I'll liaise with Detective Tuatu and ask him about the rest of the footage."

"Don't liaise," said Zero. "You can ask him about it, but that's all. You're not our emissary, and he's not authorised to tell you anything that isn't about the footage."

"Rude," I said. "I'll ask him later, then. Maybe go visit him at the cop shop."

"Make sure you don't accidentally come across anything you shouldn't see while you're there," Zero warned. "I'll be sure to ask the detective how well you behaved."

"I'm house-trained," I said innocently. "No worries."

"Hm," said Zero. "Perhaps Jin Yeong should go with the Pet if she goes on foot."

"Rude," I said again, but by then no one was listening to me, because the house was getting uneasy around us. I said gloomily, "Flaming fantastic."

It was visitors again, dead cert.

"We gotta do something about the amount of vermin in this place," I said, not quite below my breath, as the linen closet door began to open.

"Jin Yeong," said Zero beneath his breath, "look after the Pet."

"*Ye, hyeong,*" Jin Yeong said, in resigned sort of way that was flaming rich, coming from *him*, and reached out to hook a finger into my collar. "*Catchiga, Petteu.*"

He tugged me toward our usual couch, then shoved me lightly toward it until I sat down. Oh well. At least this time I'd be able to watch the show, even if I was being sent to bed like a good pet, so to speak.

They came through the door one at a time, a guard first, then the golden fae and his female lieutenant, then two more guards.

The golden fae looked around and locked eyes with me for the barest second, then passed on to JinYeong. With a faint curl to his lips, he made a dismissive gesture toward us, and all the sound in the room cut off abruptly.

"Ugh!" I said, shaking my head. If I couldn't hear my own voice, I would have thought I'd gone deaf.

JinYeong said something rude in Korean and threw himself elegantly on the couch beside me. Ah. So the golden fae had done it, and included JinYeong in it.

"That's just rude," I said, in disgust.

JinYeong shrugged one shoulder, and said so that I could understand it, "What else did you expect?"

"Is Zero gunna let him do that?"

"It is not an insult to you," he said.

"Doesn't make him any less of a prat, though," I said. I caught the eye of the female fae and gave her a grin and a thumbs up. If she could hold her own with Zero, that was impressive.

She looked amused, but wouldn't acknowledge the gesture, which was probably sensible. Her boss was hard enough to deal with already.

I pointed my chin at the golden fae, and asked JinYeong, "What's his name, anyway?"

JinYeong made a sound that was a bit like someone working up a spitball.

"I didn't ask what you thought of him, I asked what his name is. I can't just keep calling him *the galah* in my head."

"*Andwae?*"

"Well, I can, but I'll probably call him that by mistake one day, and then if he doesn't kill me, Zero will."

He said something about Zero that carried the faintest meaning that Zero wouldn't let that happen.

"Yeah," I said, slightly comforted, "but I wanna know. Was that thing you...said...his name?"

"*Ne.*"

I snorted. "What, even his own mum hated him?"

Jin Yeong made a hissing little laugh that he didn't try to hide from the golden fae, and I saw the golden eyes flash.

Disastrously clear, I heard the golden fae say, "They should have put that one down like his sister."

It came so easily through the soundproofing he'd put up that I knew he meant it to be hearable to us—well, to Jin Yeong, anyway.

There was a moment of molten silence that made it very clear to me that Jin Yeong and I were the only ones who had heard the remark: outside our bubble that had fractured with the words, Zero was still discussing something with the female lieutenant, and Athelas sat back, observing it all with a faint smile.

Jin Yeong's profile, all white and burnt-sockets for eyes that glittered straight ahead without seeing anything, hovered in front of my own face, impossible to look away from.

I felt as though I'd been shaken to my core. It hadn't occurred to me that Jin Yeong could be hurt—that he had any kind of personhood in him that could be cut to the heart or pinched to the quick. He was just a vampire—just one of the psychos.

I saw a blur of movement, and instinctively grabbed at Jin Yeong's hand. If I hadn't been still running on vampire saliva, I probably wouldn't have caught it. Jin Yeong's head turned at once, dark, liquid eyes focusing on me, and two bared incisors snarled far too close for comfort.

"You better not," I said, low and threatening. I didn't know what to say that would actually stop him, so I fell back on sarcasm, as usual. "If I bite you back in self-defence, I bet I know which one of us Zero's gunna blame."

"*Nwa*," he said, but there was some warmth of colour back in his face.

I tipped my head at the golden fae, who stood with his fingers just touching his sword and his balance all forward and low like Zero had taught me from my first training lessons. "He's just waiting for you to go after him. He wants to kill you."

"*Pft*," said JinYeong, a dismissive hiss of air. As if he hadn't just looked like someone stabbed him through the heart. Painstakingly understandable, he said, "I would kill him in a moment."

"Yeah, but then I'd have more mess to clean up," I explained. "And that's a pain in the neck. Anyway, I think Zero wants some info out of him before you tear his throat out."

"Very well," said JinYeong, his fingers relaxing within mine. "Then I shall kill him next time."

"Okay," I said. "Just make sure Zero doesn't see. I'll help you hide the body."

I let go of his hand, and he didn't try to lash out or get up, so he must have been appeased. Still, by way of distraction, I spent the rest of the meeting poking him and leaving dirty marks on his trousers until he snarled at me, and by the time the fae were moving toward the linen cupboard door, Athelas had ceased to pay attention to them and was amusedly observing us instead.

When the last fae guard disappeared from the room, sound abruptly opened to us again, and Athelas said, "What a novel way you have of spending your time, Pet!"

JinYeong glared at me and dusted his trousers off, but I bounced up, ignoring him.

"What was all that about? Are you going out again?"

"JinYeong, stay with the pet," said Zero, without answering me. "We've some business Behind."

It must have meant something to JinYeong, because he looked interested as well as faintly satisfied. He spoke in Korean, and Between whispered the meaning of, "So you got it from them at last," in my mind.

I glanced between Zero and JinYeong. "What's Zero got?"

Had he got the information he had wanted out of this

exchange? There was no way: I didn't trust the golden fae to give anything useful at this point.

"Good pets," said Athelas, "do not ask questions to which there are inconvenient answers."

"I know, I know," I grumbled, sitting down again. "I'm not supposed to ask, and I'm not included."

"I've not noticed," said Zero dryly, "that it makes much difference what you're not supposed to do."

"Rude!" I said. "I'm always an obedient pet!"

"I've not noticed," he replied again, even more dryly, "that you're always obedient. Jin Yeong, I've dealt with the banshees but I'll need to ward the house later. Make sure the pet doesn't play with anything she shouldn't touch."

"*Ne,*" said Jin Yeong, unusually obedient.

He must have seen me rolling my eyes, because he cocked one eyebrow at me as Zero and Athelas left, mouthing, "*Wae?*"

I just shrugged at him, but when the shifting of Between was done, I jumped up from my seat. "I'm going out."

Jin Yeong shook his head. "*Andwae.*"

"Zero didn't say I couldn't go anywhere," I argued. "He just said you have to go with me if I go."

"*Shilloh,*" he said, sitting down on the couch.

I didn't need to use my Between hearing to work that one out —he said it so often that I knew that meaning without assistance.

"You're a pain in the neck," I said accusingly.

"*Ne!*" said Jin Yeong smugly, crossing one leg over the other.

"Well, you shouldn't be so flaming proud of it!" I retorted. "Fine; I'll call the detective over instead."

I don't think Detective Tuatu would have believed that I was allowed to look at the footage and discuss it with him if he hadn't seen Jin Yeong as soon as he walked through the door.

He nodded warily at Jin Yeong, who smirked at him, and said, "I don't suppose I could have a cuppa, could I?"

"I'll even get you some biscuits," I said, heading for the kitchen. "I wanted to ask you about the rest of the footage and stuff."

The detective followed me. He was probably put off by Jin Yeong's unblinking stare. "The rest of it?"

"Yeah. I mean, the bloke obviously knows where all the cameras are, so—"

"We noticed that, too," Tuatu said grimly. "I've had someone combing over the rest of the footage for the last couple of days, but we haven't been able to pinpoint anyone in all five lots of footage."

"How'd he get the info on the cameras, then?" I demanded, filling the kettle.

"From the security company, perhaps. I've got someone looking into that, as well—I might have more answers for you— for *them*—tomorrow."

"Oh yeah," I said. "That reminds me. I wanted you to have a look at one of the clips—the one of the woman getting murdered. I thought I saw something there, but I'm not sure."

Not to mention the dead guy who was walking around. I wanted to ask about him, too, but not in front of Jin Yeong, who had followed us, slowly and softly, into the kitchen. That they already knew about it, I was fairly certain; that they wouldn't want me to know about, I was absolutely certain about. Maybe I'd have to text my questions.

Detective Tuatu nodded wearily, and I wondered how many times he'd looked at the footage himself. Just enough to get nightmares, or enough so that it was all a flat jumble of nasty that wasn't quite real?

"I'll bring the biscuits," I said, by way of cheering him up, and Jin Yeong made a sulky complaint from his side of the kitchen island. To him, I said, "You've still got blood in the fridge. Stop whinging."

"Blood?" said Detective Tuatu, startled, as I grabbed the biscuits and my coffee. "There's *blood* in your fridge?"

"Yeah, it goes bad if you leave it out," I called over my shoulder.

"That's not what I meant," he said, catching up with me at the top of the stairs. "Where are you getting blood from?"

"A couple hospitals, mostly," I said. "Not too much, though; Jin Yeong usually goes out and gets a bit of fresh stuff whenever he's too hungry."

There was an eloquent silence behind me before Detective Tuatu sighed and said, "Why do I even ask?"

"Dunno," I said cheerfully, switching on the monitor. "Woulda thought you'd know better by now."

I put the biscuits down beside the keyboard on his side and kicked a chair toward him. "Sit down. I've got to find the right clip and the right part of it. Plus I've got some other questions."

"Can't wait. What are the other two up to?"

I shrugged. "Dunno. They've been leaving the house without telling me where they're going, these days. Sometimes they're going to crime scenes, but I'm pretty sure this arvo was about something else. It's got something to do with Zero, and they're telling me diddly squat."

"You think it's something to do with those...people who were at the latest crime scene?"

"Definitely," I said, scowling. I'd liked the fae little enough when they came with a previous job offer for Zero; I liked them far less now that they were playing games with Zero and actively making life annoying for me. I brought up one of the files, and to my surprise, it was the right one straight away. "Here, this one. It's just before she gets done in."

Detective Tuatu leaned forward in his chair, resting his elbows against the desk. "What do you see, anyway?" he asked me.

"That's what Athelas asked me, too. Why are you lot so concerned with what I see? I'm just a pet."

"You're not a pet, you're a girl. And I asked you that because what I see is different from what they said they could see."

"How d'you mean, it's different?" Even Athelas had said he saw the same as me, and he had more of a reason to be weird than Detective Tuatu did. "It's video surveillance—it doesn't change."

"I don't know," said Tuatu. "But if you're seeing what they say they see, they shouldn't have had you watching this footage."

"You mean the bloke reaching in with his hand and tearing out hearts?"

Detective Tuatu sucked in a breath through his teeth. "That's really what you see?"

"Yeah." I frowned at him for a while, and then asked, "What do you see?"

"That's the thing," he said. "When I watched it the first time, I thought I saw a knife."

"There's no knife."

"Yeah," he said dryly. "I was beginning to think that. What is it instead?"

"Told ya. He literally punches them in the chest and pulls out their hearts. It's flaming disgusting."

The detective looked a bit sick. "I knew there was something weird about it, but I had to look at it by myself because the others wouldn't believe me if I tried to tell them. Even when I slowed it down to frames and looked them over one by one, I couldn't get a grip on it. It's like there's a fuzzy patch in my brain with a little bit of information missing, and every time I go to check on it, I forget what I'm looking at until I'm looking at another frame with all the blood."

"Flamin' Behindkind," I said. I pulled out my phone and tapped on the photos Morgana had sent me. "Oi. What do you see with this, then?"

"Looks like one of the North Hobart houses to me."

"Who do you see standing outside the house?"

"A bloke with more muscles than fashion sense. Looks like he's checking out the house."

"Just one bloke?"

"Are you telling me there are two people in this photo?"

"Yeah. And one of them isn't a bloke, either. It's a Behindkind with a moth sorta head."

Detective Tuatu sat back in his seat with a hopeless gesture and slumped there for a few moments. At last, he burst out, "How am I supposed to do any type of effective police work in a world like this!"

"Yeah, it's a pain in the neck," I said.

"Every time I think I might have a handle on it, something else comes up. I don't even know enough to know what I'm missing."

"I know the feeling," I said comfortingly. "But there's gotta be some way of fixing stuff like this—or at least of making it possible to see people like this."

"If even a camera doesn't capture them, what can technology do?"

"Breathe, it's gunna be fine. We'll sort it out. Get a Behind-kind who knows about electronics or something, I dunno."

"Are there...are there fae like that?"

I shrugged. "Bound to be. And we've got a computer here nowadays, so Behindkind must be able to use technology. Well, my Behindkind, anyway."

"Did you set it up?"

"Nah, I don't know much about computers. Jin Yeong kidnapped some techs."

Tuatu, sounding exasperated, said, "I knew it! As soon as those two came into work with dark circles to their knees and saying they couldn't remember what happened last night, I knew it was something to do with that lot!"

"He kidnapped police geeks?"

"A woman in a Doctor Who t-shirt and a man with a woodcutter's beard?"

"That's them."

"Yeah. Do they know they could have just *asked?*"

"Probably. If it helps, I don't reckon Jin Yeong bit either of 'em."

"That's a real comfort."

"It should be," I told him, grinning. "Otherwise *they* might start getting a bit peckish too, if you get my meaning."

The detective went a bit pale. "Oh. *Oh.* How do I know if—"

"Told ya. They start getting a bit peckish. From what Zero told me when I was bitten, you would have noticed by now."

"The vampire bit you?"

"He's bitten me a few times now. So long as I don't bite him back, it's fine."

"Yeah, sounds perfectly normal. What are you doing?"

"This bit," I said, rewinding the video. "This is the bit I wanted you to see. It's weird."

I'd seen it the first time I watched it: a kind of flicker to the scene. Or maybe not a flicker so much as a hesitation. I rewound the last few seconds; played them again, and the bloke flickered again, just for a millisecond.

"That," I said, pointing at the screen. "What's that?"

"A corruption in the file, we assumed."

"Yeah, but the rest of it's fine. Smooth, and high-res. It's top of the line security. It's more like, I dunno..."

Detective Tuatu sat back. "What? You think it's something to do with Behind?"

"I dunno," I said again, rewinding it once more. "But would you call that a hesitation, just before he kills her?"

"Only if he's moving at a speed faster than the cameras can pick up," the detective protested. "And it's not like that's—*is* it possible?"

"Yeah," I said darkly. "I reckon so. I would have tried to slow it right down to frames, but I don't know how to do that."

"Shove over."

"You know how without your geek squad?"

"I came up through the geek squad," he said, grinning. "Hang on a tick."

It actually took him about half an hour, but when he was done, it was all laid out there on the screen, frame by frame for us to scroll through.

"It's only sixty frames per second," the detective said. "So there won't be a lot more detail than we could already see in the video—and I won't be much use if you're trying to see the...the heart-pulling-out stuff."

"We only need one of us to be able to do that," I said. "Beauty! This is perfect."

I scrolled through them swiftly, each business-card sized frame rolling upward, until I came to the series closest to the tearing out of the victim's heart. More slowly now, I scrolled through them, and as I did there was a series of sixty or so that were exactly the same—the murderer, frozen, just before he tore out her heart. The only difference to each of the frames was the amount of darkness, and three of those frames were complete darkness just before the murder.

I studied them, frowning, and said, "He's definitely hesitating —for about half a second, I reckon. But how come some of these are black?"

"I'll ask the geek squad to look at them," Tuatu said. "It's probably just a problem with the file, like I said, but we'd better make sure."

"D'you reckon he's hesitating because she's a woman? None of the other victims on the flash drive are female."

"He could be," Tuatu said. "But I don't think so. Someone who can pull out someone else's heart isn't likely to be squeamish about killing a woman as well."

"Yeah, that's what I thought," I said, in dissatisfaction. "But he's definitely hesitating—and the shadows do something weird every time he hesitates."

"It's not when he hesitates," the detective said. "It's afterward. First the shadows are everywhere, then as soon as he does...whatever it is he's doing, they're gone."

"Does it happen in any of the others? I only remember the one from the club in Salamanca."

"Not that I noticed," said the detective. "He keeps turning off lights before he goes in, though."

"All right," I said, clicking on a random footage file. I wasn't so sure—I seemed to remember something about shadows in one of the other murders, but I couldn't remember which one.

The footage flickered up, the date stamped in the bottom left-hand corner, and I said, "Hey, this is the one after the woman got killed. How come they weren't in order?"

"They were when I sent them with Athelas," Tuatu said, frowning. "Did you reorder them by accident?"

"Heck if I know. You reckon this bloke is planning on killing someone else? He's already killed five people, and you'd think that'd be enough for one bloke."

"Those three seem to think he is. They're preparing to keep someone safe at the moment."

"Ah, so *that*'s where they've been going all week!"

Detective Tuatu said something under his breath that might have been rude. I was pretty sure he'd forgotten he wasn't meant to talk to me about any of this.

"Don't worry," I said, grinning. "I won't tell on you. Oi. Does the murderer look a bit thinner to you in this one?"

The detective nodded. "I thought so, too, but he's always wearing one of those big suede jackets, so it's hard to get a good read on size. It might just be this recording, too."

"Maybe," I agreed. "I mean, the victim's hair looks like someone put a mop on his head, so—"

"No, that's because he's wearing a wig and there's a huge lump in his skull underneath it. Apparently he had a rare type of benign tumour—he was going in for surgery tomorrow. I found out from the slab boys in the morgue this morning."

"So that's why it bulges out funny on the right side."

"Exactly. I thought it was just the shadows when I watched the footage the first time."

"Yeah, that's another thing. Doesn't it look like there's a lot of 'em in this one, too?" I asked him. "The shadows, I mean; more than usual. And they seem to move a lot, too."

Detective Tuatu squinted at the monitor. "Are you sure it's not just because the lights are out? It's pretty hard to see anything along the bottom half of the room with that floor. It could just be the blood."

"Yeah," I said slowly. "Maybe. Let's look at the one from the club house—it's all pink and white on the bottom half. Should be easier to see shadow against that, even when he turns the light off."

Tuatu switched videos with a few clicks of the mouse and brought up the exact time when the murderer entered the room.

"Watched these a few times, have you?" I said, with grim amusement. "Oi! Tuatu, his cap—!"

At the same time, the detective said, "No way."

We looked at each other, wide eyed, then back at the screen. In the club room, the murderer's right side was to the screen, his cap bulging at the side. The clothes were all the same as they had been in every other clip, but that cap...

Tuatu leaned forward and snapped down on the pause button.

"There's no way," he said. "This one is the latest murder—it's *after* the one we just watched. The bloke's dead, and he's definitely not the murderer. It's gotta be a trick of the lighting."

"Pretty flamin' specific trick of the lighting," I said slowly, my thoughts whirling. I'd seen a dead man, and so had the concierge. He hadn't taken it too well, but I knew better—I should have known better. I hadn't even double checked the footage. I said in annoyance, "I'm an idiot."

"What is it?

"You blokes thought the concierge had been drinking a bit, didn't you?"

"He smelt like a brewery and he told us he saw the murdered bloke leave the club three hours after he was dead."

"Fantastic!" I said, beaming.

"I'm glad you think so," Tuatu said grumpily. "It's not much good for us if we need to put him on the witness stand!"

"Yeah, but I saw a dead bloke yesterday, myself," I told him, grinning. "I reckon we've got a lead for the psychos."

"You saw a dead—have they been taking you to crime scenes again?"

"Nah, this dead bloke was walking around, buying smokes."

"He what?"

"He was at the cigarette counter, buying cigarettes. His name's Cameron Michaels, according to his ID."

"That makes absolutely no sense, Pet."

"You're telling me! What kind of Behindkind smokes cigarettes? I didn't think their lungs were even the same as ours. I know their blood's not."

"Talking with you is a rollercoaster, you know that? None of the murdered men were named Cameron Michaels."

"I'd look into it if I were you," I advised. "Reckon the psychos will be interested."

"Haven't you already told them about seeing a dead bloke?" There was incredulity to his voice. "Pet!"

"I thought the psychos already knew," I said. Now, I doubted it. Whatever Jin Yeong had been looking at in the street that day, it hadn't been the dead bloke. "I'll tell 'em. You just find out about that name, and who he is."

"I'll look into it," he said. "But I'm telling them when I know."

"I told you," I said, a bit grumpily. "I'll tell 'em about the bloke. Just make sure you've got the info ready when they ask."

Tuatu sipped his tea and leaned back in his chair. "They've got a name now, you know."

"You changing the subject?"

"Yes. The boys upstairs are calling them the Troika."

"I already heard," I said. "Flamin' imaginative of everyone. Oi. I didn't think there were any boys upstairs anymore."

There was a brief pause before Tuatu said cautiously, "They don't go up to the seventh floor any more, but they've got an upper floor feel to them. They're just keeping their heads down."

"Reckon that's why no one's followed up on trying to frame you? 'Cos they're keeping their heads down for now?"

"I'm still keeping an eye out for that, believe me," said Tuatu.

"All right," I said. "I better tell the psychos about it, though. They'll want to know that there's still Upper Management worming their way around in the police station."

"I'm not going to lose a limb for it," Tuatu warned me. "I'll tell them—and I won't let on that I told you. I'm pretty sure that's something I'm not meant to be discussing with you."

"Sook," I said accusatorily. "All right, you tell 'em about that. I'll let them know about Cameron Michaels. Don't go telling your boss you're looking him up, though."

"Of course, I was going to tell my boss that I'm running an address search on a dead bloke. Makes perfect sense."

"You going straight back to the station from here?"

Detective Tuatu looked across at me. "Are you kicking me out?"

"Yeah. I've got to finish off dinner yet, and they'll be back soon."

"I want to ask them some questions, too."

Oh yeah. Detective Tuatu was also investigating. "Sorry," I said, grinning. I should be the last person trying to push people out of an investigation. "You can stay for dinner, too, if you want.

It's just chilli mince, so there's a whole pot of it. You like cornbread?"

"If it's cooked, I'll eat it," he said, shrugging. I had the feeling he didn't trust my cooking.

Mind you, I've seen his place, and what there is to eat there. He couldn't do much worse, if you asked me.

"It's cooked *and* it's good," I said coldly. "C'mon; you can help me by setting the table."

"Just a second," he said. "I want to check something first."

"What are we checking?" I plumped myself back into my seat and watched him flicker over the flash drive icon with the mouse.

First he turned it into a list, then he ordered it by date.

"Nice," I said, giving him the thumbs up. "Make sure we've got the evidence in order. Good thinking."

"I have my moments," he murmured, and pressed play.

It was much more obvious watching the clips in the order that the murders happened. Still just as unbelievable, but more obvious. In the first clip our murderer was shorter than the bloke he murdered, a slightly chunky man in a big jacket and big shoes. In the second, I could see the difference in the way that jacket sat on him—the shoulders were filled out right to the seams, and if I wasn't mistaken, there was a bit more wrist sticking out from the cuffs when he punched the dead woman in the chest.

Then in the next, the jacket was barely filled, a thinner, more boyish murderer who might, I thought suspiciously, be wearing a wig, or at least tucking it up under that cap. If we hadn't been watching it in order—if we'd been watching it in the order it had come in—it might have evened out, or been put down to difference in security systems. Seen like this, it was very clear.

The fourth file was even more obvious. The lump on the side of our murderer's head, the same one I'd seen on his victim in the previous clip, was too clear to be ignored. And in the fifth clip, in the Orient Hotel, was Cameron Michaels—or a *flaming* good replica of him—sitting on a couch and waiting to be murdered.

"Unless he's doing a very good job of makeup for some psychological reasons of his own," I said to Tuatu, when the clip ran out, "this dude is changing shape to look like his victim every time he murders someone. And that last one—that's him. Cameron Michaels."

"I see it," said Tuatu slowly, "but I still can't believe it. And the name's still wrong."

"Well," I said, grinning. "At least you know that you can go back to the rest of the footage with a timeline in mind."

"You think he's going to be there in all the other footage, in order, as the last person he murdered, to scout out security cameras."

"Yeah."

"I hate my job."

"Yeah," I said again. "It's gunna be hard to bring this out in court, isn't it?"

"It won't even get to court," he said, grimly. "They'll say the evidence is doctored, and I can't disprove that. Or they'll say it has no bearing on the case, and I can't prove it does."

"Ah," I said, more slowly. "You're cranky because you have no way of bringing the bloke to justice, so you know it's going to be Zero and the others dealing with him."

"I don't like working like this."

"Yeah, but how else are you going to get justice if our laws aren't big enough to stop these people? Most of the victims weren't human, either."

"How many were human?"

"Just one. So it's kinda a Behind problem anyway, right?"

"That doesn't mean I'm happy about this."

"I know. But it's a bit better, right?"

"A bit."

"C'mmon," I said, getting up. "I'll get you more tea and finish dinner. They'll probably be back soon."

CHAPTER EIGHT

T HE PSYCHOS WERE PRETTY GOOD AT KNOWING WHEN DINNER time was when they were out of the house—good enough that I wondered whether they had some sort of spell in the kitchen or something.

Jin Yeong wandered into the kitchen as I was just about to dish out, and I felt the familiar twitch of Between heralding the arrival of the other two.

"Here they come," I said, without thinking about it.

Detective Tuatu gave me a funny look, but he jumped pretty high when the wall beside him softened and parted to admit first Zero's huge figure and then Athelas' slenderer one.

"Finally!" muttered Jin Yeong, his words caught up in the general excess of Between. "They came!"

"Ah, have we made you wait?" enquired Athelas. "And yet, it seems that the food is not upon the table."

"We found a thing!" I said exultantly, ignoring both Jin Yeong's disgruntled look and the way he stalked over to the table.

Zero didn't look particularly excited, but Athelas said, "How interesting! We, on the other hand, found very little."

"We were meant to find very little," Zero said. There was a hardness to his voice that I wondered about.

"The fae take you for a ride?" I asked them. Flaming golden fae. I knew he'd do that. Well, I had good info for Zero, and if they'd made a bargain for catching the murderer, he'd have to keep to it.

"You use the quaintest phraseology!" said Athelas admiringly.

He waited, smilingly, in silence, until I explained, "I mean, did they give you bad info?"

"It wasn't bad." Zero sank into his seat. "It's just...limited in its usefulness."

"Oh," I said. "Well, we found a thing that might help."

"I very much doubt it," said Zero wearily. "Pet, we're waiting for food."

Athelas opened his mouth to speak, but closed it again. Taking my cue from him, I too shut my mouth and put the chilli pot on the table. Detective Tuatu, looking annoyed, brought over the corn bread.

"You might want to listen to Pet," he said. "I'm off, Pet. I know what I need to do. You can call me if you need anything else."

"Thought you were gunna ask some questions?" I called after him as he stepped down into the living room. "There's dinner!"

"I've lost my appetite," he said.

"Now look what you've done!" I said accusingly to my three psychos, as the front door opened and closed. "You've scared him off again!"

"I don't think we scared him off," Athelas said. "I have the feeling the detective was annoyed."

"He'll have to learn to deal with it," Zero said shortly. "Pet, what did you discover that is so important?"

"He's changing his face every time he kills someone. Well, not his face—his whole body."

"I wonder," said Athelas thoughtfully, "I wonder just how you knew that."

"I know you lot think humans aren't that bright," I said, "but you've gotta know we'll realise it when you give us a game of spot-the-difference to play."

"We didn't expect you to be quite so perspicacious, Pet," explained Athelas.

"Why bother giving it to me to look at, then?" I demanded. I'd only half been joking when I remarked that they'd given it to me to stop me following them and poking my nose into their business. Now, I felt more than slightly miffed. They'd already known about it? "You know I'm not a dog or a cat, right?"

Zero helped himself to more chilli with the short, exasperated movements of a man who would much rather not be having the conversation he was having. "No, but you are a human. You're not expected to function on the same level that we do."

"Yeah, thanks a lot."

"If it helps, Pet," said Athelas, "I was genuinely interested in what you would see when you looked at the footage. It was also my suggestion to mix the files out of order."

Zero said around a mouthful of cornbread, "It wasn't a particularly helpful suggestion, it seems."

"Perhaps not in the event," agreed Athelas. "Well, Pet, now that you know we already know this much about our murderer, do you think we could peacefully have tea?"

"Yeah," I said, eyes sparkling, "but did you already know he's still around?"

"*We* know," said Zero sharply. "But I'm not sure exactly how you know."

"I saw the murdered bloke the other day. The last one that was murdered in the Orient." Recalling what Tuatu had said about the psychos, I added mendaciously, "I reckon he must still have someone he's going after, if he's hanging around."

Zero's eyes, cold and hard, met mine across the top of the chilli pot. I blinked back at him innocently.

"It would seem that we have a useful problem to solve, then," said Athelas. "After this afternoon, I would say that's delightfully novel!"

"No you don't," I said, hard put not to grin.

"I hesitate to contradict you, Pet—"

"No you don't," I said again, and this time I really did grin. "You're gunna say that we need to figure out who the bloke is. Well, I already know."

Zero pinched the bridge of his nose, a sure sign of exasperation. "Why do you know who the murderer is?"

"Checked his I.D.," I said.

There was a hiss of laughter from JinYeong, and a crease or two appeared beside Athelas' eyes.

Zero, through his teeth, said, "You did *what?*"

"I checked his I.D."

"Did you *pickpocket our murderer?*"

"Nah. I dunno how to do that. Just looked at his I.D. when he bought cigarettes and they asked him for it. He's not even going by the victim's name. I mean, it's not like I knew he was the murderer or anything. *Someone,*" I added virtuously, "*Someone* was making sure I didn't know what was going on. I just followed him 'cos it was weird that he had the same face as one of the victims I saw on the security footage."

Zero, frowningly, looked across at Athelas. "He's taken on the form of his victim, but so far he's made no attempt to gain information from the form—though he has once used it to gain access to his next victim."

"It's a delightful conundrum," Athelas said.

"What if it's not something he does because he's trying to get info?" I asked idly. "I mean, he's not trying to get into anyone's life, and he doesn't seem to be trying to fool anyone that he's the victim. He's using another name and he's obviously been keeping away from the family afterward—he just uses it to escape. The only time it looked like someone recognised him was the last one."

"An escape mechanism, or perhaps a by-product rather than a choice," Zero said, slowly. "Athelas, what sort of Behindkind are capable of full body transformation? I can think of a few, but my thoughts are nothing so comprehensive as we need to be. Make me a list—and in that list, separate the ones who take a full body transformation involuntarily when they kill a person, from the others."

"What, you don't know off the top of your head?"

"I assume, Pet, that you are not able to list every animal in the human world at any given time. Or even every animal that could be included under a banner of specific distinguishing features."

"Yeah, but I'm also pretty sure the other Behindkind wouldn't like you implying that they're animals."

"Perhaps not," said Athelas. "But I'm sure they'd return the favour in any case."

"Anyway, if you wanna know the name, it's Cameron Michaels."

Zero looked at me curiously. "Why would we want to know the false name of the murderer?"

"Well," I said, faintly offended to find my information disregarded, "maybe you don't. But the picture on the ID didn't look that much like him as he is now, and if he's not going by the name of the bloke he murdered, maybe it isn't a fake name. Maybe it's his real name. Well, the one he uses when he's in the human world, anyway."

"If it is his real name, what of it?"

"You know the cops can track him, right?"

"The humans have a database of names available to them?" asked Zero in surprise.

"A few," I said, trying very hard not to roll my eyes. What had Athelas been doing in the police station while he was undercover?

"If they can't get him from a previous conviction, they should be able to get him on a license or a parking ticket. He was using a licence as ID."

"It couldn't hurt to ask," Zero said, though he still looked unconvinced.

"Big of you," I said, unable to hold back my sarcasm any further. And because I was annoyed, I didn't tell them I'd already asked the detective to search the name. Instead, I asked, "You want me to call Detective Tuatu?"

"Athelas will do it."

"Don't trust me, huh?" I said, getting up to clear the table. There were a few bits of cornbread left—I'd leave them outside tonight for the old mad bloke. He was probably hungry again by now.

"Why didn't you tell me about the dead man before now?"

"Oh, right. I thought Jin Yeong told you. I was out with him when I saw the bloke. I thought that's what he was looking at in the street."

"It wasn't," Zero said briefly.

"Ohhh!" I said. "He was looking at the Sandman? Was it following me then, too?"

"*Kurae*," said Jin Yeong, just as Zero said, "There's no need to discuss it."

"That's fine for you to say," I said. "You can just strut around being all big and fae and untouchable. I'd rather know if something's out to get me so I can run and hide when I need to."

"May I also mention that since we met you, my lord has been doing a considerable amount of—how did you put it?—*strutting around*, making sure that you don't die?" said Athelas.

"And I'm grateful for it," I told him. "But it would have been nice to have a heads up before it attacked me the other day. If Daniel hadn't been there—"

"That reminds me." Over the sound of the kettle boiling, Zero said, "You've yet to tell me where Daniel is."

"I'm not ratting him out," I said.

"One assumes," said Athelas, "that that means you know where he is."

"Nope," I said, a bit smugly, pouring hot water into the teapot. "I dunno what he's up to or where he thinks he's going. I only met him the other day because he helped me get away from the Sandman, and I don't know where he was going after that."

It wasn't like he didn't have anywhere to go, after all. He wouldn't still be with Morgana, now that he had his own clothes again. Well, pack clothes, anyway.

"Anyway," I added, "does it really matter? It's not like Daniel killed anyone on purpose, and he's only just recovered from what happened to him."

"He still has to attend a Behind hearing."

I gave Zero his coffee. "Yeah? Do the Enforcers know about him, then? Didn't reckon you'd told them."

Zero took his coffee after about half a beat of silence, and that was as good as a dropped jaw. So I was right about Daniel—Zero had been keeping him secret and safe for a reason of his own. It also meant that he trusted the Enforcers even less than I'd thought.

"Maybe he'll be able to tell you a bit about Upper Management," I said helpfully. I could have told them what Detective Tuatu had told me, but I didn't want to accidently give away how much he'd told me. "When you find him again."

"Thank you, Pet," said Zero. "We'll remember that."

I grinned at him, and his eyes dropped to his coffee before the slight curve to the outer edges of his mouth could become anything more.

"So what are we doing tomorrow?" I asked. "Keeping a fae bigwig safe?"

"We," Zero said, with the suspicion of a sigh, "will be going out on business that does not concern our pet."

"Oh. Well, I might as well go to the grocery store, then. We're about to run out of toilet paper."

"You can't go out," said Zero.

"What? Is this your revenge?"

"I don't want the Sandman following you back here. I didn't go to all the effort of shielding the house from our fae visitors for you to bring a Sandman down on us."

"But I have to do shopping," I protested. How on earth was I supposed to check up on Morgana or leave out something for the old mad dude if I couldn't go out?

"One of us will go with you."

It was my turn to shut my mouth on something that would be far too revealing.

"The expression on your face is hardly complimentary," said Athelas. "One would almost assume that you find our company distressing. One would *almost* think, Pet, that our presence would keep you from some more interesting pursuit."

My eyes met JinYeong's as I passed him his coffee, and I saw the faintest gleam of one incisor. "I need biscuits," he said.

I passed him the shortbreads, and said, "Okay. I'll take JinYeong with me tomorrow."

Athelas' brows went up, and Zero frowned.

JinYeong, startled, sat up straight and said, "*Mwoh?*"

"Well, he scared off the Sandman last time," I pointed out. "Me and Daniel had to fight flaming hard to get away, but JinYeong just sorta snarled at him and he left."

"*Ne,*" said JinYeong, his poise returning to him. He sat back with his biscuit and coffee, almost impossibly smug, and said to the other two, "I am the best choice."

"I am at a loss for words," said Athelas. "Our pet, choosing JinYeong's company first!"

"Yes," Zero said, still frowning. "Very interesting."

Athelas sipped his tea. "Insulting, I would have said."

"See," I said to JinYeong. "They don't like you, either."

Jin Yeong shrugged, but his mouth was still smug.

Zero and Athelas left first the next day, presumably to make sure their bigwig was still safe. They didn't look suspicious, though Athelas threw me one last quizzical look as they left, ignoring Jin Yeong's openly mocking smile.

Still, Jin Yeong didn't comment when I turned toward the Brooker to visit Morgana, and when I said, "You better not rat on me," at him, it was more by habit than because I thought he actually would.

"*Choshimhae, Petteu*," he said to me, lazily twitching a finger back and forth. "If you are rude, should I be nice?"

"I'm cooking for you," I said. "I'm nice. I don't put holy water in your food, do I?"

To my surprise, Jin Yeong considered this sarcastic statement for a moment or two, and then nodded. "It is enough," he said.

"Yeah? Oh well, at least you don't try to drink my blood."

"Your smell is not a food smell," he said.

"Yeah? Then why do you keep biting me?"

"That is another matter."

"I think I'm working up an immunity to you, though," I said. "Last time it was only my arm and my neck that went numb. Sooner or later, it's not going to do anything."

One of Jin Yeong's brows went up. "We shall see," he said.

"Oi. Who's the bloke Zero and Athelas are looking after today?"

"*Pemil*," he said.

"Well, I know it's an important fae, anyway. But I don't get why Zero won't let me go along—it's not like it's less dangerous out here. There's a Sandman looking for my blood, or whatever it is Sandmen want, and that can't be less dangerous than snooty fae."

"There are dangers and dangers," said Jin Yeong cryptically, and after that he refused to speak with anything of Between to his words, regaling me instead with a flurry of unaugmented Korean that was far too swift for me to follow.

When we got to Morgana's house, I was still trying to prod information out of him with as little success as I would have had with Zero, though for very different reasons. JinYeong, with a perverse kind of delight, answered every one of the questions I asked him—the answers too swift and convoluted for me to even hope to understand.

"Fine," I said to him, at the front steps. "But I'm not inviting you in."

"*Sangkwani obseo*," he said, shrugging. He made a half-turn and rested his shoulders gracefully against the brickwork, and said something in Korean, tapping his watch.

"Yeah, yeah, I'll be quick," I said, and shut the door as he was pretending not to be craning his head to see inside.

When I passed through the bottom level of the house, I could hear someone moving around in one of the rooms, and there were a couple of boxes outside the door. I nearly went to have a sticky beak and find out who was moving in, but it wasn't like it was my business, after all. I'd assumed that the place rented out rooms, but this was the first sign I'd seen of anyone actually moving in.

It was good that I didn't take the time to check it out, because Morgana was already bouncing by the time I got into her room.

"I saw you come in!" she said. "Your partner came with you! Isn't he coming up?"

"Nah, he's sulking," I told her. "He doesn't like people."

"Oh. Well, I'm glad you're back, anyway! I wasn't sure you'd come back now that Daniel isn't across the road. I was just about to text you."

"Just wanted to make sure you're doing all right," I said. "Stuff got a bit hairy the other night, and I haven't been able to get back until now. Thanks for not freaking out about Daniel."

She looked surprised. "Why would that freak me out?"

"Well, he is kinda a wanted criminal at the moment."

"Yeah, but he's just scared. Whatever it was he did, it can't have been that bad."

In human terms, it probably would have been manslaughter, but I wasn't sure what you'd call it in Behindkind parlance. Come to think of it, maybe I didn't want to know.

"Still," I said. "Thanks for helping out. Things should get a bit quieter now. You get someone new moving in downstairs?"

She grinned at me. "You still want to keep tabs on Daniel, don't you? I mean, you still need to keep an eye on him for work, right?"

I had a very bad feeling about this. "Did you—did he ask you if he could stay?"

"No, I asked him. There's loads of rooms downstairs, and we're *meant* to be a hostel type thing. We just haven't had anyone for a while except the kids."

"Where *are* the kids, anyway? I haven't seen hide nor hair of them."

"They're probably keeping to their favourite rooms," she said. "They're a bit scared of Daniel."

"They're not dumb," I muttered. "Morgana, he's nice, but he's not exactly safe. It's not a good idea to let him stay here."

"He hasn't got anywhere to go right now. And I figured if you keep coming here to keep an eye on him, you'll keep coming to see me."

I couldn't help grinning, because she looked so happy and pleased with herself. "Don't your parents mind?"

"They'll just be happy we've got guests. It makes it look better to anyone who comes looking for a place, too, so it doesn't matter if he can't pay right now."

"Okay," I said. "But call me right away if anything...weird happens."

"That's what Daniel said. Why do you both think something weird's gunna happen?"

"I told you. He's a bit dangerous, and the people who tried to come after him are even more dangerous."

"Are they the ones you're really after?"

"Yeah. Right—you need anything before I go? Coffee?"

"Oh. Are you going already?"

"Yeah," I said. "My partner's waiting for me, and he'll be pretty stroppy if I take too long."

"Okay," she said reluctantly. "But next time, we have to play poker."

"Play with Daniel," I said, grinning. It would do him some good to be beaten by someone younger than him.

This time when I went past the occupied room downstairs, I poked my head in around the door. Daniel looked up from the box he was unpacking and shot a half-grin at me.

"Oi," I said. "Who said you could move in here?"

"Morgana," said Daniel, but he looked guilty. "It's just for a while, Pet. If it looks like it's getting dangerous for her, I'll leave."

"All right, but for pity's sake don't go changing while you're here!"

"I'm not stupid!" he said, indignantly. "Anyway, I can smell the vampire out there. If I change in here, he'll smell me out straight away."

"Good grief, yes!" I said, backing hastily out of the room.

"It's all right. I haven't changed again while I've been here. There won't be any scent to take back. Vampires think they're pretty good, but they aren't as good as they think they are."

I grinned. "You should hear what vampires say about you lot."

He snorted. "They're just jealous. We're warm-blooded and they're cold, so people find us naturally more loveable. Vampires have to use their control on people, but if a lycanthrope smiles at someone, they love us straight away."

"That why you never smiled at work?"

"I was going through a difficult time," Daniel said dignifiedly, after a small pause. "And I do smile, sometimes."

"No, you don't. You scowl and glare at people."

"I only scowl at you because you're annoying."

"Fair enough. I think a lot of Behindkind find me annoying." Which reminded me. "Oi. What can tear out hearts?"

Daniel frowned. "The Troika are investigating that? Weird."

"Yeah? Why's that?" I asked, side-tracked.

"Well, the fae who are being killed are high level fae."

"Yeah, I heard that. High level in what way?"

"They're all from old, *old* families—and I'm pretty sure I'm not the only one who thinks they're all linked to the Family, too."

"You mean the Family put them somewhere they'd be useful, and that's why someone is bumping 'em off?"

"That's what I think," he said, nodding. "But not too loudly. You never know who's listening."

"All right, but why wouldn't the ps—the Troika want to work on finding out who did it? Even if Zero's not on good terms with the Family, they're still dead fae."

"The Family are all about preparing for the next leader of Behind. So if he's seen to be too close to the Family right now—"

"The king-right-now will be a bit cranky," I agreed. "Yeah, Zero wasn't very keen to do the job."

"They must have offered him a lot to do it."

"Yeah," I agreed. Now that I knew exactly what it was he had been saying no to, I was certain there would have had to have been something beyond information on the murderer he had been chasing for years. Something personally important, not just catching-a-Behindkind-murderer important.

And speaking of important, I'd better get back to the point before Jin Yeong started knocking on the door. I asked again, "But what can tear out hearts?"

"Lots of stuff," he said. "Some Behindkind kill like that naturally, and some of them do it for enjoyment."

"They *what*?"

"Humans do it, too!" he said indignantly. "Behindkind aren't the only killers, you know!"

"Yeah, fair enough. But it doesn't feel like there's as many human psychos running around free out there as there are Behindkind."

"That's because the Behind courts weigh the value of any Behindkind up on charges relating to hurting humans, against the damage that's been done," said Daniel. "If the Behindkind perpetrator is valuable enough to Behind, the charges can be dropped."

There was a slight, bitter twist to his mouth, and it occurred to me to wonder exactly how Daniel had become a lycanthrope. I'd known the person who turned him into one, but that was about it.

"I got that impression," I said. "What about something that looks like a human on security footage and grabs the heart right out of someone's chest?"

"Out of a *fae*'s chest? No way."

"I saw it. Well, saw it on security footage, anyway."

"You're sure it wasn't just something you couldn't see?"

"Yeah. Athelas saw it, too."

Daniel had gone back to frowning. "You should probably stay away from it," he said.

"Yeah, that's what Zero reckons. They still got me to look at the footage, though, so that's where I'm working from."

"Okay, there's some things that could do that, but not many. Off-hand, I can think of succubi, tricksters, and perytons. Oh, and gryphons, if someone gave them a good enough cover spell."

"What about normal Behindkind with a cover spell?"

"They'd need more than a cover spell," Daniel said. "High level fae are high level because they're powerful in their own right. They've got value to the Family—or the king, if that's the way of it—because of their own power."

"So it's gotta be one of those four groups."

He nodded. "You're going to need to learn a lot more if you're hanging around those three."

"Yeah," I said gloomily. "Athelas already gave me some books to study, but I haven't had time to look at them."

"Succubi are the ones that eat hearts, but they um, get something else out of it too. And I haven't heard of them punching people in the chest, either, but I don't really know any succubi, so they might do it that way."

"What about tricksters?"

"They're awful," Daniel said gloomily. "They can do anything and get away with anything, because they *talk* themselves out of it. They're all sociopathic mongrels and they love playing tricks that hurt people in messy ways. They usually work alone."

"Can they—can they change their appearance?"

"Yep. And there's no way of telling they're not human, or fae, or whatever the heck it is they look like, because they get into your head to change the way you think about them."

"Would one of them do something like changing to look like the last person they murdered to murder the next person?"

"If they thought it was funny or ironic, yeah. Perytons go for hearts, too, though; and they do a really good human impersonation, too. The only thing they can't change is their shadow—they always have their own shadow until they kill something, then they have its shadow for a while."

"What are perytons?"

"No one really knows. They're either birds or stags, or a kind of hybrid, but they love looking like other things. *And* they're really strong magic users."

"So they change their appearance with magic?"

He shook his head. "Nah. I was told it's like a natural defence system or something; keyed into their biology. Some Behindkind can see through it."

"Which ones?"

"Dunno," he said, shrugging. "It's got something to do with how well the Behindkind can see, or something."

"How do you know if you've found one, then?"

"If you catch one long enough after it's killed someone, it has its own shadow back. If you catch it right after it's killed, your guess is as good as mine. The shadow changes to human or fae or whatever it killed last."

"Right," I said. "That's useful."

"You think it's a peryton? Why?"

I said, "Shadows. Gotta go."

And, ignoring his protestations, I dashed for the front door.

"Shadows," I said to Jin Yeong, when I got outside again.

"*Mwoh?*"

"Shadows," I said, and marched off toward the grocery store. If they were gunna be mysterious, I was gunna be mysterious.

CHAPTER NINE

"IT'S A PERYTON."

"I beg your pardon, Pet?"

"You blokes were really late getting home," I added. I felt a bit peeved about that, despite the fact that it had given me the time I needed to do my research and set up the computer. To Jin Yeong's slightly mocking amusement, I had studied one of the books Athelas gave me to look at. The best I could work out from the title, it was a bestiary, and I wanted to make sure that what I'd suspected was possible. Then I'd gone upstairs to re-watch the footage in which I'd seen the shadows most clearly, and pause it ready for them both to see.

I'd boiled the jug, too, but that had long since gone cold again after I made coffee for me and Jin Yeong.

"I fear that you're under some misapprehension, Pet," said Athelas. "It is, after all, the masters who choose their time of return, and not the pet."

"Tell that to the jug," I said. "It doesn't care about time. It goes cold anyway."

"What about a peryton?" asked Zero, slipping the yellow umbrella into the hallstand.

Huh. I'd definitely been right. They'd been out protecting someone. The question was, who was protecting that someone while Zero and Athelas weren't?

"Your murderer. It's a peryton."

"A peryton is one of the possibilities we came up with," said Zero. "What makes you think it's more likely to be a peryton than a trickster or any other of our more likely shape shifters?"

"Shadows," I said, and behind me, JinYeong *tsk*ed with his tongue as it occurred to him what I'd meant earlier.

Zero said slowly, "Shadows," and I could tell he was annoyed with himself. "Athelas, did you see the shadows?"

"Perhaps we could see the footage to which Pet is referring before we attempt to discern what is and isn't there."

"Rude," I said. "You're saying you don't believe I saw anything."

"Let us say rather that I consider you to be an inexpert investigator," said Athelas.

"Got it set up upstairs," I said. "Come and have a look."

They followed me upstairs; Zero grimly silent, Athelas with a frown marring his usually serene brow, and JinYeong chuckling beneath his breath. They watched the footage in the same way, though Zero's silence grew heavier and Athelas once said something beneath his breath that I didn't quite catch.

Once it was done, I clicked out of the footage with sense of deep satisfaction. "It is, right? It's a peryton."

"How extremely vexing," said Athelas, and there was a burr to his usually creamy voice that made me think he really was vexed. "Our pet is entirely correct."

"I dunno why you lot don't just hire me as a partner. I've flaming solved your mystery for you."

"The mystery is far from solved," Zero said dampeningly. "We were aware that it must be one of two kinds of Behindkind. Now that we know it's a peryton, we can make an attempt at finding it, but we're far from finished."

"Yeah, but you've got his name, as well," I said. "And I bet—I *bet* Detective Tuatu called while you were out, and told you where to find him."

"*Yokshi, Petteu!*" said Jin Yeong, laughing. "Such an annoying little thing."

"We went to his house earlier," Zero said. He said it on a sigh, like he'd given up on trying not to tell me stuff. "He had already gone."

"Someone tip him off?"

"We believe so," said Athelas. "Which leaves me wondering, my lord, if the Enforcers have within their ranks someone who is friendly to Upper Management, or if Upper Management are merely less inactive than our detective thought."

"Upper Management are the ones who have been killing the fae?"

Athelas, with gentle sarcasm, said, "Oh, I *am* surprised, Pet! I thought you would be sure to know as much!"

"I guessed," I said dignifiedly. "But I didn't have enough information to be sure."

"You have enough information, however, to make me wonder exactly where it came from." Zero's gaze rested on me; thoughtfully, suspiciously, consideringly.

"Athelas gave me some books," I said innocently.

"I would like to be very clear, my lord," said Athelas hastily, "that I was in no way aiding and abetting the pet! I was trying to give her something to distract her."

"Rude!" I said. "Didn't your mum teach you it's not on to shift the blame?"

I regretted it as soon as I said it, but I was too late to take it back.

"Alas!" said Athelas lightly. "My mother taught me a great many things, but that was not one of them."

"Sorry," I told him remorsefully. "Didn't think before I said it.

Oi. I've still got that really nice lavender earl grey leaf tea; I'll make you a tea cake to go with it."

"I believe we've already discussed the concept that not every ill can be fixed by the application of tea."

"Don't be prickly," I said, and hugged him.

"I stand in no need of affection, thank you very much, Pet. I believe my history is not an unusual one Behind."

"Don't irritate Athelas," Zero said.

"I'm not irritating him, I'm hugging him," I protested, but I let him go.

"I will of course accept cake and tea," Athelas mentioned. "Under the strict understanding that they were freely given and incur no burden."

"What am I, fae? I don't go tricking people into bargains."

"A shortcoming of which you should be very careful."

There was a mutter from Jin Yeong that said something about cake, and Zero said briefly, "If you've quite finished? Athelas, you didn't see the shadows?"

"I apologise, my lord. I passed the footage straight on to the pet after a cursory examination of the moment of death."

"You were acting on my orders. I should have been more specific."

"If it's a peryton, we'll need to go back to the Whiteleaf house," Athelas said. "All the peryton will need to do is murder one of the guards before they arrive, then use his face to get past. It could already have done so."

Jin Yeong made an annoyed mutter that said the house smelt like a human house and was annoying his nose, but I missed my chance to tell him it was more than his nose that was annoying because I needed to ask, "So we gotta look for a body as well as a peryton?"

"I believe we've also discussed the fact that there is no *we* in this case." Athelas' grey eyes rested on me steadily. "Your part is to stay at home. You've done enough."

"I don't know," said Zero, making my heart jump. If Athelas was looking at me curiously, Zero was looking at Athelas in much the same way. "I think that this time, at least, the pet should come with us."

"Heck yes!" I said. If only I could work this into a promise to help out Mr. Preston, too. Maybe Zero would listen to me now that I'd done a good job helping with this case.

"Do you really think that's wise, my lord?" asked Athelas. There was a note to his voice that I thought was probably surprise. "Surely the Pet doesn't need to accompany us!"

"The pet," said Zero, "seems to do nothing but get up to mischief when it doesn't accompany us. I'll make sure it stays behind me."

"I don't believe those reasons we discussed for excluding the pet have changed at all."

"The pet has earned a place with us today," Zero said. "And I'm more than slightly afraid of what it will find if we leave it to investigate by itself again."

"That's pets for ya," I said. "Always digging up stuff in the garden."

"You should be quiet now, *Petteu*," said Jin Yeong lazily.

I did my *zip the lip* motion at him, which seemed to confuse him, and shut my mouth. I didn't want Zero to change his mind. At least now I had boots, so I could go Between with them again.

"Athelas, you're with Jin Yeong; check the security feeds around the perimeter. The peryton might have been under enough of a time constraint to do something hasty. I'll take the pet and go straight to the client."

"We'll contact you when we know more," nodded Athelas. "Have a care going through, my lord. There has been more than usual goblin activity."

I saw the faint frown that came over Zero's face, and expected him to remind Athelas that he had been through Between many times before, and could deal with any amount of goblin threats, but instead, he nodded.

"Come, Pet," he said. "Bring the sword."

Well, I was a sword-bearer now. I mean, it looked more like an umbrella at the moment, all yellow silky fabric and pointed metal tip, but the handle felt like a proper sword grip instead of umbrella handle. Maybe when I got my house back I could take up a new job as someone's squire. A squire who can pull weapons out of their surroundings would be a pretty useful squire. Pity there aren't more knights around the place.

We didn't start out by going Between, this time. I mean, we kinda melted through the door, but I think that's more because my three psychos have a problem with the authority of walls and doors than because we actually needed to.

So we took to the street instead, heading down toward the heart of the city until we got to the traffic lights at the hospital, and stopped in front of the manor house opposite it.

"Huh," I said. "So this place is a Behindkind place. Should have guessed."

It was a stately house, all massive grey brick in an old-fashioned manor style, with flourishing green gardens all around it and a high wall that stopped you being able to see in from the ground. I'd seen it from up in the multilevel parking lot diagonal to it, and it had always had a closed off sort of feel to it that didn't let you look at it for too long—or wonder how such a house could have been planted there like that. And it *could* have been planted, with the huge rectangle of green it made from higher up.

"It's some sort of government property in the human world," said Zero, frowning at the gate. "Behind, it's a fae senator's residence."

"We gotta go Behind to get in?"

"Between. Then Behind—Behind *is* in."

He was still frowning at the gate, his eyes flicking up and down, seeing stuff I was pretty sure I wasn't seeing.

"You trying to pick the lock, or what?"

"Something like that," agreed Zero, to my surprise. "Anyone entering from the human side needs to find the portal and show their card."

"What card?"

"It's a sort of identification card."

"Like a passport?"

He didn't answer that, but I wasn't sure if it was because he didn't want to, or because he didn't know what a passport was. He did say, "The portal changes, and it's not always evident. If you're entering this way, you need to look for something round and convex—it could be a pebble or a decoration of the fence. Ah— there it is!"

I blinked a bit, then grinned at him. He was teaching me stuff. Not just how-not-to-die stuff, but useful Between stuff. I might not have been investigating with the thought of a trade, but in another way that wasn't quite the fae way, I was being recompensed. I would have liked very much to know whether Zero had done it consciously or not.

"We're going Behind soon," he added, as the gate opened, wafting out the scents of a garden and the chilly feeling of deep Between. "Don't let go of my pocket, and when we're there, be careful who you speak to. Janna Whiteleaf isn't a person you should talk to more than necessary."

"That's the person you're trying to keep alive?" I asked in a hushed voice, as we stepped across the shadowed threshold.

"Yes. Mind the step."

It wasn't quite a step; it was more like a missed step. I felt the human world diminishing behind me—or maybe that was just my imagination because the world got so suddenly dark—and the smooth, changing darkness of Between around us, then we were back in a garden, almost as if we'd never left.

I shivered a bit and inched closer to Zero. It might have looked like the same garden, but there was a coldness to it that was frightening and when I looked up, there were stars in the suddenly sable sky.

"Wait, it's night here?"

"Yes. It's always night here, in this part of Behind. That's why we came here immediately."

"Yeah," I said soberly. In a place that was always night, it was going to be pretty hard to keep an eye on shadows. "We're here to make sure the house stays well-lit so we can still see shadows?"

"That's a part of it," agreed Zero. "If the peryton has murdered someone in the last day or two, he'll have a human shadow, but he won't be one of the staff. If he hasn't killed anyone in the last few days, his shadow will give him away."

"So if he's killed someone in the last couple days, Athelas should catch him on the cameras as an unfamiliar face. If he hasn't, we won't be able to spot him until he's somewhere light enough to see."

"Exactly so. Pet."

"Yeah?"

"Remember to mind your tongue."

I didn't let go of Zero's pocket until we were through the front door, and even then I almost wished I hadn't. He didn't give me a chance to grab him again, though; he started off at a good stride down the hall and took the stairs of the grand staircase four at a time. I followed at more of a jog than a trot, which made it easier to ignore the fact that the walls seemed to be living and were *definitely* moving. There were probably things in there, too, but I didn't look closely enough to be sure.

We went at a good pace until we were at the top floor, and stopped outside a set of double doors guarded by two fae. The guards bowed to Zero and stood aside, though I could feel their curious eyes on me as I walked between them.

I looked around at the bit of the room I could see from

behind Zero, and saw four huge windows along the far wall, matte with silver-speckled darkness. It wasn't going to be easy to keep the room lit up if someone cut the power. Mind you: did Behind have access to electrical lighting?

I squinted up at the lights, but I couldn't tell if they were electrical or some kind of magic. I was looking around for a light switch to be sure when a cool, female voice said, "I hear there has been a development."

I craned my head around the other side of Zero, and saw her sitting there behind her huge, ancient desk. At first I thought she was a human woman; old, white-haired, and elegant. And that was weird, an old human woman being here, Behind. Then she gazed at me with the same kind of what-is-this-bug grimace that the golden fae usually gives me, and I looked a bit closer.

It could have been the crown around her brow that gave it away, all silvery and moonlight—something like I'd once seen on Zero when he came from Behind—but the kind of otherness that was almost Between but not quite made me very sure. Was I seeing actual magic?

I glanced at Zero, and saw that he was watching me carefully. Right. Don't talk about the visible stuff that might be magic. Maybe don't talk at all.

"Yes," Zero said. "We've reason to believe it's a peryton."

She stiffened just a touch. "I beg your pardon?"

"Whoever wants to kill you is using a peryton to do so. We know where it was up until a couple of days ago, but we've no idea where it is presently. My steward and my assistant are downstairs going through your security footage and your staff."

"I see," she said. "How did you happen to lose sight of it?"

"Our investigation process isn't for you to discuss and dissect," said Zero. Oh, he really didn't like her. "I'll start in this room and work outward, setting up lights. Pet, find the light switches."

That made the old woman look at me with an almost offended

look. "First you bring that abomination to my house, and now this?"

"G'day," I said, hunting for light switches. They weren't hidden Between or anything, just behind stuff. "Don't mind me."

"What," said the white-haired fae, in a glacial voice that was even sharper than Zero's ice, "is it?"

"This is my pet," said Zero. "Send it for drinks if you need anything. Don't call your own staff until we clear them to come up to you. JinYeong is working on that at the moment, so it shouldn't be much longer."

"Very well," said the woman. "But if it makes a mess, I will have it put down."

"If my pet requires putting down, I will put it down myself."

There was no emotion to Zero's voice; not even respect or interest. And yet, that lack chilled me less than the off-hand way the woman had spoken about killing me.

He added, in her general direction. "You're not to leave this room. If the lights fail here, use the electronic ones from the human world: we will be working at putting up a failsafe while we're here. How many switches are there, Pet?"

"'Bout six. Two near the door, a couple opposite each other near the desk, and a couple down this end of the room."

"Unacceptable," said the fae woman. "I refuse to sully my rooms with electronic lights."

Zero ignored that. He said, "If the power goes off on the human side, rely upon the lights I'm enchanting now. They're not the most powerful but they'll be enough to offer evidence."

"If they're being used to offer evidence it will be because I am dead," said the woman. "That is also unacceptable."

"You'll need to speak to the Family about what is and is not acceptable," Zero said. "I'm not your servant or your man. I'll protect you where I can, but if I can't, the lights will see that we're able to bring the matter before our courts. It is important for you to remain in this room, however."

"I'm a very busy person, Lord Sero. I can't remain in a single room for an entire day."

"You did so yesterday," he said briefly. "If you have paperwork to do, do it. If you don't, sit quietly regardless."

"I will make a complaint about your conduct, Lord Sero."

"As you wish. Pet—Athelas and JinYeong are in the security room. Check to see if they want refreshments and bring a tray up here. Make sure you prepare it with your own hands."

I wanted to ask where the security room was, but with the way Janna Whiteleaf or whatever her name was, was looking at me, I decided that it would be safer finding my own way, even if I was Behind. I obviously couldn't expect any help from Zero, who had gone into a state of iciness I had never seen from him, even when I first met him. If it hadn't been for the warning he'd given me before we walked in, I could have thought that he'd just gotten really good at pretending to put up with me.

The walls were still moving a bit when I got out of the room, though the bits nearest the two fae guards didn't move much— like they were afraid to play up too close to the guards. I had much the same feeling, so I just sort of nodded at them and nipped down the hall toward the stairs. The walls undulated with a rhythmic, wave-like motion on the second floor, and when I passed the round hallway mirror halfway down, I saw a face that was almost mine but not quite.

It put me off, so I stood staring at it for a few seconds before I croaked out, "Oi. Where's the security room?"

A hand rose into the frame of the mirror and into view, fingers pointing down the hall, though the face didn't change at all. Ah. I'd walked past it already.

"Thanks," I said, and backtracked. I didn't want to look at that face that wasn't quite my face for any longer than I had to.

A very tall Behindkind with straight, thick brows opened the door and looked down at me when I knocked at the door to the security room.

"G'day," I said again.

He looked at me with a faint, distant frown. "I think you're lost."

"Not at all," said Athelas' voice. "That's our pet. Allow it in, will you?"

The Behindkind looked down at me, frowning, then jerked a thumb toward the inside of the room, but didn't move, so I pushed past him.

"'Scuse me, mate." The faint smell of fish, or maybe just the ocean, followed me; a weird kind of 3D scratch and sniff. At least Athelas and Jin Yeong were in sight, and that was a relief. I asked them, "Want coffee?"

"Tea, thank you, Pet," said Athelas pleasantly. He didn't need to tell me that—I already knew he drank tea. So *that* left me wondering why he said it. If it had been anyone else, it wouldn't have bothered me, but since it was Athelas, it did bother me. Obviously we were still being careful in front of the rest of the household, not just the woman upstairs.

"*Ne*," said Jin Yeong. The woman in front of him, a brunette in a maid's uniform, blinked a little bit as he looked away, then grew wide-eyed again when he looked back at her. Interrogation? Was she Behindkind or human? Did the vampire wiles *work* on other Behindkind?

More importantly, why did the fae who'd let me in look like he was just barely holding back on punching Jin Yeong? I mean, I felt like that a lot, but I had to live with Jin Yeong and the fae didn't. Did this fae hate vampires, too, or was he watching the woman Jin Yeong was interrogating?

"What's she?" I asked Athelas, who was sitting in front of the security screens.

"Human, naturally," he said, without looking away from his screen. "What else would she be? She's one of the staff here; other than the guards and the steward here, each of the staff is human."

"Yeah, can't have Behindkind servants in a Behindkind house," I muttered.

The tall Behindkind looked curiously at me, and Athelas said, with a kind of poisoned honey to his voice, "Exactly so. Do attend to your work Pet—I would hate to send Jin Yeong with you when he's otherwise occupied."

He didn't look away from his screen, but I met his eyes in the reflection of the screen, and they were all warning. Do not be cheeky, Pet, those eyes said. That was a bit of a relief. I knew that things tended to change with Zero and Athelas when other Behindkind were around, but I still wasn't entirely sure why it happened. I threw a look in Jin Yeong's direction, and saw that he, too, was watching me through his eyelashes.

Good grief. If they thought it was this bad, they should have warned me before I got here. Mind you, maybe they were hoping to remind me to be careful what I wished for. Whatever it was, it left me with the feeling that here in this house, I was as likely to be killed on the spot as I was to be held in indefinite, indentured service with no hope of escape.

And I was left with the feeling that, as close as I technically was to the human world, I was also immeasurably far away from it.

I found my way to the kitchen more by good luck than good management, and maybe there was some kind of messaging system I didn't know about, because nobody tried to stop me moving around the place, even though I passed about three people on my way there. There were three in the kitchen, too; one washing up, one putting the finishing touches on a meal that I assumed was for her upstairs, and one polishing silver. Humans, of course. I tried to look at them covertly, but after a while I just looked at them because they didn't seem to be capable of doing or seeing anything except what they were doing.

They didn't stop me making tea and coffee, and they didn't stop me taking a tray out, either. Just sorta did what they were meant to be doing, with glazed eyes and movements that were just a bit stiff—or maybe sticky. I trotted back to take Athelas and JinYeong their refreshments, feeling more chilled than I had before, then headed to the top floor to take Zero and Janna theirs.

Janna refused to take hers from me—refused to look at me, even, so I left it on the desk for her, biscuits sitting next to the saucer. I hadn't gone even a few steps away when she said, in icy fury, "How *dare* you!" and something closed around my neck, tight and choking.

I gagged, clutching at my neck, but there was nothing there. Spots danced on Zero's back, but I couldn't get out a word to call him for help, or a breath to survive on. When the darkness crowded in at the edges as well, I gave up trying to find something to tear away from my neck, and reached out as far as the restriction around my neck would allow me.

Leather, between my fingers. I tugged on Zero's jacket, the faintest pinch and pull that I lost after a moment, and he looked around. The pressure around my neck released in a moment, and I collapsed on the floor.

"What are you doing to my pet?" I heard him ask, as I gasped for breath on the floor.

"It left *crumbs* on my *desk*," she said coldly. "If you've not trained it better, you should expect someone else to punish it occasionally."

Zero said, "No one trains my pet but myself. Remember that. These lights are tuned to you especially—they won't turn off unless you die. If your own lights fail and the human lights fail, these will stay alight."

"I've told you that it will not suffice."

"Get up, Pet," said Zero, without looking at me. "We're done here."

Janna sat up straighter, and I swear her nose got thinner. "Do you mean to say that you are not even going to *remain with me?*"

"Do you not trust the Enforcers and your guards? Do as I've told you: let no one in or out of this room. The others have orders not to let anyone in or out of the house."

"I assume that I am not included in those orders."

"You are included," said Zero. "I've given orders that you're to be returned here if you attempt to leave. As I've already told you, Senator Whiteleaf, I do not answer to you; my concern is only to catch this person and keep you alive if possible. Come, Pet."

I DIDN'T FEEL REALLY SAFE UNTIL I WAS BACK HOME WITH Zero, stepping back into the kitchen through the wall with a good grip on his leather jacket.

Then I blew out a relieved breath, clicked the kettle on, and started to get out the stuff I'd need to make Athelas' teacake.

"A little less enjoyment than you expected, Pet?" asked Zero. It could have been meant as a gentle dig, but there was a tiredness to his voice that left me feeling that he was just as weary as I was from the expedition.

So instead of answering in a straightforward way, I said, "There were humans back there. Running the house, I mean."

"Most of them."

"She keeps Behindkind as slaves, too?"

"The steward is enslaved, too," said Zero. "Behind has laws about slavery, but only to ratify what can be done. The senators are allowed more leeway than most because they provide power to the king."

"That's gross and unfair," I muttered, spooning coffee into three mugs.

"Yes," he said. "But that's what happens Behind. To the powerful, more power is given."

Without surprise, I said, "You don't like that much, do you?"

"There's very little I can do about it," he said, his voice hard.

It made me wonder, that tone of voice, exactly how much he'd tried to do about it, and how badly it had gone.

Pushing things a bit, I asked, "What about Mr. Preston? That's a thing you can do something about."

"Don't worry about Mr. Preston," said Zero.

"Yeah, but I can't help worrying about him. Maybe I could try to help by myself—I can do some stuff now."

"Your help isn't needed or useful."

Rude, but not unexpected. "All right," I said. "But if you're protecting scum of the earth like Janna Whitenose or whatever her name is—"

"Janna Whiteleaf."

"Yeah, if you're gunna protect scum of the earth like that, I don't see why you can't protect scum of the earth like Mr. Preston and stick out your tongue at the system at the same time."

"Mr. Preston is a human, and I feel no need to stick out my tongue at the system."

"I'm human, too. You still brought me along."

"You're not like other humans. You've earned a place here."

"You don't know any other humans," I said gruffly. I could feel how warm my face was, just like my heart. "I'm pretty much standard. You lot just have a warped view of humanity."

"So you say. I'm quite well enough acquainted with humanity, thank you, Pet. I've met the best as well as the worst, and I don't believe you're the standard."

"Oh. Where am I on the spectrum, then?"

"Neither best nor worst."

"Told ya—I'm average."

"You're not average."

"I would tend to agree," said Athelas, appearing around the door. Jin Yeong followed him; a lean, hungry figure, and I tossed him a blood bag from the fridge. Whatever it was that had gotten him so hungry for blood, it was best to get rid of the urge before he started baiting Zero or going out on the hunt.

"Are you finished already?" There was a frown in Zero's voice.

"Jin Yeong has vetted each of the present human staff, and I've checked the last shift of guards that took over via the cameras."

I made a mumbling sort of "pft" noise.

"Yes, Pet? I trust you're not sulking about your time in the house, since you worked so hard to get there."

"Nah," I said, even though I *was* a bit miffed, actually. "But Janna Snotnose—"

"Whiteleaf."

"Whatever. She's pretty snotty about humans and using human stuff for someone who has a whole room full of security feeds and computers."

"There are certain facets of humanity that are more useful than others," said Athelas.

Jin Yeong, sucking on his bag of blood, watched me as I stirred sugar into my batter. Goodness knew why he was interested—it wasn't like I was making blood snacks for him or anything.

"There's a lot of humanity that's useful," I said, as he got up and padded around the bench. "You lot just don't wanna admit it. You just keep using the useful stuff and snarking when you don't like something."

"*Igae mwohya?*" muttered Jin Yeong, and cool fingers twitched my chin up to let the light play on my neck. I kept stirring the batter, sprinkling blueberries into the mix, and said, "Janna Needlenose—"

Zero sighed.

"—choked me a bit because I left biscuit crumbs on her desk."

"Perhaps it would have been good for you if you had remembered your place, Pet," said Athelas. "Senator Whiteleaf is not best known for her love of humans."

"Seems like she's got a lot of company," I said, elbowing Jin Yeong away so that I could pour the batter into a tin. He moved, but kept watching me over his blood bag.

"You are sulking," Athelas said. "How very unlike you! Pet, you should remember that humans are distinctly weaker and less intelligent than most fae. It is important that such people remember their place when Behind."

I frowned. "I'm not trying to say we're not physically weaker. I'm trying to say that being physically weaker doesn't make humans less valuable than you lot. And you keep saying we're less intelligent but I haven't noticed it. You've just got access to more information than we have."

"Pet...!" said Zero, and I didn't know if it was frustration or anger in his voice. "I don't want to argue about this!"

"You never want to argue about it," I said flatly. I slid the cake into the oven and slapped the door shut. "You just strut around being strong and invincible and humans die around you."

"If humans interfere with Behind business, they can only expect to be injured. I can't play nursemaid to beings who are too stupid to keep out of trouble."

"They're not stupid, they're ignorant!"

JinYeong made his little *tch*! of amusement, and I glared at him. He only raised a brow at me and went down into the living room with his blood bag.

"JinYeong apparently believes that you are not championing your cause in the best fashion," said Athelas.

I glared at him, too, for good measure. "Someone being ignorant isn't an excuse to kill them—*or* to blame them for being killed! Anyway, if they *are* ignorant, whose fault is that? There's no flaming Bureau of Fae Affairs to tell humans what to watch out for!"

"In fact, there is a so-named Bureau," Athelas said mildly. "But it has nothing to do with informing humans of our business. Pet, perhaps you should remember it is not an insult to mention the fact of superior fae intelligence."

"Pretty sure it is," I muttered. "And I'm also pretty sure you lot just got outwitted by a human, so maybe you shouldn't be so flaming condescending."

"In what fashion have we been outwitted, Pet?"

"Well, I figured out your murderer before you did," I pointed out. "Anyway, I didn't ask you to do something about Mr. Preston this time. I said *I'd* do something."

"You will do nothing of the kind," said Zero sharply. "I've told you not to worry about Mr. Preston."

"You can't *tell* someone not to worry about something. You can't control other people's feelings."

"I can do that," demurred JinYeong from the living room, annoyingly understandable.

"Perhaps not," Zero said, with finality, "but I can tell you to stop talking about it unless you want me to lock you out of the house. Make coffee."

So I made coffee, while the blueberry teacake began to smell like hot berry around me, and Zero and the others sat waiting in the living room, oppressively silent. My thoughts, as oppressively noisy, buzzed against each other in the confines of my mind. I had to do something about Mr. Preston. Someone had to do something about Mr. Preston. But Zero had told me not to worry about him, and that meant he was doing something, right?

No, he'd do it. I didn't need to do anything. If I did something, Zero really would kick me out, I knew. I couldn't be kicked out. My parents' house, and—and—the life I had here now—I didn't want to lose them.

Zero would do something. He always did something. Even when he said he wouldn't help out, he helped out. All I had to do was sit and wait, and not get myself thrown out of the house, and Mr. Preston would be okay, too.

CHAPTER TEN

ZERO AND ATHELAS WERE GONE WHEN I WOKE UP THE NEXT morning. I wouldn't have admitted it if they'd asked me, but I was a bit relieved: I didn't want to go back to that house Behind. I didn't want to see thin-nosed Janna Whiteleaf, and I didn't want to see the dead-eyed human slaves walking around her house when I couldn't do anything about it.

"Oi," I said to Jin Yeong, who was the only one left. "We're going out for a walk."

"*Kurae?*" said Jin Yeong, raising a brow, but he got up anyway. "Where shall we go?"

"Gunna visit my friend," I said.

"*Shimshimhae*," he muttered, pouting. "Why should I go?"

"'Cos sitting around here is more boring," I said, grabbing his jacket sleeve. "C'mmon, we'll get coffee or something on the way home."

He mumbled something like *nonsense*, but let me pull him out onto the street, and he didn't saunter as much as usual, either. Maybe that was because I was still pulling him along. I let him go when it looked like he'd keep going under his own steam, and trotted on ahead more quickly. Truth be told, there was no reason for me to be in a hurry, but after yesterday I felt subtly as though I'd like to see a human who *wasn't* under thrall to the fae. Maybe there was a slight pang of fear that Morgana wouldn't be safe by the time I got there, too.

Whatever it was, it had me charging up the stairs to get in the front door with Jin Yeong on my heels, and it was only at the top step that I remembered to turn and frown at him.

"Where are you going?"

"Invite me in, *Petteu*," he said. "I will drink coffee."

"You can't come in," I told him. "My friend is human. You're not allowed to go near her."

"Your friend will like me."

"No she flaming won't!" I said firmly. I still remembered the reverential note in Morgana's voice when she first saw Jin Yeong. There was no way I was exposing her to him at close quarters.

Jin Yeong pursed his lips, but he didn't seem exactly sulky. "I will come back," he said, instead of protesting again, like I'd half expected he would.

I breathed a sigh of relief and shut the door on him, but as soon as the door was shut, I saw a shadow moving by the stairs. I jumped and reached for the nearest thing that could be a weapon: a walking stick by the door, sticky with ancient dust.

"Pet!" said Daniel's voice, indignant and slightly shocked. "What are you doing? You can't do that!"

I looked at him down the length of the rustiest sword I'd ever seen, and said, "Sorry. Thought you were a peryton or something."

"Yeah, but you can't do—" he stopped, looking indignant. "I wouldn't let a peryton in here."

"What, could you stop one?" I asked sceptically, putting down the rusty walking stick again.

He settled his shoulders a bit. "Probably not. But I'd make a pretty big mess, and I don't think it'd get much further than the stairs before I got reinforcements."

"It'd make a pretty big mess of you as well, I reckon," I said.

The bestiary Athelas had given me agreed with Daniel that there were two forms of peryton: one of them was a giant bird of prey with stag antlers, and the other was a stag with bird of prey wings, antlers, and a giant beak on its otherwise stag body. Either of those forms would cause a pretty bit of damage, I was certain. Especially considering it was only the appearance of the beast that changed, and not the actual body of it. The books had said something about a kind of outside façade that flickered through time and reality and could deceive even most Behindkind eyes, which was scary enough without being a stag-bird hybrid in reality. Daniel had been right: it was possible to see through a peryton's façade, if you could see accurately—or, I was beginning to suspect, *fast* enough—and that, coupled with the frame-by-frame study of the surveillance footage with Detective Tuatu, had left an interesting idea tickling over in the back of my mind.

"They're big, but my jaw's strong, and my teeth are sharp," said Daniel. "Why are you here, anyway?"

"Came to see Morgana," I explained, propping the rusty sword back against the wall, where it became distinctly more walking-stick like. "The others are off doing stuff, so I thought I might as well. Why? Are you trying to kick me out? I met her first!"

"It's not that," he said, following me slowly as I ascended the stairs. "It's just...what do you know about her? Morgana?"

"Not much," I told him. "I was just using her place to check up and see how you were going."

"No one needs to check up on me," he said indignantly. "If anyone should be checking up on anyone, I should be checking up on you! You're part of my pack."

I didn't tell him that I was no longer part of his pack, even if it was true. Instead, I asked, "Why are you asking about Morgana?"

He looked uneasy. "I don't know. She's—well, no one checks in on *her*. For humans, that's weird. I haven't seen her parents once since I moved in there."

"Oh." I had to think about that for a moment. "I haven't seen them, either. What about the kids?"

"What kids?"

"She's always talking about the kids who help her with stuff. They set up her mirrors and rigged everything just right. I reckon they check in on her."

"I haven't seen any kids."

"Yeah. She says they're hiding at the moment because you're scary."

"I'm not scary!" he said indignantly. "What did I do?"

"You're scowling right now," I pointed out, heading for the stairs. "And you always look like you're about to tear out someone's throat. Or maybe snap at them."

"Oh."

"Yeah, oh. Anyway, I haven't met Morgana's parents, but she did say she's sick all the time, so maybe not many people know she's here. Some humans just live like that."

"All right," he said reluctantly. "But for humans, it's weird. You should ask her about it."

"Oi!" I said. "I'm a human too, you know!"

"Yeah, but you don't act like it. You're more like...I dunno. But you're not like a human—you're more like us."

"Us?"

"Behindkind."

"Rude!" I said indignantly. "I'm nothing like you lot! I'm a human!"

"All right, all right, no need to get your knickers in a twist!"

"Shush," I told him. "She'll hear you."

"What will I hear?" asked Morgana, as soon as we were in the door.

By way of revenge, I said, "Daniel's saying bad stuff about you."

"I was not!"

"He was talking about you, anyway."

"Pet!"

"So long as he's talking about making me a coffee, I don't care," Morgana said.

"All right, I can take a hint," said Daniel, and skulked over to the kitchen.

I sat down on Morgana's bed with her, and for the first time noticed that her usual gothic getup was a bit more gothic than usual. She usually just had a black t-shirt and the black lipstick and eyeliner, dark and dramatic. Today, she had little black wrist-ruffs as well, and the t-shirt she wore wasn't oversized and carefully ripped—today, it was black and lacy, with small puffed sleeves and a ruff high at the neck to match the ruffs at her wrists.

It prompted me to ask a question I'd been meaning to ask for a while now. Making a vague gesture that included all of Morgana's makeup and the pretty black ribbons around her wrists, I asked, "How come you wear all that, anyway?"

"*Pet*!" growled Daniel from the kitchen. "You can't *ask* girls stuff like that! I'm not even a—a girl, and *I* know you can't ask stuff like that!"

"Oh," I said, taken aback. What a traitor! He was the one who'd told me no one checked up on Morgana or asked how she was. "I didn't know. Sorry."

"It's okay," said Morgana. "I don't care. Don't make faces at her! If I say it's okay, it's okay! Mind your own business!"

To my surprise, Daniel only grinned at that. "All right, sorry," he said.

"I've worn it since I was twelve," Morgana told me. "That's when it got so I couldn't walk anymore."

"Did you have an accident?"

"Normal people don't ask other people stuff like that, either," Daniel said, but this time he said it with less of a commanding tone to it.

Morgana's thin face became less certain. "I don't really know," she said. "I don't remember that time very much. I used to have some memories of it, but I figured out they had to be a dream, so now I know I don't really remember. Not what actually happened, I mean; I still remember the dream."

"What sort of dream was it?"

"A bad one," she said, shuddering. "I woke up one night, and someone was opening the door to my bedroom."

"From the corridor?"

"Yeah. That was the worst bit. I don't think I would have been as scared if it had been someone from outside."

"What about your parents?"

"They didn't wake up," she said. "I mean, I know now that it was a dream, so it makes sense that they wouldn't, because there was no one actually there. But for a couple days after I felt really resentful anyway because it was such a horrible dream and they didn't wake up."

"What happened?"

"It wasn't a someone, it was a monster. It stood over the bed, but sort of surrounded it as well, all inky black up to the ceiling with too many eyes. It said, 'Call for help,' but I was really scared, so I couldn't make a noise. Then it said it again, really softly, and I screamed for my parents."

Caught up in a memory of my own Nightmare, I asked quietly, "Did they come for you? In your dream, I mean?"

"No one came," she said. "I remembered thinking, even though I knew it was a dream, that there wasn't anyone to help me. And the monster said—really calmly, like it didn't matter —'They chose not to save you. From now on, you're dead. If you make too much noise, you'll regret it'."

"You don't have to tell me if you don't want to," I said. She was shaking, and if it wasn't for the bubbling of the kettle in the background, I think I would have been able to hear the little black beads on her wrist ruffles tapping against each other.

"It's all right," she said. "I don't remember anything after that, anyway. I got really sick afterward, and when I got better, I couldn't walk anymore. My parents called in some people, but no one can really say what's wrong. I just...get sick a lot."

"Coffee," said Daniel, shoving a cup at her. Morgana took it, smiling a big, black-edged smile at him, and he passed another mug to me. "Are you two finished talking about makeup and stuff now?"

"Nearly," she said. "It sorta stuck with me, what he said. *From now on, you're dead.* So when one of the kids brought me some stuff one of the lady boarders left behind, I sort of just went with this style. I like it. I might look like I'm dead, but I'm not: it feels like I'm saying *so there* to the monster."

Good for her. I wish I'd been able to do that to the Nightmare, instead of just screaming and flailing.

"You don't look like you're dead," I said.

That made her grin. "Yeah, that's the joke," she said. "Hey. How come your partner is staying outside?"

"I told him he wasn't allowed to flirt with you," I explained. "Is he still sulking around the front door?"

"Yeah—well, he must be. I didn't see him leave yet. Do you have to go away again straight away?"

"Nah, he can wait. He doesn't want to get back to work, either."

"Is your investigation going badly?"

"It's a bit tricky, that's all. We've got some footage that isn't moving fast enough to catch what we need it to catch."

She nodded knowledgeably, taking me by surprise. "Yeah, security cameras aren't the best. They're usually only sixty frames per second because the human eye can't see faster than that anyway; they like to concentrate on clarity instead. What do you need to see that's faster than that?"

"What would I have to use if I wanted to capture something that moves faster than the human eye can see?" I asked, dodging the question. "Like a hummingbird or something."

"Yeah, well, you can't capture stuff like that on a security camera," Morgana said. "You need top class equipment for that. Even the high-end security cameras focus on high resolution rather than frames per second—they only need it to capture motion as fast as the human eye can capture it."

"What about non-human eyes?" I muttered to myself. To Morgana, I said, "So if we wanted to capture something that moves more quickly than we can see, we'd have to buy—"

"—a *really* expensive setup with slo-mo capture," she said, nodding.

I didn't think Zero was short of money; he could probably afford something like that. Janna Whiteleaf *definitely* could, and if the camera was being used to catch the Behindkind who was trying to murder her, it was a fair charge.

"I'll tell 'em what they need to get," I said. It would mean getting Jin Yeong to take me down to Janna Whiteleaf's house, but at least then Zero and Athelas could catch the Behindkind and get away from the place. I wanted to make sure that Mr. Preston was given as much time and attention as he needed, too.

"Actually, I think I've got one around here," she said. "I was going into photography for a while, and I tried a bit of videography, too. Have a look in that sports bag that's inside the cupboard over there, the one with the buttons on it."

I found the bag and brought it back to the bed with me. Inside was a sturdy bag with a telescoping tripod strapped on the side, and packed inside that was a black camera that I might have mistaken for a normal camera if it wasn't so heavy.

"It's a micro studio camera," Morgana said. "I only used it once or twice. It's pretty heavy, but if you use it with the tripod, you won't have to worry about shakiness or anything."

I stared at her. "You mean I can just...borrow it?"

"Yeah. I don't use it anymore. Just bring it back when you're done so my parents don't notice it's missing for too long."

"Are you sure? Do you just loan your stuff out to everyone?"

"I don't see everyone," she said simply. "Just you and Daniel. I mean, *and* the kids, but that's it. Who else is going to use it?"

"Okay. I'll tell my bosses to look after it."

"There's an app, too," Morgana said. "Give me your phone."

I passed it to her cautiously, but she didn't try to get into anything else, just went to the app store and downloaded something with a couple swipes of her finger.

"It's nothing like as good as the camera," she said. "But if you don't have the other one set up and you need to catch something in a hurry, you can get some really good footage with this one."

"Thanks. You sure about the camera, though?"

She shrugged. "I'm not using it. Anyway, if I loan it to you, you'll have to come back," she added, grinning. "I need someone I can beat at poker. Daniel's too good."

"Knew there was a reason you liked me visiting," I said accusingly. "All right, I'll play one game of poker, then I'm off. They'll need me back home soon, I reckon."

I left her playing poker with Daniel and trotted back downstairs with my booty, feeling bright and hopeful. There was no guarantee I was right, or that the stuff I'd borrowed would work, but I was pretty sure I was. I wasn't looking forward to visiting Zero and Athelas at Janna Whiteleaf's place to take them the idea, but it couldn't be helped. Whatever it was that was so important to Zero, I wanted to make sure he got it.

When I got outside, Jin Yeong was propped against the stones beside the door, looking at his watch with a cocked eyebrow. Since I knew he must have heard me coming, I guessed he just wanted to remind me that I'd been in there nearly an hour.

I stuck out my tongue and shoved the camera bag at him.

Jin Yeong lifted an eyebrow, but he took it. "*Igae mwohya?*"

"It's a camera," I said. "Reckon Zero's gunna find it useful for catching that peryton. Just a guess I've got."

"Good *Petteu*," he said. "We will visit them."

"Coffee first," I told him. "If I gotta go back to that place, I'm gunna need coffee."

It was a good day for coffee. Especially coffee I didn't have to make. I had money in my pocket to replace the baking things I'd used to make Athelas' teacake, but I didn't feel like going to the grocery store again, and it wouldn't hurt to use a bit of it on coffee for Zero and JinYeong, anyway. I could be generous. I'd solved their mystery for them, and probably made it easier for them to catch their murderer.

I mean, the day would probably have been a lot better if it wasn't for JinYeong sauntering along by my side, doing his impersonation of a model as usual, but I couldn't have everything.

"You wait out here," I said, scowling reflexively at him.

He shrugged, but settled against a nearby window, smiling serenely at an old woman who was so dazzled that she nearly walked out into the road instead of over to the crossing. I went on to the café, rolling my eyes.

I didn't particularly want to go to that house again, but I was pretty sure Zero would want the camera as soon as possible if my idea was correct—and I was very sure it was correct. I turned my head to tell JinYeong, "You fae really need to start keeping up with the times", before I remembered I'd left him back at the last window.

Oh well, there was still good coffee to look forward to, even if I couldn't be snarky at JinYeong. I pushed through the glass door, happily anticipating that my second cup of coffee from the place would be as good as the first, and walked right into trouble.

I came through the door, looking up to the back of the café for the counter, but there was somebody between me and the counter. It was a man in a wheelchair with black curls, straight, thick eyebrows that looked permanently a bit worried, and an olive complexion that seemed to have seen a lot of time under an Italian sun. But it was his eyes that caught me. He looked over naturally at the opening of the door, just as I was looking up, and our eyes met. His were probably brown, but mostly they looked kind and bright, and his lashes were the longest I'd ever seen.

I don't know if I stood there for as long as it felt like. I hope not. He smiled at me, and a crease appeared along the top of his left cheek; a dimple in the wrong place and around the wrong way. I couldn't help smiling back—even Zero couldn't have resisted responding to a smile like that—and that shook me free. I made a bee-line for the counter, trying not to look at him again as I went around his wheelchair. I couldn't afford to be rooted to the spot by someone's eyes.

Especially not with one of the psychos outside.

I ordered my coffee, keeping to the counter and trying not to look around, and when the coffee came up I headed for the door pretty quickly, too. I think he smiled at me again as I left; I gave him another half-smile that I reckon was closer to a grimace than a real smile, and hastily nipped out the door.

Jin Yeong was waiting for me by the lights when I stepped onto the street, but maybe I was still walking a bit too quickly, because his brows lifted a little when he saw me.

"*Petteu*," he purred, as I approached. "*Musen il?*"

"What? Nothing's up. Just got coffee, here's yours." I shoved his cup at him and hoped I didn't look as red as I felt. Good grief, it was ridiculous! It wasn't like I hadn't seen a good-looking bloke before!

"*Kuroji?*" remarked Jin Yeong, tilting his head to the side with narrowed eyes. "*Aninko.*"

"What do you know, you're just a vampire!" I snapped.

Jin Yeong's eyes hovered on my face for a few moments before they flicked over to the café windows. I saw the faint movement of his foot to go toward the café, and started walking away.

"Coffee's gunna get cold," I said, as nonchalantly as I could.

To my relief, that seemed to work. It was bad enough that

Jin Yeong was following me around; to have him poking his nose in on this would have been unspeakable.

"Then we will go," he said. *"Caja, Petteu!"*

CHAPTER ELEVEN

"HOW LONG WILL THIS TAKE?" DEMANDED JANNA WHITELEAF.

"Dunno," I said. It wasn't as if I knew what I was doing, or anything. Actually, I was just lucky Zero was letting me play around with it. I could tell he wasn't convinced by my explanation, but there must have been enough to it to make him allow it.

I fiddled with the adjusting screws on the tripod, which nearly sent the whole lot plummeting toward the ground, and Janna said sourly, "Do you know what you're doing, human?"

She might as well have said, "filth" instead of "human", because that was the expression on her face.

I adjusted the tripod a bit and tilted it, catching a brief flicker of Janna's narrow, unpleasant face on the screen.

Immediately, her eyes narrowed at me. "Do not point that thing at me! I refuse to be made a suspect in my own building!"

"Sorry," I said. Hopefully I sounded sorry enough, because I didn't want another run-in with her. I mean, I was *mostly* feeling safer. Mostly, because Zero had pulled me aside while Jin Yeong distracted Janna Whiteleaf, and dabbed a spell on one of my ears. Not quite wholly, because I didn't put it past her to go for me with her letter opener or something, and Zero and the others were down in the lower levels, clearing more staff to come back to work.

But I was comforted, anyway. Comforted at Zero's brief explanation that the spell was something to keep Janna from working any more magic on me, comforted by the fact that he was trusting me to set up and try out the camera *at all*—comforted even by Jin Yeong's normal, irritating saunter as he walked out the door, complaining about the smell of human chemicals in the house.

I'd finished setting the camera up through a series of calls to Morgana by the time they sent up one of the vetted staff with a tray of food and drink. It should have been about midday in the human world, but here where everything was moonlight and darkness it was hard to tell if I was being fed a snack or supper. The girl who gave it to me was human—the same one I'd seen the first day being checked by Jin Yeong. Unlike that time, her eyes were completely clear, and she shook her head very slightly as she passed me a cup of tea. I took the tea, unsure if I'd really seen what I thought I'd seen, and again she shook her head, then looked directly at the tea.

Don't drink the tea, then.

"Thanks," I said, grinning at her. "For the tea and biscuits."

"It had nothing to do with me," said Janna. She must have thought I was thanking her. "Your owner must have arranged for them to be sent up."

"That's weird," I said, watching the human woman leave as unobtrusively as possible. She hadn't left biscuit crumbs on Janna's desk, so I suppose she was better trained than me. "Usually I'm the one getting tea and coffee for them."

"Are you going to be much longer?" she asked. "I have important meetings to get to, and I've already had to lose a day's worth of important business due to this ridiculous charade."

Well, pardon us *for trying to keep your skinny carcase alive*, I thought. I was bright enough not to say it aloud, mind you.

"Reckon they're checking the second shift at the moment," I said, just as the power went off.

It wasn't just the Behind lights that went out, either—it was the human lights, too.

"What the heck?" I said, as the softer lights Zero had installed bloomed into florescence.

"Someone has hijacked our defences," said Janna. "From the human side and the Behind side at the same time, it appears. Perhaps we had better leave."

She said it as the door opened, and Zero came swiftly into the room, JinYeong half a step behind him. "Do not think about leaving," he said to her. "We're going to check outside; everyone has been completely vetted downstairs. Pet, stay *here*. Don't do anything stupid."

"I never do stupid stuff," I told him. "I'm just always in the wrong place at the wrong time."

JinYeong, a slim, snarky twin to Zero's warning, twitched his forefinger at me and followed Zero back out the door.

"How utterly ridiculous!" snapped Janna Whiteleaf, sitting back down with a jerk. "Why should I be left here with a human pet while my house is overrun with criminals?"

"Hey, at least I'm not a criminal," I said.

"I have no knowledge of that," she said, with no less of a snap to her voice. "Your tea is growing cold. Why does it take humans so long to do things?"

"Yeah, I don't drink tea."

"Why would they get you tea, then?" she demanded.

She was far too annoyed about it to be normal. Even for being annoyed at Zero and JinYeong, she was too het up. What was the bet she'd ordered the doe-eyed staff downstairs to mickey-finn anything sent up to me? Which begged the question of why the human girl who'd given it to me *hadn't* been doe-eyed—and more importantly, why she'd warned me at all.

"Dunno," I said, lifting my phone to check the camera view.

Oh yay. Janna Whiteleaf, nice and clear. I'd already set up the proper camera, but it would be nice to have my own phone set up in the app, too, even if it wasn't as good. "Probably 'cos one of those three told them the wrong thing."

It was Athelas, I'd bet. He would have very carefully told them the wrong thing, just in case this happened, and then left it up to me to be sensible. He'd warned me, after all. They'd all warned me.

I still wondered what I would have done if the human girl hadn't warned me directly not to drink the stuff.

Janna glared at me in smoothly digital pixels, and I put my phone down on the table beside me. Cranky old fae. It wasn't like I was filming her, after all. I just wanted to set up the app.

Oops. Looked like I had filmed her, after all. Not on purpose or anything, but there was a short, thirty second clip stored away in the app. Maybe I could look at it later when I wanted to give myself a few more nightmares. At least these ones would be in slow motion, so I might have a chance to get away from them.

"What were you doing with that?" she demanded. "Were you filming me?"

"Why the heck would I film you?" I demanded, forgetting that I wasn't talking to fae who would excuse me being cheeky up to a point.

"Humans are always filming on their dreadful little hand-held devices. I refuse to be filmed. Give it to me."

I grabbed the phone, instinctively holding it against my chest. "You can't have it. Zero gave it to me."

"I will not," said Janna Whiteleaf, rising from her chair, *"ask you again."*

Ah heck.

Clutching my phone, I scrambled to my feet, and retreated behind the couch I'd been sitting on. Janna meant business; she came out from behind her desk, and her shadow came with her, fluttering wide with too much edge and space and feather for a human shadow.

Ah heck.

We were too late. We would always have been too late. Janna Whiteleaf wasn't antsy because she had somewhere to be, or because she had a natural aversion to being filmed, she was antsy because her shadow was starting to change back to look like her actual form instead of the human façade.

Janna Whiteleaf wasn't Janna Whiteleaf.

"You really shouldn't have tried to film me," the peryton said with Janna's mouth, but now the speech pattern and expressions were completely different. "Now I've got to kill you. I would have been happy just to get away."

I saw the darkness of the peryton's shadow ripple across the wall in the softness of Zero's backup lights: wings with a spread wider than a delivery van, antlers stretching high and spindly across the roof, and the rounded, inky suggestion of stag haunches behind that. But in front of all that was the beak that was curved, sharp, and bigger than my head.

I bet if I saw it on security footage it would have looked normal enough; an old, white, thin nosed woman backing a younger woman across the room with the sheer force of her personality. But I saw it in the screen of the slow-motion camera as I backed away; an earlier, slower capture of Janna Whiteleaf's body flickering in and out of sight. And every time it flickered out of sight, I saw the peryton instead of a human, joining seamlessly with its shadow on the floor as it moved inevitably across the floor toward me.

I looked away from it and around for weapons instead. I didn't know how it worked here. I could grab stuff in the human world and Between because it was something else here Behind. What was I supposed to do when I was actually Behind?

What could I do?

Talk. Yeah, I could talk.

"You're crazy," I said, backing away. "They're gunna know what's happened as soon as they come in and see my body on the floor."

"I've already got one body hidden here, and they didn't find it."

So *that*'s why JinYeong had been complaining about human chemicals for the last couple of days! There was blood around here somewhere, and even though she'd managed to clean it up, there was still a bit of it somewhere, mixed with whatever she'd cleaned it up with.

"You put it in the freezer, didn't you?"

The peryton smiled. "It gets rid of the smell completely and has the added advantage of taking care of the corruption that a vampire might smell, too. It's a good thing this stupid fae keeps a lot of human things around her house. Bleach is such a human thing, but it's so useful. Fae don't know what they're missing out on by clinging to their old ways."

"Yeah," I said. "But I reckon you might have forgotten about the freezer when you made the power go off. How long d'you think it'll take the smell to start being noticeable for a vampire?"

I mean, I hadn't seen her turn off the power, but she was the only one who could have done it—who would have *wanted* it to be done.

She stopped—*it* stopped—comprehension flitted across the living dead face of Janna Whiteleaf. "Then I'd better kill you quickly," it said. "If I throw your body out of the window it'll give me enough time to slip away while they try to discover what happened to you."

"Yeah? That's gunna be hard if you can't put a glamour on my body," I said. "Zero already put a spell on me that stops you from being able to use magic on me."

"I'll throw you beyond the wall," the peryton said. "I'm not usually vindictive, but you're a real pain in the neck."

"You could pass as a human," I said. There was nothing of the stilted speech of Zero, nor the flourishing vocabulary of Athelas. "Not like that lot."

The peryton smiled again. "That's because I'm not bound by tradition like the fae. Not all Behindkind are."

"Like Upper Management," I said, throwing it out on a chance.

It stopped, then grinned; a very odd expression to see on Janna's pinched white face. "They were right about you," it said. "You're not just a pet, are you?"

"I'm a pet; I'm not stupid. You lot always think you're so flamin' clever, so you don't watch what you say around humans."

"This fae might have believed that," the peryton said, gesturing toward its body, "but I'm not that gullible. I've heard about you. I've heard about the Troika—their business, their links, and their rule-bending for their little human pet."

"Suit yourself," I said. "But that's more than I know."

Janna Whiteleaf's head tilted, displaying interest and amusement. "You really don't know!" the peryton said in wonder. "It's almost a shame to kill you, but I need to get going before that lot finds out who I am. I've got the feeling that it'll be much easier to leave the house as you. I would have been tempted to keep you alive if they hadn't shut up the house. Upper Management is really interested in you."

"Yeah? Well, they can mind their own flaming business," I said, edging back again.

"Stop looking around for weapons," said the peryton. "I'm a killer by trade—did you think I wouldn't notice?"

"Telling me you're a killer isn't likely to make me stop looking for weapons," I pointed out. I dodged to my right to get out of the corner the peryton had been slowly nudging me into, sprinting along between the couch back and the windows while shadows and huge feathers I couldn't see flipped and slapped as the peryton made a hasty turn to face Janna Whiteleaf's desk.

C'mmon, Jin Yeong, I thought desperately. *Hurry up and smell the body. Don't be a pain in the neck all your life.*

But there was no sound of footsteps outside the door, and the peryton was already stalking toward the desk. "If you'd just drunk the tea, it would have been a lot easier for you," it said.

"Thanks, but no thanks," I said, and ducked behind the desk. Why was I Behind? I couldn't even fight properly here! It didn't help that the stapler was old and huge and looked a bit like a cosh, or that Janna Whiteleaf's paperweight looked like a gun if you looked at it from a level point of view.

Hang on.

Hang on. If I could use stuff from Behind in the human world by bringing it Between, why couldn't I use stuff from the human world by bringing it Between? I just had to see it the right way, right?

For instance, the paperweight that looked like a gun from my crouching position behind the desk—who said it had to be a paperweight when it was Behind? What if it secretly wanted to be a gun?

"You're a gun," I said to it. "You're not fragile and glass, you're metal and plastic and deadly."

"Now that'd be a real trick," said the peryton, looking almost interested. "Go on, pick it up. I want to see this."

"Don't reckon ya do," I said, because I could already feel the cool certainty of a gun butt against my palm.

Ah heck yes! Human world for all the firepower!

I picked it up, tilting to check for the safety, and flicked that off. Then I touched my finger to the trigger, light and slightly damp with sweat.

The peryton said something that was definitely more human than Behindkind, and stepped forward, so I shot it. It wasn't my best shot, but I hadn't been to a gun range in years. Still, it copped him in the shoulder, throwing out quicksilver blood that mutated in the air to become invisible and wriggled away into the carpet without a trace.

The peryton staggered back a step with its hand over its shoulder, glimmering around the fingers with that quicksilver blood. The image of Janna Whiteleaf flickered and died, then expanded into the shape of a stag with wickedly sharp hooves, its wings monstrous but not so frightening as the black-tipped beak.

"Ow!" it said, shocked. "You little—"

"Pet," Zero's voice said. "Duck, please."

I ducked behind the desk and peered through the lower half of it, my heart thundering in my ears. Something bright and stinging flared over the whole room, smacking stickily against the desk and narrowly missing my face, and a mad tumble of teeth and steel and beak screamed into being.

By the time it was settled, and I came out with my gun at the ready, the peryton was on the carpet, enmeshed in the stickiness of something that wasn't rope, struggling but contained. Zero was sporting a blue-blooded slash across his upper left arm and JinYeong's suit coat was in tatters from what looked suspiciously like bird claws. Athelas, touching the tips of either sword to the carpet beside him, seemed to glisten just slightly at the temples in the soft light. Had he been sweating?

"Pet," he said, rather breathlessly, "perhaps you could do me the goodness of not imperilling your life every other week."

JinYeong spat an "*Aish!*" at the far wall and ripped off his suit jacket. "*Ah, mangyeosseo! Petteu! No daemuniya!*"

"*I* didn't rip your jacket!" I protested. "And I found the murderer for you!"

"I knew sooner!" he shot back, Between edging the words. "I found that body. I was *coming!*"

I stuck my tongue out at him. "I didn't need you, I had Zero."

"*Hyeong!*" protested JinYeong. "Punish the pet! She disobeyed orders!"

"I was a good Pet," I said smugly. "Stayed exactly where you told me to stay, didn't I, Zero? I can't help it if you lot left me with a murderer again."

"We do seem to be forming troubling habits," murmured Athelas. He cleaned his twin blades on JinYeong's ruined jacket, drawing a snarl from the vampire that made his eyebrows rise in amusement. "Pet, perhaps you would be good enough to see if JinYeong's jacket can be saved when we get home. He seems to be more than usually concerned about it—I assume it was a favourite of his."

"Fine," I grumbled. "You okay, Zero?"

"I am damaged," said JinYeong, very clearly. "I need to be fixed."

"There's nothing that'll fix what's wrong with you," I told him. "Are you even bleeding?"

JinYeong snarled and turned his shoulder on me, but Zero, interrupting us, asked, "Pet, where did you get that gun? Where did you learn to *use* it?"

"She told it to be a gun," said the peryton. It was shaking, but I was pretty sure it was shaking with laughter. "So it became a gun. You're playing a very interesting game, Lord Sero!"

"I was under the impression that it was Upper Management who was playing games," said Zero.

"You can't tell me you didn't know she could do that!"

"It," said Zero, chillingly. "This is merely a human pet."

"Is that why it has the feeling of vampire to it?" asked the peryton. "Or why it had a magic-repelling spell on it?"

"Oi!" I said, insulted. "I don't smell like a vampire!"

The peryton clicked its beak. "I didn't say—"

"Enough," said Zero, with finality. "I'll have something to discuss with you soon enough, bird. Athelas, keep everyone out of the freezer—when the Enforcers get here, we'll need to direct them to their latest body. JinYeong, you stay with me and guard this one until the Enforcers arrive. They'll want to question it."

JinYeong's brows rose. I didn't even have to try to understand him, because his words were clear. "Really, *hyeong*? You're going to pass it to the Enforcers without talking to it first?"

"No," said Zero pleasantly. "I'm going to have a talk with it first. Then I'll call the Enforcers. Pet—"

"I know, I know—coffee!"

He stared at me. "No. We don't need coffee. But you need to go below stairs and wait until we're done up here."

"You gunna kill it?"

Zero looked over at the peryton, which had gone very still and watchful, the single liquid eye in view unblinking. "I haven't decided yet. Go below stairs."

"Yeah, but it was talking about Upper Management and stuff, so there's probably some things it can tell you."

"There are many things it can tell many people," said Zero. "Go below stairs, Pet."

I went, because I'd protested long enough to be believable, and for Athelas to be busy in the freezer. There was something else I had to do before I left this house, and it wasn't something I could let my three psychos see me do.

WHEN I GOT DOWN TO THE KITCHEN, THE GIRL WITH THE wide-awake eyes was there already. Beside her was the tall fae who had been in the security room the first time I'd come to the house.

"What's happening?" she asked.

I couldn't help glancing at the tall fae.

"It's all right," she said. "He's why I'm like this and not like them."

"Yeah?" I looked suspiciously at him. "You sure about that?"

"Very," she said. "What's happening?"

"Short version—Janna Whiteleaf is dead, and the Enforcers will be here before too much longer."

"We should go now," said the tall fae.

"Not before you get all the others," I said sharply.

"I don't care about the others," the fae said. "Just this one."

"I'll get them," the maid said. "I'm not leaving without them. If you leave without them, you leave without me."

He sighed in frustration, the whisper of it a familiar sound. "They'll need to be disenchanted. We don't have time."

"Then we'll take them with us as they are and *make* time," she said. "Wait here if you don't want to help me fetch them."

"I'm coming," he said. "It will be quicker with two of us."

I was nearly dancing with impatience by the time they got back, shepherding nearly a dozen humans, each with that glazed look to their eyes. "Hurry it up!" I hissed, opening the front door. "The Enforcers will be here any minute."

I opened the gate for them as well, but I don't think I was the one who opened the way back to the human world. That was the fae, who went in the lead, humans following obediently like a row of ducks. The maid stood by the garden gate with me as they passed by, watchful and bright eyed.

I couldn't help saying, "You're going to stay with him, aren't you?"

She nodded, her eyes still on the humans.

"You sure about this?" I asked her. "He doesn't care about any of them except you."

"I know," she said. "But that's enough for now. If he loves one of us, he can't hate the rest of us. He wasn't like this when I first met him, and if he can change so much since then, I know he can change more."

"Yeah," I said, a bit gloomily. "That's what I keep hoping, too. If they can get fond of one of us, they should be able to get fond of the rest."

She gave the smallest of nods, perhaps a remnant of her training with Janna Whiteleaf. "They just need time. Give it time."

"Reckon that's something we've just run out of," I said. I felt a stirring somewhere within the house—the same sort of feeling that the psychos gave off when they were coming into the house through Between. "Reckon the Enforcers just got here."

"It's time to go," said the tall fae, returning to pluck at her sleeve.

"Good luck," she said. "Don't take this the wrong way, but I hope we don't see you again."

"I get that a lot," I told her cheerfully. "Good luck."

I was just inside the door again when Zero came down to get me.

"Pet," he said, his eyes going from me to the front door. "What are you doing?"

"Just coming up to meet you," I said, trying not to pant. "Had to um, tidy up the kitchen."

"Is that why I can now only sense a single human in the house?"

"You can't tidy up humans," I told him. "Not like crumbs. You can brush crumbs into the sink and under the table, but you can still see humans if you try that."

"Don't try to talk me out of questioning you."

I looked at him unblinkingly, aware of Jin Yeong padding down the stairs behind him, eyes dark and amused. "I can't do magic. It wouldn't be much use letting them go if I couldn't really release them, would it?"

"That much is true," said Zero, though I wasn't sure if he was agreeing with my argument or telling me he believed I was telling the truth—up to a point.

"Well," I said, allowing the indignation to creep into my voice, "how come you're so flamin' suspicious, then?"

"Experience," Zero said, unperturbed. "Jin Yeong, is Athelas ready to go?"

"*Ye, hyeong.* The others have come."

"Tell them to come down and meet me. I'm not going up to them."

Jin Yeong didn't have to tell them: the next thing I saw was the golden fae flouncing down the stairs with his usual cohort behind him and Athelas threading gently through them to join us.

Without bothering to greet Zero, the fae demanded, "Where is it?"

"It put up a good fight," said Zero, and I knew that they'd killed the peryton.

And yeah, I know it was a murderer, and I know that they had their own legal right to kill it, but it still made me feel hollow and wobbly in the stomach. Detective Tuatu probably wasn't going to like it much, either.

The golden fae said furiously, "You *killed* it?"

"There was no choice," Zero said flatly, and I heard the truth in there. Whatever else the peryton had or hadn't told Zero, it had been enough to seal its fate in one way or another.

"You were specifically tasked to capture it alive! How can we interrogate it if it's dead?"

"You can't. You'll have to find someone else if you wish for information about Upper Management."

"That was not our agreement."

"Our agreement was that you would provide certain intelligence, and we would provide certain investigative services. We found and executed your murderer in accordance with the agreement *and* Behind law, but you have as of yet given us no useful intelligence."

"Your father will be very displeased," the golden fae said evenly. "I hope you don't regret it, Lord Sero."

"My father is always displeased with me."

"Despite that, he wished to make sure you are aware of certain developments."

"The only developments I'm interested in are those relating to the information I was promised," Zero said.

"You should look closer to home, I think," said the golden fae.

"A significant event has occurred while you've been chasing your tails."

"If we'd been given the information I asked for in the first place, we would have done significantly less chasing," said Zero, his voice a threatening rumble.

"Your father was saddened by the fact that you were not able to make as good a use of the news we gave you as you would have liked."

The fae lieutenant flicked her eyes toward the ceiling briefly. That, coupled with Zero and Athelas' reactions when they got home from that particular trip last week, left me feeling like the information they'd been given had been deliberately not very useful.

"Your father wished to make sure you knew that while you've been busy protecting fae, the murderer has killed again—an heirling, this time. You'll need to be prepared."

"I've got no business with heirlings apart from catching the murderer if he's murdered one."

"I think you do."

"Then you should mind your own business and stop telling Zero what *his* is," I muttered.

To my surprise, Zero didn't tell me to shush. All he said was, "Where is the body?"

"Then is our business concluded with this exchange?"

"I think you'll find I can discover the body by use of my own resources," Zero said. "There's no clearing of the debt owed."

I know I must have looked smug, and Jin Yeong definitely looked smug. Even Athelas had a faintly irritating air of amusement to him, and all three of those combined must have been too much for the golden fae.

He snapped, "Then I bid you good day!" and marched off toward the nearest door.

Unluckily for him, that was the cleaning cupboard, which, unlike the linen closet in our place, didn't take him anywhere. He marched back out again, his nose very pinched at the nostrils, like he was trying not to smell something dreadful, and led his sparkling cohort out through the proper doorway instead.

As soon as he was gone, Zero said softly, "Pet, call Detective Tuatu. He'll know if there's been another murder."

I obeyed, and the detective picked up on the second ring.

"I can't talk, Pet," he said. "There's something going on."

"Let me guess. You've got another body like the one you found outside my window."

Silence. Then, "How did you *know*?"

"These three want to come and see."

"Okay. We won't be moving the body for a while yet. They might as well join the circus. I'll text you the address."

"Catch ya later," I said, and hung up. To Zero, I said, "Yep. They've got another one."

"Very well," he said. "Let's go."

CHAPTER TWELVE

THE BODY WAS HANGING FROM THE POWERLINES WHEN WE GOT there. I think we were in Claremont by then, but it was kinda hard to tell, because Zero took us Between to travel there. It might be quicker and smoother for travelling, but it doesn't help when it comes to my sense of direction.

Detective Tuatu was waiting for us, but when he made a protest about my presence that Zero summarily ignored, he tightened his lips and left the psychos to it.

"I'll be over there if you need me," he said to me, heading back to his co-workers.

Zero and Athelas circled the body, much like they'd done the first time I'd laid eyes on them. It wasn't strung up outside of someone else's window this time, so I suppose that was nice. That was the only thing that *was* nice about it, though. It looked the same as the last time I'd seen one of these bodies: throat cut, stomach slashed open to dangle entrails on the lawn. The head wasn't hanging, at least; it sorta drooped sideways, its dead eyes staring straight toward the house it dangled in front of. Even the bloke looked familiar, but it wasn't until I got a proper look at his face that I knew why.

"Oh, for pity's sake!" said Zero impatiently, at the same time. "It's the human from across the road again! How many bodies will we find with his face?"

"Last time it wasn't a body," Athelas pointed out. "It was more a pile of ashes and a few body parts. Are you quite sure it's the same one? He looks somewhat more...dishevelled than the first time we saw him supposedly dead."

"That's just all the beard and hair," I said, with a leaden stomach. Despite the heaviness, I couldn't quite believe he was dead. Like Zero, I'd thought him dead twice before. "It looks like him, all right."

"Interesting," said Athelas, his eyes dwelling thoughtfully on me. "So he escaped once, but he couldn't avoid the murderer twice."

"Yeah," I said, shoving my hands in my pockets. "Looks like it."

"Now that you mention the hair," he added, his voice growing chilly, "I'm almost certain I saw someone similar outside the house a few days ago. If I'm not mistaken, our leftovers were left out for him."

I coughed.

Zero said icily, "We will discuss that, and the fact that you seemed not at all surprised that he's been alive, later."

"Okay," I said, my voice barely a mutter. He wouldn't kick me out of the house for this, would he? I'd known it was a risk to keep quiet about the old mad bloke, but how could I tell them about him? I couldn't lose the house for this. I'd clung to it for so long now, and I *couldn't* lose it. It was home, and safety, and comfort.

Jin Yeong, ignoring us all, crouched beside the bloody body and touched one finger to the dead man's blood-soaked cheek, then to his tongue.

A soft hiss of laughter escaped him. *"Ku saramun aniya,"* he said. *"Ah, nomu jaemi isseo!"*

"I *beg* your pardon?" Athelas said.

Zero, sharply, asked, "It's not him? Again?"

I could have laughed my relief if it wasn't for the fact that someone actually was still dead—if it wasn't for the fact that I was still in trouble. "Did someone do a glamour again?"

Zero stooped for a closer look at something I couldn't see, his eyes running over the corpse from head to toe.

"It's really not him," he said. "It's a glamour again. This one is fae, I think."

"It can't be a fae glamour," said Athelas, rather grimly. "I would have noticed it this time."

"It's not fae magic," Zero said. "It's human. The *corpse* is fae, but the magic is human."

"Hang on, *humans* can have magic?"

None of them answered me. Jin Yeong laughed again, his eyes bright and malicious, and said something I couldn't follow.

"Indeed," agreed Athelas. "Perhaps our murderer would have better luck picking someone at random this time. He doesn't seem to be able to keep up with who is his intended victim and who is not."

"He's broken his pattern again, too," remarked Zero. "Perhaps that will be useful to us."

"Or he knew the bloke was fae again," I said. All three of them looked at me, and I added defensively, "Well, you said there would be one human murder and four Behindkind ones. Maybe he knew this fae was pretending to be human. Maybe he didn't care about what games they were playing. It could be the start of one of his rampages, again. If it is, there should be two more Behindkind murders and a dead human somewhere, right?"

"Perhaps," said Zero, but there was a worried line between his eyes. "But I find myself doubting it. I've never seen him do something like this before. We've found the fae bodies before the human bodies at times, but that was merely a matter of us coming across them at the wrong times. What's made him change his pattern now? Why this fae—or human, if he thought it was a human? And most importantly, why did the Enforcers think this is an heirling?"

Athelas laughed suddenly, a bright, amused sound that was more than his usual soft, chuckle. "Ah, this really is a puzzle! My lord, has it occurred to you that this human who seems to keep being murdered could be a harbinger?"

"What's that?" I asked.

"Trouble," said Zero briefly.

"For the Family and the crown, certainly," said Athelas. "Not something that need trouble us, however."

Jin Yeong only grinned, but he's mostly trouble in a suit himself, so it was probably just fellow-feeling.

"So the old mad bloke is a harbinger?" If the old mad bloke was a harbinger, what did that mean?

"It seems likely," Zero said, surprising me by answering. "Your neighbour across the road has been surrounded by trouble, attracts danger, and has escaped death multiple times. Not unusual when you deal with Behind, but to survive it all and still be drawing trouble would suggest special status."

"So it's what, a special position Behind?"

"Something like that. But it's a born position, not a given one."

"What's a harbinger do?"

"Sow discord, bring rebellion, attract danger—and heirlings," added Athelas. "How very interesting, my lord! If a harbinger has indeed shown up, it would seem that you have less time than you hoped."

"You got any idea what they're talking about?" I asked Jin Yeong.

He shrugged and said in Korean, "I'm too young. There is one ruler Behind since my turning."

"What use are you, then?" I demanded in disgust, and went

back to listening to Athelas and Zero. Even if they talked in circles, at least they knew something.

JinYeong made a sniffy little laugh and crouched beside the corpse again.

"Do you mean we're gunna have heirlings appearing all around Hobart?" I asked Zero. "Is this the Behind apocalypse or something?"

"The apoc—well." Zero stopped, and I saw him glance at Athelas, who was still looking distinctly amused. "It's a fairly accurate summary, if it comes to that. When the full cycle of a ruler's reign comes about in Behind, the world itself works together to shake off the old for the new. heirlings begin to be born, and a harbinger works his way through the cracks to draw heirlings to himself."

"So heirlings are potential Behind leaders, and the harbinger is like the guardian of them all?"

"The harbinger is perhaps closer to being a catalyst," Athelas said. "I find it interesting, my lord, that our contacts told us about this death in particular. Do you think they knew the significance of it?"

"They might have thought he was a harbinger," Zero said, nodding once. "If so, they're probably the ones who tried to kill him."

"Hide a body in a graveyard," said JinYeong, still clear to understand, shrugging one shoulder. "It is sensible."

Good grief, no wonder the old mad bloke was as mad as he was. I'd already thought it must have taken a toll on him, always being surrounded by weird stuff happening everywhere, but if he was a harbinger, it had probably been weird since he was a kid.

I asked, "What if he doesn't want to be a harbinger?"

"He has very little choice in the matter. Even were he to give up the position, it would be difficult to convince anyone that he'd done so."

"But he can give it up?"

"Indeed. One assumes he does not wish to do so."

"Reckon I would, by now."

"Perhaps he's of your mind, Pet," suggested Athelas, with a gentle humour. "Perhaps he feels that heirlings as well as other humans ought to be protected. Perhaps he sees it as his duty to them."

"That one should stay away from our pet, then," said Jin Yeong, startlingly understandable. "Our pet is protected."

"And not an heirling," Athelas said, with slightly more pointed gentleness.

"Yeah," I said. "I don't want it!"

"Being an heirling isn't something a person can give up," Zero said. There was a heaviness of experience in his voice. "You can run away from the expectation of it, but it follows in one way or another."

"Indeed," murmured Athelas, and I thought he laughed, though it could have been sorrow I saw in his eyes, too.

"I will take the blood," said Jin Yeong. "What else, *hyeong*? *Nan Petteuleul daerigoyo?*"

"I don't want to go with you," I told him indignantly. "I'll go with Zero."

Jin Yeong made a *pft* sound that managed to be disparaging and sulky at the same time and disappeared through a writhing of vines on the wall beside him.

"Should I see what there is to be seen at the police station?" enquired Athelas.

Zero said, "That will likely be troublesome for the detective."

"No worries," said Tuatu, approaching us. "They've already connected me with you. It won't be any worse if he comes with me."

"You gunna be all right?" I asked Athelas.

"Certainly. This time I shall not permit myself to be captured."

"Not being captured is a good choice," I said, even though it wasn't exactly what I'd meant. To Detective Tuatu, I said, "You better make him a nice cuppa. And give him some of the bikkies you keep in your desk drawer."

"How do you know what I keep in my desk drawer?" demanded the detective, startled, but Athelas, pinching the sleeve of his shirt, drew him into Between through a slight ripple between the gate before I could answer him.

I heard the faintest echo of his voice saying to the detective, "We have some matters to discuss, I think," and that was worrying enough to make me gaze after them for quite some time.

"Athelas will manage," said Zero's voice. "There's no need to worry. Follow me; I'm going to see how far I can track the murdered fae Between before I lose the trail. If he's fae, he came from somewhere Between. We might be able to identify him while the glamour wears off."

"Okay," I said. "But if dinner is late tonight, it's your fault."

I don't know whether Zero was sniffing him out or following a trail that only he could see, but it took us inside the house we'd found the body outside. We paused briefly at the stairs, and didn't go Between until we were in the kitchen, where there was still a cup of tea sitting with the milk making a scum along the top.

"Who lived here?" I asked. "The fae? Did a human glamor him, or did the murderer?"

"If the murderer glamoured him, the murderer is a human," said Zero. "And considering most humans don't even know about Between and Behind, I very much doubt that. I've also seen his work Behind, and I'm certain a human couldn't manage that."

"Yeah, but it's not like it's particularly reasonable that a human is going around putting glamours on people, either. Hang on, though: what if the human knew he was going to be murdered and didn't want to die?"

"You think your old neighbour glamoured the fae."

"Don't tell me you didn't think the same thing," I said. "So this human"—the old mad bloke, but somehow I didn't want to think about that—"this human didn't want to die, and he knew there was a fae here, so he glamoured them and ran away before the murderer got here."

"The interesting thing," Zero said, opening the pantry door, "is that if it's so, this human has to be a harbinger. We were told the body was an heirling, but I'd give a lot to know whether the Family knew it was false when they told us."

He stepped into the pantry as he said it, and I followed, tripping over a huge bag of flour and leaving a few white footprints behind as I staggered Between.

"How do you lot know who are heirlings and harbingers, anyway?"

"By the way they interact with the world around them. And occasionally, the amount of dead bodies around them."

"So you look at the old mad bloke and see all the deaths and the magic that someone's doing, and you say, *yep, that one's a harbinger*!"

"Something like that," Zero said, as the shelves turned to a ladder by his shoulder. "Up we go, Pet. Follow me closely."

I did so. I didn't like the way the darkness above us swallowed up the ladder, not to mention Zero's shoulders. We went rung over rung until we reached a ledge, but the ladder began again after that, a bit wider. It wasn't the easiest climb I've had, but we'd only seen one person—creature?—going down while we were going up. Most of the things I met Between were actively trying to kill or imprison me, so I was pretty pleased with that.

I was a bit slower this time in following Zero, which was lucky, because just as his boot came level with my face, a little trapdoor opened between the rungs, and a goblin head popped out.

It grinned at me with murder in its eyes, and put a single, knobbly finger up to its lips. Then it raised its hand and stabbed its needle through Zero's boot.

"Don't do that!" I said, and punched it in the face.

It squeaked and dropped its needle setup, and fell onto the

ledge. I heard it a moment later, wailing at the top of its lungs as it ran for cover, and saw a last flash of wide, rolling eyes as it disappeared into the shadows. I might have felt sorry for it if I hadn't seen the gleeful murder in its eyes as it stabbed Zero's foot.

"Those won't kill me," Zero said, dropping back down to the ledge.

"I know," I said. "You told me ages ago. They're for knocking people out."

"Bring them," he said, and stood up again. He turned on his heel and went on along the ledge instead of up again without waiting for me. I scrambled for the needles and hurried after him, stuffing the tiny apparatuses into my front pockets.

"Hang on, I know they're not gunna kill you, but are they going to do anything to you?"

"Yes," said Zero, even more briefly. "We need to be home before that happens."

"Okay," I panted, "but don't forget that your legs are a lot flamin' longer than mine!"

I don't think he actually remembered, because it didn't slow him down much. He didn't ever let me drop out of sight, but he didn't give me any chance to breathe, either; he forged a path through Between at a lope, his leather jacket a patch of darkness to follow in the changing world around me.

Sometimes I can sense we're about to get home just before we do, when it comes to Between. Sometimes. This time, I don't think we were even halfway there when Zero stopped suddenly, causing me to walk into his back, and turned sharply to the left.

That took us into a walk-in freezer that must have been in someone's restaurant in the human world. Here, it was neither freezer nor something else, just cold and weird and slightly slimy.

"Oi," I said, startled. "What are we doing?"

"Shut the door," he said, swaying.

I shut it, pulling back on the emergency open to do so, and

there was a cavernous sort of boom as it sealed. There must be a heck of a lot more to this place Behind than there was in the human world. Fortunately, there wasn't as much cold here Between, and the walls were solid enough when I looked around it.

Zero pushed me gently to the side and ran his hand around the inside seal of the door. Straight away, things got a decent bit cooler, though still not as cold as they would have been if we were right in the freezer, and the outline of the freezer walls got clearer.

Still swaying in a way that worried me, he walked along one of the walls with his hand trailing through the frost until he reached the far end, and sat on the floor with his knees bent and his forearms resting on them.

"Hang on, what are you doing?"

"Sitting down," he said.

I followed him. "Yeah, I can see that, but *why?*"

"I'm about to be slightly drunk," he said.

"Behindkind can get drunk?"

"Anyone can get drunk, if you've got the right kind of stimulant. Those needles don't knock me out, but they do...make havoc in my body."

"What, you don't want people to see you stagger?"

"Call Athelas. Tell him he needs to come and get you."

"What, you're a nasty drunk? Rubbish!" I knew a few things about people who got drunk, and the most important thing I'd learned was that the drink didn't change them; it just took away their inhibitions against doing whatever they wanted to do. People who were nasty deep down got nasty. People who weren't, got happy.

"I'm not—in this state, I can't keep you safe, and the Sandman is still lurking. Sit still and call Athelas."

"We're in a freezer," I said, wiggling my phone at him. "There's no signal."

There was silence for a few moments before Zero gave a huge sigh that gusted around us. "Of course there is not," he said.

"Oi," I said, sitting down next to him. "You sounded like a human then."

"I am part human."

"Yeah, but you don't usually sound like it."

"Are you trying to irritate me, Pet?"

"Athelas says that it's being part human that makes you able to be an heirling."

"Ah, you *are* trying to irritate me."

I grinned. "I would never."

Zero might have given the smallest grin, but he tilted his head back to rest against the wall so that I couldn't see it, and when he next spoke, it was to say, "You didn't call for me."

"Knew you were coming," I said, but that wasn't quite true. I'd also known JinYeong was coming. Was it the fact that I hadn't been as much frightened this time? Or maybe just the fact that I hadn't been *acting* in mindless fear?

"I see," he said. "Next time, call anyway. Pet, how long have you known the harbinger was following you?"

"Since I was a kid," I said, my grin fading away. This was the bit...this was the part where he would kick me out of my house.

But he didn't sound angry, just tired. "How long have you known he was still following you after we thought he was dead the second time?"

This time, my voice was only a mutter. "The whole time. After we found the bits and pieces of his body, and the ash, I saw him alive. He wanted me to see him."

"You need to talk more."

I meant to say *sorry*, but I said, "That's flamin' rich," before I could stop myself, instead.

A soft, deep disturbance of sound shook Zero's shoulders for a moment, and it took me far too long to realise that he was laughing. By the time I realised it, he was serious again.

"There's no necessity for me to talk," he said.

I wanted to protest that, but I'd already been cheeky instead of apologising, so I said, "Sorry."

"I can't protect you if I don't know what's happening around you. Next time...just tell me."

"I know. I was afraid you lot might kill him."

"We would have discussed it," Zero said. "But I doubt we would have decided to kill him. Perhaps we would wipe his memories to be safe."

"You gotta catch him first."

"Indeed," said Zero, and there was a thoughtfulness to his voice. "He is...oddly difficult to catch, for a human."

"Maybe Athelas is right, and he's a harbinger."

"I hope not, though it does seem likely."

"Anyway," I said, "I'll tell you next time I see him."

I said that because I *couldn't* tell him that I wouldn't hide something like that from him again; not when I was still not planning on telling him about Morgana. There had to be something that this Behind-tainted life of mine didn't touch, and it was far too late for the old mad bloke. If there was one thing I was going to keep safe from Behind and Between, it was Morgana. It was bad enough that she'd already seen Jin Yeong —*and* that she was currently sharing her house with a lycanthrope.

"Oh yeah," I said, and I couldn't help the stray thought that fluttered through my head—the one that said if I told him *this*, he would trust me more, suspect anything else less. "Full disclosure, though; I'm researching what it is that could be after Mr. Preston."

"I know," he said; and though he was short, I was pretty sure he was pleased that I'd told him.

Was it Athelas in my head, so approving while I felt guilty? Or was I changing in ways that I hadn't expected? Changing like the old mad bloke, maybe.

"You don't need to worry about Mr. Preston, Pet," he added, as if he hadn't meant to say it.

"Okay," I said, and there was a warmth in my heart that made the guilt worse. I had been right: he really was doing something about it. And I was still lying to him—or at least, not telling all the truth. "It's because you don't want people to get hurt, isn't it? The reason that you fight so hard against helping humans?"

"Helping humans never stops at the act," Zero said. I don't think he noticed, but he automatically shifted his arm across to let me lean against him. "I helped a human once, and that turned him into a vampire. From there, his sister was turned, and died."

"Yeah, but it's not like that's your *fault*," I protested.

"The fault can only rest with me."

"'S'pose you think Athelas is your fault, too," I muttered. He'd gone all stately again—though his arm was still around me, so that was something.

"Athelas *is* my fault," said Zero. "He was sold to my family with the intention of being given to me when I was born."

"*You* didn't turn him into a creepy old tea-drinker."

"That was—Pet."

"What? You're not gunna try to tell me he's not a creepy old tea-drinker, are you?"

Zero's eyelids flickered for an instant, and his eyes grew bluer. "Don't say that where he can hear you."

I grinned. "What am I? An idiot? You know you can't take the responsibility for how everyone turns out, right?"

"Athelas had no chance. He was bought from his parents when he was five and trained from that time with my father to kill, protect, and serve."

"Yeah, but that's still not your fault."

"For my sake, they trained him to fight by giving him something to love—a small creature, or a human friend—and then sending something to kill it."

"That's..." I swallowed a bit. "They gave him humans? Like a pet?"

"Something similar. Some of them he protected, but he couldn't keep them from the Family. As soon as he became too fond of anyone, the fae made him kill them. If he didn't, they took them and played with them until he did. It taught Athelas how soft things can die painfully, and how to kill cleanly and quickly."

It was funny, I thought, how sick you could feel about something without even seeing it. A bit thickly, I asked, "What about you?"

"What about me? I lived an easy life. I'm the heir—and an heirling."

I looked up at him, surprised to find tears in my eyes, and saw that he was gazing at the freezer door without really seeing it. No matter what he said, the same childhood that had scooped Athelas inside out had cut deeply with Zero, too. The coldness and the pushback against anything soft or human or emotional—I thought I might understand it a bit more.

"It's not your fault," I said again, fiercely.

"Because of who I am, Athelas was made into who he is."

"Now you're just being silly."

Zero laughed in a huge, short rumble. "Is that so?"

"Oi."

"If you think I'm going to answer all your questions because I'm drunk—"

I blinked a bit. "You're actually drunk? This is you drunk?"

"The fae version of being drunk," said Zero, shrugging. "I told you it would affect me."

"You can say you're not gunna answer," I told him. "I'm just gunna ask questions. Same as usual. You can answer or not, just like usual."

"Thank you," said Zero, settling back against the wall again, "for your permission. Go ahead."

"Your family—they were trying for an heirling, weren't they? That's why your mum was human."

"Yes," he said, baldly.

"Did she—what happened to her?"

"She died giving birth to me."

I looked up at him again, and saw the deep line that cut between his brows. He didn't believe that; it was another of those things he blamed himself for. For a fae who touted his unemotional faeness to the detriment of his more emotional human side, he was carrying a heck of a lot of baggage.

"You reckon someone killed her?"

Zero's sigh almost sounded like a whisper of laughter. "Ah, Pet! How do you still have so many questions!"

"Well," I said. "We're family now. We should know at least that much about each other."

"We're not family. I know what happens to family."

He said that, but his arm was still around me. I was pretty sure that was his chin resting on the top of my head, too.

"Yeah, but you still need family," I argued. "Look at me; I had a family, and I turned out all right. I'm still alive."

"You're a pet."

"Well, yeah. But I don't go around being rude to everyone."

A breath of laughter stirred the hair at the top of my head. "Yes you do."

"Okay, but I don't go around being *nasty* rude to people. I'm a good pet."

"You're a troublesome pet," he said. "Please...please stop trying to die. We can take care of the Sandman, the perytons, and the Mr. Prestons. There's no need for you to die, too."

"Too late," I said. "Athelas already killed me six times. Anyway, you said that if I stayed behind you, you'd make sure I didn't die, but these days you keep going out and leaving me at home. How am I supposed to stop dying if I can't be behind you?"

"I know," he said. "But that was...necessary."

"Yeah, I figured. How come?"

"I'm slightly drunk, not very drunk."

"Wanna know what I reckon?"

"No more suppositions, Pet," Zero said, but I felt him laugh even though I didn't hear it.

"You should be drunk more often," I told him. "Oi. You said that if the Behindkind is important enough, charges get dropped in Behindkind courts."

"If they're ever upheld to begin with," Zero said. There was a kind of quiet futility to the words that almost made me regret asking him about it. He'd been happy a moment before—or maybe just amused, or content.

"That's why there was someone," I said, because it was too late to stop the frown from deepening between his brows. "That's why there was someone, like Athelas said. Someone going around making sure people were brought to justice."

"For a time, there were two. The Behindkind law wasn't able to do anything about the two of them because it was lawful for them to do what they were doing. But it wasn't popular."

"Someone killed them, I suppose," I said gloomily.

"One died. The other...well, I suppose he died, too, in a way. No more, Pet," he added. His voice had a sticky, almost sleepy sound to it, but it was final. "That is enough questioning. Enough talking."

"Yeah, don't want you to injure yourself," I said. "You didn't even stretch first."

I hoped that would get another deep rumble of laughter, but it didn't. The only rumble I got was a faint snore from where the heaviness of Zero's head leaned against the top of my head.

____

CHAPTER THIRTEEN

____

IT WAS TOO EARLY IN THE DAY WHEN SOMEONE KNOCKED AT the front door, but at least it wasn't a knock at the linen closet. After the other night, Zero had woken up with what I guessed must be his version of a hangover. He shouldered his way back to our house without speaking a word, me trotting after him as usual, and brought us back into the human world to face the raised brows of Athelas and the scowls of Jin Yeong.

For the rest of the morning, he alternately moved around the house without speaking a word more than necessary, ignored me almost completely, and sat in his chair, sharpening knives.

I didn't like to think what he'd do to visitors coming through the linen cupboard door.

Come to think of it, I didn't fancy the chances of visitors coming through the front door, either. Not even ones who had been polite enough to knock.

None of the psychos told me not to open the door this time, though, so I went to open it and found Detective Tuatu outside.

"Hey," I said, opening the door. "You got a death wish today, or something?"

"Someone gave me a little tree that looks after me," he said. "I'm fine. Why? Are they particularly annoyed today?"

"You know the dryad only works at home, right?"

"Yeah, but I figure if you can live with those three, I can come and see them every now and then. I've got a few questions for them, anyway. Officially."

"Come in, then," I said, and yelled down the hall, "Detective Tuatu's here! Officially!"

Jin Yeong, who had just descended the stairs, made a disparaging sort of noise that might have been some kind of greeting, and continued on to the kitchen. He was probably going for one of his blood bags—he always did drink more when he was annoyed. That meant he was going to be more irritating than usual tonight. Jin Yeong starved of blood was dangerous and snarly, all liquid eyes and flashing teeth, but Jin Yeong when he had just fed was more irritating—warm, invasive in a deliberately provocative way, and inclined to purr destructive comments into the warm living room to stir up whoever was most likely to fight back.

Neither Athelas nor Zero replied at all, but Athelas at least looked up when we came into the living room.

"How delightful to see you again," he said. "We have something further to discuss."

"Do we?" asked Tuatu, looking uneasy.

I didn't blame him—I felt pretty uneasy myself, but there was nothing I could do about it. Detective Tuatu had hastily said something when he first met Athelas that I had reason to think he'd regret before long. I mean, I wouldn't want to be in debt to any fae, but I definitely wouldn't want to be in debt to Athelas.

"Certainly we do," said Athelas. "I'll remind you of it again, one of these days."

"Thanks," Tuatu said, and he still sounded like he wasn't sure about how thankful he ought to be. "Anyway, I've come to ask you a few questions about a body we've found."

"How uninteresting!" Athelas sighed, but he looked amused.

Undeterred, the detective said to Zero, "Someone had been watching him for a while—we found their little lair this morning. There were photos all over the wall, and an itinerary of his usual movements."

"What has that got to do with us?" asked Zero, without looking up. "I've told you—"

"I know. You investigate the crimes you want to investigate," Tuatu said, his voice rougher with the same kind of annoyance that made my own heart burn. "But he came here before he died. He was here for a while, too, if the pictures are anything to go by."

A glossy photo caught the light as he pulled it out of the inner pocket of his jacket.

"Give it to me!" said Zero sharply, but it was too late.

I'd already seen it. I'd seen the receding hairline, the threading of grey, the unpleasantly pinched expression of the man's face.

It was Mr. Preston.

"He's dead?" I said, in shock. He couldn't be dead, because Zero had said...Zero had *said*—

"Perhaps it would be helpful if you fetched tea and coffee, Pet," said Athelas' voice, low with warning, though I wasn't sure if the warning was for me or for others in the room.

"That's Mr. Preston," I said to Detective Tuatu, and it wasn't a question. "He's really dead?"

Tuatu turned his gaze on me. "Did they know him as well? Is that why he's dead?"

"Didn't you—" I stopped, thoughts and emotions swelling. "No, but I thought you *sent* him. And how is he dead? Zero—"

"Get him out," Zero said, his voice icy. He had gone back to his knife sharpening, motions short and gritty against the knife.

Jin Yeong left the kitchen in two light steps to seize Detective Tuatu by the collar, and dragged him, backwards and protesting, right through the front door.

"Oi!" I yelled, and started toward the door. It was already too late, of course; I felt the movement of Between as Jin Yeong drew the detective right into it, and all sense of them disappeared completely when it shut itself.

I stood staring at the shut door while anger grew and heated behind my eyes. It seemed that I could hear, as a kind of a refrain to the constant, rhythmic sweep of a knife being sharpened, Zero's voice saying *You don't need to worry about Mr. Preston, Pet.*

You don't need to worry.

No need to worry.

And suddenly, in the quiet comfort of my house, a sickening change was growing.

"Pet."

I turned on my heel, ignoring Athelas, who had spoken my name, and stalked across the carpet until I was in front of Zero.

You don't need to worry about Mr. Preston, Pet.

My voice sounded choked when I said, "I trusted you!"

Zero refused to look away from the knife he was sharpening, and somehow that made me angrier.

"I told you I wouldn't help him."

"You always say that, and you always help."

"I've only helped you. One human. We have a deal."

My throat hurt with an ache that was sharp and deep. "You were supposed to be better than that."

"You were supposed to follow orders," said Zero, so quietly I almost couldn't hear him.

"Pet," said Athelas, his voice silky with warning. "Now is a time for tea, not talking."

"No tea for you!" I said hotly.

Zero's rumble shook the table. "Pet, *coffee.*"

"I'm not going to make coffee for you!" I shouted at him. "You let a bloke die! You were supposed to be better than that!"

Zero looked up, and his voice was more hasty than icy when he said, "If you feel as though you can't restrict yourself to my orders, perhaps you should leave now."

"Yeah?" I said, and I wasn't sure if the molten heat I felt in my stomach was the fury of disappointment, or just actual fury. "Maybe I should."

"*Mwoh?*" said Jin Yeong's very startled voice, from the hallway. "*Petteu, mwoh hae?*"

"Be very careful what you say from now," Zero said, after a staticky kind of silence. "If you utterly refuse to do as you're told, our contract ends now."

"Pet, I really do advise—"

"You gunna tell me to ignore someone who needs help again?" I asked.

"That's my right. If you want your house, it's your duty to obey."

"Can't do it. You might as well—" I stopped and swallowed against a sharp pain in my throat. My house. I had to keep my house. But how could I? "You might as well just kick me out now. Because next time someone asks for help, I'm gunna give it to them."

"Humans are not our concern!"

"Maybe not yours, but they are mine."

"Pet—"

"There's gotta be *someone* looking out for them. You lot sure as heck aren't doing it."

"You don't have the skills to look after anyone," Zero said. "You've barely stayed alive by the skin of your teeth these last few months."

"Yeah, 'cos there was someone looking out for me," I said. "I might not have the skills, but I've got some of the knowledge now —and if I see something and don't do something about it, how am I better off alive instead of dead? What's the good of me if I don't do what I can do? I already lived like a rat in a hole for four years."

"Pet," said Zero, his eyes lightest blue and mesmerising. "Tell me you'll obey me."

I looked into those eyes and saw a message there. Echoing it, Athelas murmured, "All you have to do is say you'll obey my lord, Pet."

And in Athelas' smooth murmur, I heard the promise that so long as I wasn't caught, I could keep doing what I wanted to do. I could speak my obedience, and keep doing what I thought best, safe in my protection.

I laughed a bit, taking myself by surprise, because it was so much like Athelas.

"I'm not here to help humans," Zero said. "I won't throw away the time, or lives, or—or—"

"Emotion?"

"*Energy*. I won't throw away the energy I could use to do something else, into saving creatures who will die a day later doing something stupid."

I pressed my palm against my chest, just below the collarbone, where it ached. Wish it wouldn't hurt so much. "So then what stops you from telling me to kill someone next time?"

"I won't tell you to kill someone."

"Might as well," I said, and there was just a thread of voice left to me. Ah heck, I was tired. "If I'm gunna agree to not helping people who're going to die if I don't help, might as well kill 'em myself."

"*Petteu*," said JinYeong, from across the room, his voice as commanding and clear as the words themselves. "I wish to eat. You should make kimchi rice."

All the blood in me tugged me toward that voice—or maybe it was just the vampire saliva still in me that drew me—and I nearly took a step in his direction. I looked up and saw his eyes on me, liquid and dark and pleading where his voice was demanding.

"Don't do that," I said, shaken. "Don't try and make me do stuff I don't want to do. You're not my pack."

"*Yah, Petteu. Wae gurolkka?*"

"Eat before you go, Pet," said Athelas, the quiet voice of reason. "We'll discuss it over a meal."

"Nah," I said. If I didn't go now, I'd give an excuse, and then another. If I wanted to keep my humanity—if I wanted to be able to do the right thing—I had to go now. "Lost my appetite."

I passed Jin Yeong as I went down the hall to the front door, and there was the faintest tug at the cuff of my hoodie. I twitched away from it without stopping, and his voice said, still shocked, "*Non kalgoya? Chinchalo?*"

I didn't stop for that faint tug, either. I just said, "Yeah, looks like I'm going."

I don't remember if I opened the door or if Zero opened it for me without crossing the room—or even if I walked right through it, Between. But I was out on the street a moment later, the brightness of early evening a shock all around me, and a huge, hot wetness behind my eyes.

Zero had done nothing. He'd told me I didn't have to worry, and then he'd done nothing.

But the worst of it, the most awful part of it, wasn't that Zero had done nothing. It was the fact that *I'd* done nothing. I'd been in a position to help—had the knowledge to help—and I had tucked my head in and listened to Zero when he said to leave it alone. As much as my psychos, I'd let a bloke die because I hadn't cared enough to say *no* to Zero when I should have. I was the human; I was the one with human feelings. I should have been strong enough to do that, at least. No one expected psychos to have feelings or act on feelings.

And for the first time since I'd met them, thinking of them as my psychos wasn't comforting.

I didn't cry as I walked downtown, but I had to keep clearing the catch from my throat, and I might have blinked a bit more often than usual. I was gunna buy myself some coffee. Birthday coffee. I caught sight of the *open* sign on Kalbi's door as I passed the magenta pub walls over the road, and changed my mind.

Nope, I was gunna buy myself some birthday kimchi jiggae. Use up the last of the shopping money I still had on me in one hot, sniffle-inducing meal.

I sniffed again, reflexively, as somebody drew shoulder to shoulder with me and stayed there. I didn't have to look sideways, because I could already smell his cologne, but somehow I looked, anyway.

JinYeong sauntered by my side, lips pressed together in a smug *moue*.

I threw him an annoyed look. "Go away."

"*Shilloh.*"

"I don't want you! Go away!"

"*Shileundae, nega wae? Olma chul kondae?*" JinYeong sang, mockingly.

There was a feathering of Between around the words, and I got the impression of *Won't. Can't make me. How much you gunna pay me?*

I stopped short, hands on hips. "How about I don't kick you in the shins?"

He took a swift step backward, but his mouth didn't look any less smug. Maybe I should just kick him in the shins anyway. It wasn't like he could bite me while we were out in public, anyway. Zero would have something to say about that.

Zero would—

Yeah. It wasn't as if Zero cared about that anymore. Probably hadn't cared from the start, just like Athelas had told me. It wasn't as if Zero hadn't told me himself, either—he'd told me he was only protecting me because we had a deal.

And now I'd gone and broken it.

"*Wae?*" said JinYeong.

"I couldn't do anything else, anyway," I said to him, without meaning to say it aloud. "I can't stay if you lot are going to let people die when you could save them."

"*Tangyeonhaji*," Jin Yeong said, with agreement in his voice, and I knew that word.

It meant, *Of course*!

The smug little bloodsucker was mocking me.

I looked at him for a ragey moment, then kicked him hard in the shins and crossed the road while he was swearing in Korean behind me. I shoved through the restaurant door in a whirlwind that probably worried the other diners, but Jin Yeong followed me in before I could shut the door in his face.

I sat down heavily, tiredly, and he dropped into the seat opposite me. I stared at him in bafflement. Why the heck was he following me? Just to annoy me?

Oh wait.

Nope. He was definitely following me to annoy Zero.

"You're getting in the way of my view," I said sourly.

His Korean edged with Between, Jin Yeong said, very clearly, "I am the view."

I made a very realistic chuck-up noise that caused the man who came to take our order look alarmed. "Sorry," I told him. "Felt sick suddenly. I'll be right."

That didn't make him look too relieved, and Jin Yeong took the opportunity of reeling off an order to him, which he wrote down automatically.

I glared at Jin Yeong. "I'm not buying your lunch!"

He shrugged one shoulder and said, "I am able to pay."

"You better," I told him, and put in my own order. I mean, technically speaking, it was Zero's money, anyway, but I'd cooked their meals for long enough that it was probably more like a pay packet, anyway.

That's one thing I'd renegotiate if it ever came back to another contract.

Hang on. Why was I thinking about next time? There was no next time, just me on my own again—this time without my house.

Maybe I was thinking for too long. Across the table, Jin Yeong narrowed his eyes at me, and said so that I could understand, "Do not bite, *Petteu*."

"Wasn't gunna," I said wearily. "I'm not gunna bite anyone. I'm just a Pet without a pet house."

His look turned speculative. "Not angry?"

Was I angry? Mostly, I was pretty sure I was too exhausted to be angry—exhausted and confused and disbelieving. Everything I'd had, I'd lost; and it was my own fault. My own fault that I didn't have a house anymore. My own fault that I didn't even have a pretend family.

"Just eat, and we'll get out of here," I said as the food arrived, exhausted all over again. "I gotta find somewhere to kip for the night."

I DON'T THINK I HAD THE PURPOSEFUL IDEA OF GOING TO Morgana's place. I was just walking, trying to ignore Jin Yeong, and then somehow I was facing the Brooker and its skyline of old houses, strolling down Morgana's street.

I mean, it wasn't stupid—there was a whole lower level of the house where I could camp out in a room—but it wasn't something I'd done deliberately. Jin Yeong seemed faintly approving, though what it had to do with him, I didn't know. It wasn't like he was going to go back and report to Zero, though, so at least there was that.

And I knew that, because I asked him when we got to the front door.

"Oi." There was no way of telling him what to do and making sure he did it, but I said, "You won't go telling Zero where I am?"

He shrugged. "There is no fun in that."

I mean, it wasn't like Zero would ask unless he was trying to make sure I didn't tell anyone about him and Between and was going to send Athelas to take care of me or something. It struck me suddenly to wonder if he and Athelas and Jin Yeong would have a discussion about me, like they would have had about the old mad bloke—whether or not to kill me. Whether or not to take away my memories.

Was that something they could do?

"All right," I said, but there was a chill of fear behind the words. "Make sure you don't."

"*Yaksok*," said Jin Yeong, shrugging.

Well, a promise from a vampire was about all that was standing between me and potential brain-wiping or death. That was nice.

"You better go before Zero gets really cranky about you leaving," I said to him, instinctively still concerned with keeping the peace between them. Stupid, that. It didn't matter to me whether or not they tore each other to pieces, now.

Jin Yeong cocked an eyebrow at me, and I had the feeling he'd expected me to say something else. Maybe he wanted me to invite him in. I wasn't stupid enough to do that; not with Morgana and Daniel in the house as well.

Still, he dropped down one step, then another, and sauntered off toward the front gate with his hands in his pockets. Nice of him to do what he was told for once.

I let out a faint breath of relief, or something else that hurt a bit, and put my hand on the door knob to swing the door shut.

"*Ah, cham!*" said Jin Yeong, turning on his heel.

"What?" I said, as he came back up the front stairs, lightly and swiftly. "You forget something?"

"*Ne*," he said, pausing just the step before the threshold. Pushing through Between, the meaning of his words said, "Invite me in, Pet."

"Heck no," I said. "I don't want you here; why should I?"

If I could remember the little ditty he'd sung at me earlier in the day, I would have sung it back in his face. Maybe I could look it up on my phone later on. And that thought was another one that hurt unexpectedly.

One hand on either side of the doorframe, Jin Yeong tilted his head, eyes narrowing. "*Musen il, Petteu?*"

"Nothing's wrong," I muttered. "Just gotta get a new sim card when Zero stops paying the phone bill."

I should probably give it back to him—should have already done it. Thrown it at his head or something. But the truth was, I needed it. It connected me to Detective Tuatu and Morgana— even to Daniel, now. I needed that connection, just for a little while. Not as much as I needed my boots, that other gift from Zero, but still enough to make me unwilling to send it back with Jin Yeong.

I couldn't help looking down at the toes of those boots, already scuffed and comfortable, and Jin Yeong muttered something beneath his breath. Probably still complaining about me not letting him into the house.

I heard something that might have been a mutter of "Then if I cannot come *in*, you must come *out*," and Jin Yeong's slender fingers curled unexpectedly around the nape of my neck and drew me to the threshold.

I took a breath to say, "What the *heck?*" but never got the chance to say it.

Jin Yeong, just a step below me in a dreadful convenience that meant his nose was exactly level with mine, leaned forward with hypnotizing slowness and nudged his lips against mine, warm and soft.

Surprise fizzed at the back of my mind, momentarily paralysing me.

Why was a cold-blooded vampire so warm?

Why were my eyes closed?

Oh, hang on.

Hang on.

Why was I being given vampire spit *this* time?

Jin Yeong didn't seem to be in any hurry to stop, either. I felt his thumb slide up behind my ear as he shifted a little, his lips more than a soft nudge now, and it tickled. I reflexively turned my head against the tickle, feeling the brief warmth of his cheek pass mine, and found that my palm was against his chest.

I used that hand to push him away, and he stepped back at once, eyes half-lidded and catlike, as though he'd just been drinking blood.

I blinked a bit, then protested, "What the heck! What was that for?"

"*Saengil sonmul*," JinYeong said, looking far too pleased with himself.

"How'd you know it's my birthday?" I demanded. "And how is that a birthday present? I didn't want it! If you're gunna give me presents I don't want, you should give me a receipt with them!"

"*Wae?*" murmured JinYeong, one brow cocked; and then, startlingly understandable, "You want to give it back? I'll accept it."

"Stop saying stuff in weird ways!"

"You prefer I should bite you?"

"No, I don't prefer you bite me!"

"'Sup, Pet?" said Daniel's voice behind me. "You need a hand?"

JinYeong, eyes glittering, made his usual, sultry *moue* and took one step up and across the threshold and into the house. "Why is the dog still here?"

"'Cos he needed somewhere to stay," I said. Thoughts were moving very swiftly through my mind now. I said explosively, "Birthday present, my eye! If I've got some of your spit, you can get in without an invitation, right? I'm right, aren't I?"

"*Yokshi, Petteu!*" purred JinYeong. He twitched one long, slender finger at Daniel, and said, "*Noh—choshimhae.*"

"Is he threatening me?"

"Oi," I said to JinYeong. "You forgot to switch on your translator."

"*Naeil bwa,*" he said. One incisor showed in a mocking smile, and I swear one eyelid dropped in a wink as he turned to go.

"I better *not* see you tomorrow!" I yelled after him, but he had already been swallowed by Between, and I doubted my voice could reach him. More annoyingly, he was gone before I remembered he hadn't really answered any of my questions.

"What's with him?" asked Daniel.

"Beggared 'f'I know. He followed me here."

"Why are you here?"

"What?" The sudden energy that had come with the vampire spit sank a little. "Oh, there's some trouble at the house."

"What sort of trouble?"

"I'm not your pack, you know," I said defensively.

"Yes, you are," he said. "Pack is always pack. Did they kick you out?"

I cleared my throat instead of sniffling. "Yeah."

"Got any clothes?"

"Nah."

"Money?"

"A bit."

"Did you come to ask Morgana to let you stay for a while?"

I had to think about that. I hadn't started out for the place with that idea directly in my mind, but there was a big raw patch of me missing, like I was a snail with no shell, and I had wandered to the one place where I felt there was still a little bit of home.

"I could do that," I said. "Maybe for a day or two. If she says yes."

"She'll say yes," he said. "I don't know about her parents, though. They don't seem to care one way or another, but they might change their minds one day. How will you keep your cover?"

"That? I'm not going to keep it exactly."

"You can't tell her, Pet."

"Don't try to tell me what to do," I snapped. I'd had enough of that for the time being. The sound of my own voice fell harshly in the room around us, and I said, more quietly, "Sorry."

"She's human."

"Yeah, I know."

"And things get dangerous once humans know about us."

"Yeah? Why are you staying here, then?"

Daniel looked uncomfortable. "I'm being *careful*."

"And you're like me; you've got nowhere else to go."

"I've got somewhere else to go," argued Daniel. He added, more honestly, "Just not yet. There was a Sandman out to get me, Pet. I know what that means."

"Yeah? What does it mean, then? 'Cos it looks like it's after me, too, and I'd like to know what to watch out for."

"It means that Upper Management is trying to make things quiet. They're cleaning up the mess they started at the Police Station, and I'm part of the mess they need to clear up."

"How am I part of that mess?" I demanded. "It's not like I was colluding with them or anything."

"*I* wasn't, either!" shot back Daniel. "It was Erica!"

"Yeah, nah, sorry," I said. "I didn't mean you were involved, I just meant why me? I can understand 'em going after you, because you took over after Erica, and I s'pose they think you know too much."

"If I know too much, you definitely know too much. Well, you know the wrong kind of people."

"Zero."

"Lord Sero," Daniel agreed. "But no one apart from the Family likes Athelas, either, and even the Family hates Jin Yeong."

"Yeah, I got that impression," I said. "So why not come after them?"

"Killing you *would* be going after the Troika," said Daniel. "Well, that's what I think, anyway. I think they know they can't touch those three, so they're trying to give them a warning by bumping you off."

"Great," I said. Perfect timing. Just as I left their protection, I was about to need it the most. "Reckon *I'm* dead, then."

"Nah, I've got some ideas about that," he said. "Don't worry,

Pet. I'll look after you."

"You should look after yourself first," I pointed out. "They want you dead, too."

"I've got some ideas about that, too. Don't worry, we'll be fine. It's Lord Sero who should be worried."

Sharply, I asked, "Why should Zero be worried? What's it got to do with him?"

"Because Upper Management have been murdering Family affiliates around Australia. If they're doing that, it's for a reason. Usually, that means someone's trying to challenge the succession."

"You mean the heirling stuff?"

"Yeah. Heard they'd found out there's a harbinger around, too. So things will be pretty interesting from now on—and if the harbinger doesn't take a shine to Zero, there's no way he's going to end up running Behind."

"What, the harbinger picks the next leader?" I hadn't gotten that impression from Athelas at all.

"Nah. It just...happens a lot. Unless someone finds out who the favourite is and kills them, anyway. So if there is really a harbinger out there, and the Family or Upper Management knows who they are and who they've been hanging around, a few more bodies might show up soon."

"You just said it was too dangerous for them to try and kill Zero."

"I said that they wouldn't try to kill the Troika. If they want to go after Zero as an heirling, that's a different thing. They'd have to think the risk was worth it, though."

I had my phone out before I realised it, with the instinctive thought that I should warn Zero.

"He already knows," Daniel said. "He knows the signs. He probably knows 'em better than most people: he was around last time this happened."

"What happened last time?"

"Last time everyone died, even the harbinger, and the king

just kept reigning. There was a lot of talk that he'd done the killing himself."

"What a surprise," I said. Everything I'd heard about Behind was that it was savage and cruel. Even the brief experiences I'd had there had been horrible. The superiority I'd felt from most Behindkind toward humans was irritating like that—what was the point in being supposedly more intelligent or stronger than humans when there was no kindness or compassion with it? What was better about being more intelligent if you were also more cruel? What was the point in being more logical and unemotional if that just made you a psychopath?

Daniel, frowning, asked, "You okay, Pet?"

"Yeah," I said. "Just...flaming tired. I'd better go up and see Morgana."

"All right," he said. "But be careful what you say."

"I'll tell her what I need to tell her," I told him, and went up the stairs ahead of him. They still echoed as though the house was empty, a booming of loneliness I'd never liked, and even Daniel's footsteps seemed to blend with mine.

No wonder Morgana looked like a goth princess most of the time. She'd probably caught it from the house as much as from her nightmare.

She was waiting for us when we came through the door

"There you are!" she said, bouncing a little. "You got here *ages* ago! What were you two talking about down there?"

"Hi," I said, short and awkward because I couldn't answer the question.

"Did something happen at the police station? How come your partner didn't come up? I saw him as well—he stood in the doorway for a long time."

Daniel's eyes fixed on me, more yellow than brown, anxious and warning at the same time.

I took in a breath and let it out. Then I said, "There's some stuff I gotta tell you."